ACCLAIM FOR THE WORK OF RAFAEL ALVAREZ

"Rafael Alvarez knows Baltimore like nobody else. He can winkle a delicious story out of every cranny in this town."
—**Madison Smartt Bell, author, *All Souls Rising***

"Only Alvarez with his alley smart style of writing can allow one to feel Baltimore with all five senses . . . "
—**Mark Alan Noone, rock star emeritus, The Slickee Boys**

"Rafael Alvarez gives us a glimpse of Baltimore drawn from the heart. No city has ever had more of a crusading champion. Read this book, and join him on a journey into a place that no one knows better or loves more.
—**Mark Kram, Jr., author,
Like Any Normal Day: A Story of Devotion,
PEN/ESPN winner, 2013**

TALES
FROM THE
HOLY LAND

STORIES BY
RAFAEL ALVAREZ

Perpetual Motion Machine Publishing
Cibolo, Texas

Tales From The Holy Land

ISBN: 978-0-9860594-0-7

2nd printing

www.PerpetualPublishing.com

Cover Picture by Leo Ryan
Jacket and Interior Design by Lori Michelle
Edited by Max Booth III
Copy Edited by Jay Reda

FOR
PHOEBE

TABLE OF CONTENTS

THE BASILIO STORIES

INTRODUCTION

CITY OF IMPOSSIBLE MIRACLES

ON THE FICTION OF RAFAEL ALVAREZ

IF YOU LOOK at Baltimore on a paper map and not a computer, you can study it the way the powers of heaven must do when they are shifting people into the different vortexes that shape their lives.

It is a city with early origins in the Port of Baltimore at Locust Point, where the military presence at Fort McHenry held the British back in the War of 1812 as our former colonizer tried to retake its former prized possession. It is a city with a history of slavery and a deep southern consciousness, a city that is the site of the first Catholic cathedral in America; that counts as one of its native sons Joe Gans, the black boxer who became the first American champion and is still referred to as the "old master."

It is a city of confluences and contradictions and the richness that comes from those intersections, a large Jewish history in a city that was once the East Coast's second largest intake port for immigrants. It is a city with a history of hard knuckle politics as well as the mansions in Eutaw Place that once counted the Fitzgeralds among their residents.

Baltimore is a treasure of a city only now being properly inscribed in American literature as the writers who proudly call themselves Baltimoreans embody its real presence.

Rafael Alvarez is devoted to that embodiment as few are. He weaves through the layers and interstices of the city to create characters that have their eyes on the sparrow of redemption through the unwavering promises of goodness, a goodness that both acknowledges difference and looks through it to the indelible presence of the soul and soulfulness.

These are stories with phrasing and syntax that dart through the contexts of his emerging narratives to show us strength where we would not expect it, courage where the heart would seem to fail, and a spiritual essence that transcends the most ardent skepticism but without a blind condescension. Revelations of identity in his characters are subtle. The

i

reader is invited to believe the characters as the sum of their actions as opposed to what we might construct from sociological clues.

These stories are about what holds human beings together, what John Coltrane would call a love supreme.

In "The Sacred Heart of Ruthie", doubt is suspended as an African American doctor who bears the name of Thomas and an unlikely Catholic upbringing spreads the full powers of his gift as a cardiac surgeon to save a young white woman who has fallen victim to drug abuse and is in labor with a child whose health is endangered by her own endangered health. It is the stressful air of emergency rooms in any big city in America where lives lived in extreme marginality hang precariously while all the spheres of life spin around them and professionals with their own full and pressurized lives work to save lives that come from all parts of American society.

Alvarez draws the heart as both physical and metaphysical, the throne of a love that has no choice but to be supreme.

He is a writer in love with his city, its landscape, the facts of its history, the ways in which it seems to promise eternities in spaces that appear limited. Baltimore was the point of departure for the domestic slave trade from 1800 until 1860, when black folk were marketed within the U.S. borders, sold down south in sweep of history caught in the spiritual "Many thousands gone."

The name "Patapsco" is from the Algonquin language of the Native Americans who lived in the area when European colonists and later enslaved Africans arrived, and the river which takes the name "Patapsco" flows into Chesapeake Bay and forms Baltimore harbor.

The native word means "backwater," or "tide covered with froth."

The emerging history of Baltimore, a city with echoes of old European cities, comes in singular phases. Alvarez meshes the distinctiveness of the city into his fiction with characters that embody its history.

In "Aboard the Miss Agnes", there is the Greek captain of the tugboat named Agnes that could have been Athena, and the Polish boy who loses his virginity and his freedom piloting a boat without a license.

Baltimore is the quiet but solidly American presence sitting between the nation's capital to the south, and what could have been the nation's capital to the north, Philadelphia the poor sister swinging her legs as she sits on the edge of the Mason Dixon line. Alvarez is Baltimore's guardian of letters, a writer who sits at the gates to posterity recording it in fiction

ii

that lines the ineffability of a city's spiritual sepulcher, namely the lives of the people who call it home and those who pass through with varying degrees of admiration or disdain.

Faulkner embraces a region, Morrison embraces a culture that is regional in size but national in historicity and resonance, Ellison embraces a consciousness, Fitzgerald a nation's troubling temperament while Alvarez embraces the solid fact of a city that has yet to be recognized for its greatness.

He believes in that greatness and he uses that faith to paint the figures in a fiction that I believe will endure and grow. Despite the news of its contradictions and failures, it is Baltimore's time now, and few people know that as well as Alvarez, who understands the character of a Fredrick Douglass who escaped enslavement in the city and returned to Maryland after the Civil War to forgive the people who once owned him, but not to lay down his project of pushing democracy to meet its claims and prove its own legitimacy.

In "The Ganges of Baltimore", there is a line that is the emblem and shield of the hand of the writer and the man: "If a great man were to paint a landscape of the 200 miles between the City of Baltimore and the far reaches of Western Maryland, where might the line fall between braggadocio and despair?"

There is a magic in Baltimore, and Alvarez lives inside of it. He breathes it. He abides in its faith.

AFAA MICHAEL WEAVER
SIMMONS COLLEGE, BOSTON
JULY, 2013

8

1
TT: 10:40
AQUALUNG
CROSS-EYED
 MARY

3
TT: 11:35
MY GOD
HYMN 43
SLIPSTREAM

2
TT: 10:19
CHEAP DAY
 RETURN
MOTHER GOOSE
WOND'RING
 ALOUD
UP TO ME

4
TT: 10:24
LOCOMOTIVE
 BREATH
WIND-UP

ABOARD THE MISS AGNES

*"**No one has** ever come back to explain how it works. You polish something over here but it is something over there that becomes shiny . . ."*

Gibby Lukowski lost his virginity in the galley of a tugboat called the *Miss Agnes* one fine summer night in the dank and enchanted City of Baltimore.

It was late July of 1977 and Gibby was fifteen years-old, a ticket to see Jethro Tull in the pocket of his dirty dungarees and no way of knowing that one day a tugboat would be the cudgel with which he would kill a man.

On the other side of his manslaughter conviction—shipboard negligence, dope in his piss, the privilege of going to sea taken away for life—Gilbert Gregory Lukowski would grind his teeth into paste trying to make peace with the struggle. Abiding the torment would be the only lasting relationship he'd ever know.

But not tonight, not for many thousands of nights beyond it.

Beneath the glow of 410 light bulbs that spelled CITY PIER BROADWAY, the boy with the curly mop of blonde hair was on the nib of an all-night fling that would handcuff the hands on the clock and make Baltimore shine like Paris.

The *Agnes* was a "bum boat," the harbor equivalent of a junkyard pick-up. She was built in the Sparrows Point shipyard after World War I and named for a Pratt Street barmaid. Fired by coal (feeding the boiler was one of Gibby's many jobs, his shoulders and biceps as big as his thighs and strong as oak) the creaky tub towed scows of scrap and bunkers of fuel oil from one side of the harbor to the other, hauled barges of muck down the Chesapeake on dredging jobs. She hadn't docked a ship in forty years and was one barnacle away from sinking.

To Gibby, whose family had worked the waterfront in Crabtown for a hundred years—Polack stevedores, deckhands, line handlers, *busias* running boarding houses, all the legacy of a sea captain from the days of sail—the *Agnes* was home.

Home, a spotless cracker box on an alley called Chapel Street, not a mile from the pier, was no place he wanted to be.

It was a little after seven with no work scheduled when the Greek went ashore for dinner; leaving his livelihood—which he intended to rename the *Athena*—in the care of a kid who didn't have a driver's license.

Papageorgiou let Gibby live on the boat, paying him next to nothing and all he could eat to work as an unlicensed deckhand, coal tender, first mate and wiper, teaching the boy everything he'd learned on waters from Piraeus to Rotterdam to Baltimore.

Papa made a good omelet and kept the galley stocked with "deals" he got from wholesalers who serviced the city's Greek diners. When he and Gibby heaved lines, turned wrenches or scraped rust, the old man—every minute of a hard and hearty fifty-five—would beat his chest and say: "This life makes me strong . . ."

The Greek told Gibby he was "going up to Prevas' to have a few" and made the short leap to the pier.

"Keep a good eye, Junior. Something on the radio, come find me."

"Okay, Cap," said Gibby, watching the skipper pound his way up Broadway. He hated when the old man called him Junior and, having witnessed the Greek in more than one bar fight, bit his tongue instead of calling him Zorba in return. There were a lot of men in the neighborhood, most of them drunks, who'd gladly take Gibby's place.

Tull was set to go on in a couple of hours and sometimes *Papageorgiou*—who also believed that a man with a fat wallet could always get lucky—forgot to come back.

"Don't get lost," yelled Gibby, waiting for the Greek's dismissive wave before heading aft to smoke a joint.

He kept a small cassette player under a canvas tarp and set it on a capstan. Then he leaned back on a fat coil of hawser, slipped Tull into the box, brought a match to the reefer and hit play.

First song, side one of the new album: "Songs from the Wood."

A copse of flutes and mandolins wafted across the oily sheen of the Patpasco, the massive neon of the Domino Sugars sign glowing in the humidity, its double reflected across still, brown water. Gibby was high. The closest he'd ever been to a forest was a stand of peach trees in Patterson Park, a bulwark against the British in 1814, the oasis where his parents courted on a boat lake when "Ebb Tide" was a hit.

All of the cobblestone streets around the pier were given proper English names when the Limey's founded Fells Point as a boat-building village in the 17th century—Lancaster, Thames, and Shakespeare; Gough and Aliceanna—and as Gibby took a monster hit from the joint, the sky broke with rain.

And then it poured: a sudden summer storm: cats, dogs, rats and frogs blowing in from the east, the temperature dropping by 20 degrees. Gibby pinched out the joint, put the boom box under his shirt and moved up the port side to the galley.

As he pulled the hatchway closed behind him, a voice called out from the dock.

"Hello?"

It was a man with a camera around his neck, standing three feet away and drenched. Next to him was a woman in a white blouse, long skirt and a huge purse made out of rope. She was also soaked.

"Can we come in?" she asked.

Gibby, just inside the hatch, was confused.

"Come aboard?"

"That's it," said the man with an accent Gibby didn't recognize. "May we come aboard?"

Mimicking a line his mother used to use when Gibby's father still came up behind her for a kiss, he said, "Permission granted."

The tourists tried to keep their balance in the galley, soaked and dripping onto the gray steel deck, steadying themselves on the table edge as the storm rocked the Agnes port to starboard, the hawsers tying the boat to the pier whining in rhythm each time the slack gave out.

"Thank you mate," said the man, his British accent unlike Gibby's beloved rockers: not Townshend, not Trower, not Tull. Wiping his wet hands on his wet pants, the man reached toward Gibby and said, "Elroy. Elroy Court."

Stepping aside in tight quarters, he said, "And this drenched daffodil is Edith."

Gibby figured the man was maybe twice his age. The only Ediths he knew were old ladies. This one looked like a college girl who didn't go to school.

She took off her straw hat with soiled pink ribbon and nodded; her light brown hair shorter than Gibby's, damp cotton blouse clinging to her breasts. There was a small gap between Edith's front teeth and her tongue filled the space as she spoke. Gibby wasn't sure what she said. He was stoned and trying not to stare.

Aside from being able to pilot a tugboat from Baltimore to Hampton Roads and back, Gibby didn't know much. But he'd known from the cradle when people had been drinking and these two smelled of booze. It stunk on the man and lay softer on the woman. Gibby passed her the blue and white dish towel hanging from the spigot. As she dried her face, he asked if they'd like to see the boat.

The man beamed and held up his camera. "All right to snap?"

"Snap away," said Gibby, leading them back out on deck. The storm had passed over to the cemeteries of East Baltimore—his father there, his mom not far behind—and the air carried the scent of sidewalks cleansed by the pounding rain. He walked them mid-ships to the hatch that opened onto the engine room.

Gibby stood aside and the man went in first; Edith lightly touching his wrist as she passed, launching a thousand guitars in his head. Maybe the Greek would get half-a-bag on and stay out all night. He fantasized about losing the goof with the camera—people fell overboard all the time—and taking Edith to see Tull.

He followed inside and told them to be careful as they stood on a catwalk looking down on the original 1919 steam engine and the filthy bin of coal that fed it.

"The engine room is the largest area on a tugboat," said Gibby, immediately feeling ridiculous, like a tour guide at Poe's grave, which he'd visited the year before with the 9th grade, his last day at school before quitting to make his way on the water. "This one was Army surplus from . . ."

"The first world war," said Elroy, fascinated.

"Three hundred-and-thirty two horsepower," said Gibby quickly.

"The Jag's got more horses," said Elroy, leaning far over the rail to get shots of the fickle beast that pushed the *Agnes* from Curtis Bay to Locust Point and back to Broadway, exposing the crack of his pale and splotchy ass above a half-pint of peach brandy. Edith plucked the bottle from his bottom, winked at Gibby and nodded for him to join her out on deck.

"He'll be in there forever . . ."

What fifteen year-old can fathom forever? The Greek would not be happy to see a stranger swinging from the engine room monkey bars. And while *Papageorgiou* might smile at Edith, he'd be scowling at Gibby the moment after asking her, kindly, to leave. The teenager's friends were

14

already gathering for the concert, more than a dozen kids meeting up in alleys and corners to get high and gulp cheap beer before walking downtown to fill the entire eighth row of the Civic Center.

Before Edith could speak, Gibby pulled his Jethro Tull ticket from his pocket—$6.50 worth of engine room sweat, enough money in his pocket to buy another one at the door—and held it before her.

"Wanna go?"

Edith plucked the ticket from Gibby's hand, read it and, when he tried to protest, hushed him with a fingertip.

"Go back inside, shut the door and wait."

"But . . ."

Gibby reached out to take the ticket back from her but she hid it behind her back.

"Do as I say . . ."

And Gibby did.

-o-

In a moment, a second storm rocked the *Agnes*. The hatch to the engine room banged three times (less rust to scrape, thought Gibby, hoping it would fall from its hinges) and Elroy's voice roared against the corrugated tin watchman's shack on the pier. Just like his old man's used to shred the rooster and sunrise wallpaper in the kitchen on Chapel Street.

Anger, by any other accent . . .

He didn't hear Edith's voice and when the quiet became too quiet Gibby stuck his head out of the galley to see if she was okay but didn't see anyone. Turning toward Broadway, he found Edith on the prow, kneeling above the frayed hemp "whiskers" that cushioned the tug against bumps and blows.

A flesh and blood figurehead with her arms outstretched toward Elroy on the concrete edge of the bulkhead, Edith's blouse was unbuttoned to her navel as he snapped a dozen shots a minute.

Gibby walked up behind her, a little stunned and thinking it best to stay out of the way. He stopped when Elroy put his camera down and began waving at him, holding the Tull ticket high above his head.

"Thanks mate!" he said as Edith climbed down from the bow and turned toward Gibby as she buttoned her blouse, leading him back to the galley, her eyes following the clouds.

"Did you see that?"

Her breasts? Or his Jethro Tull ticket headed up Broadway with a foreigner who could get killed between Fells Point and downtown with one wrong turn?

"Did I see what?"

Edith was chatty now, as though they'd known each other for years, not forty minutes.

"The storm," she said. "The storm changed direction. It rolled in from the east, hovered over us like a spaceship and sailed back the way it came."

Gibby followed her into the galley, repeating "a spaceship," swallowing the word as Edith took his face in her hands and began kissing him this way and that—in his mouth and outside of it, over his collarbone and behind his ears, kissing like none of the neighborhood girls—not even Dirty Arlene—could; his anvil-hard *kielbasa* chafing against the inside of his zipper (he never wore underwear), suddenly aware that he was about to go all the way for the first time.

His Jack Purcells were the first to go, then his pants. Gibby had his hands all over Edith but Edith still had on all of her clothes except the straw hat, which sat atop her rope purse on the table. Gibby couldn't believe he was about to get laid in front of the pot-bellied stove where the Greek fried steak and eggs, tried to say that he had a bunk back aft and stopped trying to say anything when Edith put every finger of her left hand in his mouth, running her right up and down his cock.

Out beyond the breakers, Gibby got an idea that wasn't quite his own, probably something he saw in one of the titty magazines strewn about the boat. He turned Edith around, bumped her up against the table, lifted her damp skirt above her hips (fingers staining the cotton) and pulled down her panties.

[For years afterward—sleepless and confined to the shore, lucky he wasn't confined to a cell—the aging Gibby would try and fail and try again to conjure the precise shape and shade of her rear-end; wished that he'd slowed down for something that only happens for the first time once.]

Reaching behind him to the wire shelf above the stove, he grabbed a bottle of the Greek's prized olive oil and dribbled it across the small of her back, watching golden rivulets cross and trickle into the crack of her ass.

Edith's ideas were not only her own, but fixed. Reaching around for Gibby's cock, she guided it in and the boy knew, just for a moment, the source of numbers.

-o-

Edith's hat was back on her head as they sat barefoot and cross-legged on the small deck above the wheelhouse, side-by-side with their backs to the city—the great dome of Johns Hopkins behind them, the Proctor & Gamble soap factory rumbling across the channel.

Back and forth: the half-pint of peach schnapps from Elroy's pants and the fat nub of the mangled joint Gibby'd been smoking when visitors arrived on the storm. Silent between them, the banged-up and paint spattered cassette player. Gibby reached out to push "play" but Edith beat him to "eject."

She read the label, grinned and set the tape in the apron her skirt made between her knees. *Anderson's artsy-fartsiest artifact yet . . ."* is how a journalist lover in London had disparaged it.

"No music."

"No music?"

Edith sipped the schnapps and exchanged it for the reefer.

"It's nice like this."

Gibby had never known nice like this, never would again.

"Ever hear of ball lightning?"

Hear of it, thought Gibby, stifling a playground snigger with a belt of schnapps, I was just hit by it.

"Uh-uh."

"Very rare and mysterious," said Edith, flicking the roach overboard and reaching for the last sip of booze. "They ride violent thunderstorms . . . orbs of light—blue, orange and white, the size of bowling balls—floating through the air, passing through windows."

"You saw it tonight?" said Gibby, wondering what else he'd missed, taking the empty schnapps bottle from her and setting it aside. He'd retrieve it later, keep it on the shelf above his bunk until the Greek died and he was old enough to get his seaman's papers.

"Once back home, a shower of them flew into Daddy's factory. Bouncing between the machines, a deluge of sparks and *poof*—gone. That's how the fire started but no one believed it."

"Your father owns a factory?"

"It only lasts two or three seconds," she said. "Impossible to photograph."

"Even for your friend?" asked Gibby.

Near the foot of Broadway, some thirty yards from the tug, Papageorgiou was coming back from supper, a toothpick in his mouth.

High above the *Agnes*, a full and buttery moon compelled the Greek to take out the opera glasses he used to check on barges in tow. Though lenses ground in Athens: the boy and a good-looking woman below the rising, rendered orb. She was running her fingers through her hair.

"I'll be-a goddamn," said the Greek with a smile, folding the glasses and deciding to have another beer.

"When will you see him again?"

"Not tonight."

It was half the answer Gibby wanted, the inferred portion an agitation, his Polish grandmother's voice squawking in his head: "Ain't you a glutton for punishment . . ."

"When?"

"Probably back in Africa," she said. "Unless I go to L.A."

Gibby took Edith's hand from his hair and held it tight.

"Is he your husband?"

"God, no."

"Boyfriend?"

Edith was feeling anger. Tugboat or bobsled, why was it always like this?

"Don't you want to know who I am?"

Gibby began to kiss her and she kissed back, but not like before. He stopped and asked again, believed he could not defend himself from a personality—childish, grandiose, sensitive in the extreme without any constructive outlet—that would cause so much suffering in years to come.

He took the Tull tape back from the folds of Edith's dress and said, "He's sitting in my seat."

"How do you know you're not sitting in his?"

"Who is he?"

THE AISHE COOPER STORY

LEINI WAS A pretty girl, a beauty not seen in the Holy Land until the great-granddaughters of the Diacumacos brothers served chili dogs on Eastern Avenue long after Leini was dead.

But it was not Leini's gaunt good looks, her curiosity or the awkward grace that always spilled soup over the lip of the bowl that drew Orlo into the signature narrative of his life on a Friday evening in September of 1926.

It was tragedy—pure, ghastly and criminal.

Unlike the slow, corrosive hardships that buffeted Leini over her long decades in Crabtown—the discovery that she'd been traded for sewing machines, an arranged marriage to a monster, her only son killed in the war—the catastrophe Orlo found behind the broom factory took place in less than five minutes.

BOOM-CHAKA-CHAKA-CHAKA-BOOM-CHAKA-CHAKA-CHAKA-BOOM.

Machines slapping broomsticks into place, steel wire spinning 'round a head of straw, the only sound in a vacant lot of weeds on the far reaches of Toone Street when Orlo discovered the body of a twelve year-old gypsy girl named Aishe Cooper.

Raped and murdered, still bleeding but not breathing when Orlo climbed down from his cart to look.

Flies buzzing, gulls circling.

BOOM-CHAKA-CHAKA-CHAKA-BOOM-CHAKA-CHAKA-CHAKA-BOOM . . .

-o-

Orlo galloped off to find a cop he knew, a detective from the pickpocket squad, and told him what he'd seen.

"My God," said the junkman, turning his wagon for home. "Even in Verdun, I never saw anything like it."

Clip-clop down to the end of Clinton Street, a ride that usually took twenty minutes today lasting more than an hour as Orlo stopped again and again—knees knocking, ankles sore—to check on a whole lot of nothing glinting beyond the machine shops and fertilizer warehouses, hopping down from the wagon just to feel his legs move beneath him.

Passing Ralph's Diner—beyond it, big white letters spelling SALVAGE HOUSE on the roof of the only place he'd ever lived—all-of-a-sudden famished. He tied his horse to a tree near the clearing where Ralph Rafailidis slaughtered hogs on a stump and hobbled inside, feeling old at twenty-nine.

The Feast of the Holy Cross.

The birthday of Eleini Leftafkis.

Magic Hour.

-o-

Wash and blanch four pigs' feet.

Wrap in cheesecloth and cover with water. Bring to a boil. Reduce heat immediately and simmer for four hours, uncovered.

In the last thirty minutes of simmering, add: a pound of fresh green beans—snipped and snapped—one head of cabbage and replace one quart of water with one quart of stewed tomatoes.

Season with fresh basil and cracked peppercorns.

Serve hot.

-o-

Orlo ordered the special: stewed pig feet not long from the stump, fresh trotters that distinguished Ralph's among the stevedores, laborers, barge men, pipefitters and railroaders who worked the length of Clinton Street.

Black and white, Bohunk, Polack and Kraut, men who had their choice of a half-dozen gin mills for a meal between shifts—Girlie Hoffman's, the Tip-Top, Aggie Silk's—chose Ralph's because they knew he butchered his own hog meat.

The girl who brought them a deep bowl of stew, half-a-loaf of black bread and tall glass of beer had served Orlo lunch or dinner or both two and three days a week since she was old enough to carry a tray; the heretofore predictable charge of hard-working Greeks who could not have children of their own.

Turned seventeen that morning, Leini remained forbidden to go anywhere alone except church and the library, both of which she turned into rocket ships. Aishe Cooper was twelve and dead, dead, dead and Orlo Pound, the junkman of Clinton Street was about to forfeit a lifetime friendship with Mr. and Mrs. Rafailidis.

"Thank you," he said, pushing his chair an inch away from the table to give her room, touching her hand with his fingertips as she wiped a spot where the stew had spilled.

Leini looked at him with surprise but did not move her hand. Orlo pressed her hand and the girl shifted her weight from one thin leg to the other.

"Yes?"

Orlo lowered his eyes and picked up a spoon. Looking into the stew—*a travers le miroir*—he followed shining drops of olive oil as they drifted across the surface of the broth. Knew what he was doing and did it anyway.

"Take a ride with me."

Leini mistook the tear in his eye for steam rising from the bowl. At age nine, she'd crossed the ocean. For the past four years, she'd gone through pre-determined paces—school, work, church, rinse and repeat—along a rough stretch of Baltimore waterfront with the knowledge that the Ralphs had bought her for a crate of sewing machines, the kind you worked with a treadle.

She had read enough to know that the answer to Orlo's question was not: "Where?"

Leini took a cloth-bound book from her dirty white apron. The novel was new, celebrated; the fallen Eve on the cover in a green robe, slumped beneath a tree without leaves. She'd finished it in the kitchen just before Orlo walked in, a fresh smudge of grease on the page where a bloody ear is passed from the ring into the stands.

Setting the book next to the bowl of pig feet, she said, "This has to go back to the library before noon tomorrow."

-o-

It took nearly three years for Orlo and Leini to lie down together for the first time; three years and a couple of hours for him to tell her what he'd seen before walking into Ralph's on the day that changed everything.

Until then, arguing with her on the balcony of a room he'd had built for them in Cabbage Alley—after the nap that followed their bath over a long and promising afternoon—no one but the dick from the pickpocket squad knew it was Orlo who'd found the girl. The papers attributed it to "a passerby."

"Impossible," said the detective the next day when he saw Orlo with a girl in his wagon who looked an awful lot like the one in the morgue.

"How so?" said Orlo, eager to ride off.

"The word *cooper* cannot be translated into gypsy English. It just can't," said the cop, rattling on in the way that know-it-all policemen often do: "All the stuff we use every day? Buckets? Tubs? Barrels? Them *Romas*—that's what they are you know, call 'em a gypsy is like callin' 'em a nigger—they don't have a word for any of it. Maybe that's why they're filthy."

Orlo tipped his hat and headed off to savor what remained of the half-hour Leini had lied to acquire; no need to explain the crude anthropology lecture because she'd decided to spend their first day together (if a half-hour can be construed as a day) listening.

Only to hear it blurted out in anger three years down the road, on the eve of a looming Depression no one knew was coming, a collapse that would trump every coming decision.

"Do you know why? Do you? Know why I *needed* to show you something bigger than a shithole Greek diner?"

But Leini wasn't putting up with it anymore. Come hell or Hoovervilles. She stamped her bare foot and played an ace.

"Your Baltimore is a good story . . ."

And it was. A pretty one, secret rooms walled and carpeted in new velvet, a skylight made of broken transoms that made up half of the roof, a bathtub built for two salvaged from a wrecked mansion uptown. Treasure from the debris of other people's lives. Just a story.

"Mine is real," she said, her hair still damp, the evening breeze giving her gooseflesh. "It's real and it hurts."

Leini asked him to run away with her, made the distinction between taking her and going with her. Said her toddler son was close by with a friend and she had $500 pinned inside of her dress.

"Tonight—now," she said. "Or I'm going back to Greece."

And he rewarded her with the Aishe Cooper story, cooking the details until they boiled.

Said he wasn't sure what was in the weeds but was certain it wasn't good, the horse skittish, leaping. That for an awful moment he thought of ignoring it. How the gypsy caravan was halfway to Cecil County by the time he found a cop.

Told her that when he walked into Ralph's he sat down to the best *les porcs pieds* of his life but felt like a cheap hunk of *braciole*.

"Not Sunday *braciole* up on Conkling Street," he said, attacking with the thing they loved best, chaste meals shared in confidence for thirty-six long months. "Peasant shit, Len. Wooden hammer playing 'Oh Susanna' on pork belly. Flattened me out good."

24

He'd never seen a casualty in the Great War as dead as the girl in the weeds behind the broom factory when the beauty of Clinton Street—Aishe Cooper in bloom—served him the Friday special.

Leini stamped her other foot and held her ground, leaving the coward Orlo Pound alone to watch the sun set behind a plaster Statue of Liberty high atop the Tutti Frutti ice cream factory.

-o-

It was destined that there would be an Orlo Pound from the time the English set up colonial shipyards along the Patapsco River.

That there existed a Leini was proved with a sales receipt for fourteen sewing machines the girl found in a button tin on the day she first got her period.

But if not for the fate of Aishe Cooper—ripped apart like a cantaloupe, cold butter tearing through a thin slice of soft bread—there never would have been an Orlo and Leini.

-o-

It is the last hours of the final day of the cursed year of 1963 in a far corner of Baltimore.

The coffee cup warming Leini's cold, aching hands was salvaged decades earlier by her lover from the ruins of the waterfront diner where she'd grown up, a simple lunchroom of chrome stools and wooden booths that burned to the ground on her wedding day.

A teenager married off in fear by those who knew better. No pregnancy to account for the haste. Orlo sat on his roof across from the reception, his back against the chimney of the Salvage House as he watched the blaze, the cause of everything across the street except the fire, though he'd be questioned about it often and at length.

The fire department pumped water onto the building straight from the harbor and into the harbor would go the embers. While hokey-men raked the rubble, Orlo did what he did best: rooted around in the debris for a shimmer or a glint.

And found an unblemished button tin, a soggy album of photographs from the old country and the coffee cup Leini used every night before going to bed.

-o-

Five minutes before the hour of witches, Leini stands in her kitchen across from the Ponca Street bus yard with a hot cup of Lipton and lemon and the head of a pig boiling in an iron pot on a back burner.

Its snout just above the film, water as clouded as the midnight sky across the Holy Land, the head had simmered for souse across a long and throbbing New Year's Eve.

Leini had bought the *tete* in the morning, bringing it home from Pratt Street on the bus in a canvas bag, unaware—as she would be for two days—that while she was haggling over the price, her husband was blowing his brains out in a seaman's tavern a quarter-mile from the market.

She left it covered and cooking on the stove with cloves and peppercorns and locked the door behind her, back downtown for a New Year's stroll to see once more how the other half lived, stopping at a bus stop bench to share a bag of late afternoon fruit with Orlo.

[The junkman had an orange in the pocket of his pea coat and they watched and smelled the citrus spray as he held the rind at arm's length and squeezed it in the cold.]

Arrived a bus whose doors would not open, or perhaps they wouldn't close, the same measure as the distance between the jangled eyes of Leini's illegitimate daughter. The moment before the bus spooked Leini in a way that was foreign to a woman who'd been within a mile of hell and back.

The day she'd found proof of purchase in the button tin—fourteen American sewing machines exchanged for one nine year-old Greek girl— and the afternoon of the suspicious fire that devoured her wedding reception seemed like the work of people playing with string.

But the fucked-up accordion door on the bus that stopped at the peeled orange bench (it flopped before her like a broken arm) seemed to come from below, rattling Leini as deeply as the death of her son at Normandy two decades before.

She refused Orlo's offer of a cab and made the rough walk home around the harbor rim, about four miles from the corner of Pratt & Light to the corner of Ponca & Eastern, and made a cup of tea without taking off her coat.

Alone now, or so she believes.

The tea and the *cochon* steamed the kitchen as though in harmony. Leini sips the last drop but does not rinse the cup and put it away, going to the china closet for the nub of a candle, half-a-thumb's worth of wax.

She lights the candle from the blue flame beneath the stew pot and the wick sparks in the transfer. Putting the candle in the cup, she sets the votive on the sill of a window that looks down into the backyard of the apartment she has long rented with a husband who is never home.

More than once: "I might as well be a widow . . ."

[And Orlo too much of a coward to bring her the title.]

In the window, Leini sees the candle's flicker and her face at fifty-four: once beautiful and now handsome, the drawn, creased reflection of a woman that anyone can see had once been beautiful and others still see.

The "Magic Chef" electric clock, its red and white dial built into the stove, hums into midnight with Leini—still in her coat, unable to shake the chill—grateful that the world and its party is on the outside.

Once all of the flesh separates from the skull, Leini will strain the broth and set it aside for stock, waiting 'til morning to pick through the meat for bones, chopping the ears as fine as rice before mixing everything with dark vinegar and sage.

Early tomorrow, as others ate black-eyed peas for luck, Leini would pick through the carrion of her own fortune while packing the devil into a mold of a baby pig, dusting the delicacy with paprika and slide it to the back of the fridge to gel.

Orlo liked his souse on black bread and Leini liked to watch him eat.

Tomorrow, just a shout away.

Tonight, regarding herself in the black mirror, Leini is enveloped by a humid perfume of onion and sea salt and accepts that she has nothing to show for being the smartest kid ever born in her village.

Neither poet nor teacher nor librarian.

Not much of anything but a hardened, stubborn gourmand with soured secrets in the street and a sandwich to spare.

She begins to address the woman in the glass—*"I forgive you . . ."*—when the window shatters and something unseen yanks her from the sleeves of her coat like a shot from a sling.

Tiny shards of glass pepper her face as Leini hits the wall, the candle beginning to burn her black peasant dress as the big hand joins the little hand and gunfire and rockets erupt outside.

Leini looks up and thinks she sees the scalded head of a pig dancing in the air, leering at her through empty eye sockets.

Struggling to her blue, swollen knees, her thin back pulsing as though broke, she crawls toward the stove as the pig slowly circles her like a rapist.

Holding onto the oven to raise herself—thinking there was a leak, she had to turn off the gas—Leini brings her brow above the burners as the empty stew pot flies off the stove and cracks her across the temple.

27

Blood leaks into her eyes and she falls in a puddle of gelatinous pork liquor.

"I'm frightened," she cries. "Yia-Yia . . . Orlo . . . Mama . . . I'm frightened."

The pig laughs and Leini wets herself, urinating into a pool of broth beneath her bottom, extinguishing the small fire burning her dress.

Did someone fire a gun through the window?

An idiot on the street hurl a cauldron at the moon?

She calls again for her grandmother, for Orlo, for her mother but as the blood drains from her head she calls on George, her husband and father of her dead soldier; George the drunk who sometimes hit her and today was George the alcoholic suicide.

Sometimes George saw things that weren't there. Swore that he did and Leini never believed him, used it as an excuse to spend more time with Orlo.

"George," cries Leini before passing out, all of the heat and steam sweeping into the night, the house like ice again, the pig skull—whistling with a bullet hole the size of a half-dollar—between her legs.

The phantom nibbles and is gone, down the sink to course through the bowels of Baltimore before seeping into a sleek bed of chrome and magnesium on the bottom of the Patapsco River.

JUNIE BUG

"This isn't a set . . . people live here . . ."
    —John Waters to Pia Zadora during the filming of *Crybaby*.

YOU THINK YOU know Baltimore because you own a television? Can recite Poe? Maybe a distant relative had some rare and awful thing cut out of their brain at Johns Hopkins Hospital and lived to eat the best crab cake of their life before flying home.

Who doesn't believe they are smarter than Pia Zadora?

This story is about the other Baltimore, a city that once made nearly every bottle cap in the world; a place where each narrow block has a tavern on one corner and a church at the other, promising that anything was possible in between.

This is the tale of a middle-aged miracle with a shovel in his hands named Junie Bug.

Junie was seven when he began digging for his father's body with broken garden tools, got started the same day he heard a homicide detective tell his grandmother—neither the cop nor Mom-Mom aware that the kid was listening under the table—that the body of Tilghman Reed, like so many others, had probably been dumped in Leakin Park.

Running out the back door with the cop still in the house, Junie raced a half-mile from his grandmother's house to cross into the thickets of the largest urban forest in the United States for the first time; two thousand unbroken acres of wild growth, meadows, streams, and abandoned mills; a jungle of untended woodland once known as Dead Run Valley.

When Junie crossed that threshold it began an ignorant kid's lifelong campaign to find a father he believed might only be hurt and not dead; his first cut of earth into a clump of weeds as tall as he was, brambles glinting in the sun from the cracked mirror of a broken make-up case.

Junie was a scrawny kid, but not for long; his shoulders, forearms and chest spreading with muscles as he dug hole after hole, thousands of holes. He drank lots of water and used sunscreen. Learned the apiarist's art by watching others, rescued a dog that saved his life more than once and cleared a secret spot big enough for a kitchen table, four chairs and china closet, all salvaged.

Hole after hole. Passed up cartoons on TV and neighborhood games and dug; dropped out of school and dug; forgot what day it was and fell into reveries so deep he forgot why he was digging. And kept digging.

Junie made maps in his school composition books as reminders of where he had already prospected; each hole—more wide than deep, the bad men of Baltimore never going to too much trouble to hide their work—marked in a series of hand-drawn maps drawn in ink and shaded with colored pencils.

The first books were his own, scribbled with spelling and math assignments [buy for one, sell for two] and then, after quitting school, he made maps in new ones from the drug store or barely used ones tossed out by kids who hated school the same way Junie did couldn't see a better way to go.

Junie became enlightened about things he otherwise would not have known, garnering enough knowledge from observation and cross-referencing what he saw at the public library to qualify for a degree in botany.

He saw people having sex but they never saw him. Watched a young girl give birth and leave the baby where it landed. He took the infant to the closest fire station and said he found it crying in a trash can.

He was in the park just about every day for three decades and up until today, almost no one noticed him.

Today—the solstice and his birthday, a boy named for the month of his arrival; the park a refuge from apprentice sociopaths who needed no more reason than a funny name to give a kid a daily beating—Junie had no more inkling of where his father might be than the week he disappeared.

On this midsummer's eve—the park quiet and cool in the early evening, the soil soft from two days of rain—Junie had on new work boots, a straw cowboy hat and sported a state-of-the-art metal detector, all of it (like his property taxes, his food, books and paints, his beekeeping equipment—paid for with things he found in the park, cleaned and repaired and sold at flea markets.

"Your daddy wore a gold cross around his neck, I gave it to him when he made the altar call," Mom-Mom had told Junie on her death bed. "Unless them evil hoppers yanked it from his neck, he's wearing it still."

Seven people were shot or murdered in Baltimore over the summer weekend in 1973 when Tilghman Reed left home to see a woman who was not Junie's mother and never came back. All but one either went to the hospital or left their bodies on the street as proof of misadventures that ranged from jealousy to a misunderstood remark. Junie's father did not.

In the thirty years that Junie had been digging, homicide in the United States had moved beyond a time when killers took pains to hide their victims to one in which dead men remained where they fell.

The West Baltimore Tilghmans—some carried it as a last name, some their first—were descendants by blood or property of the Revolutionary War planter for whom an island in the Chesapeake Bay is named. They were also kin to the founding members of the pioneering doo-wop singing group known as the Orioles.

For all the bird watching Junie did over the years (three stout jars of "Jay Bug's Baltimore Brown" honey traded for a fine pair of binoculars) he never saw the state bird in the park.

Like simple solutions and easy answers—Baltimore had the highest taxes and the most entrenched poverty in Maryland—the Oriole was virtually non-existent in the city which gave the bird its name.

"Well what do you know," said Junie, the detector putting out a staccato beep across an area fourteen feet long by about six feet wide. "What do we have here?"

Junie Bug Reed never wanted much—not in the way most people had lists of things they had to have to be happy—and in return the park provided all that he needed.

There, Junie sacrificed his life, found his life (which revealed itself as both a gift and invention) and worked to protect it as the ceaseless drama of Baltimore City rolled on with the seasons.

His humility was rewarded with a stubborn health—he never caught a cold and the allergies and asthma that once dogged him faded away— and an eccentric prosperity.

In the summer, he grew bell peppers and tomatoes, harvesting enough love apples to eat them on white toast [light mayo, a pinch of salt] through the end of September. Herbs he'd never known or tasted until middle-age were sold downtown at the farmers' market.

In fall, he picked wild berries. And when the ground was frozen, he collected pine cones and sold them to stores specializing in Christmas decorations and cut down one Scotch pine a year for the Baptist altar where his grandmother had worshipped.

For every meal Junie ate in Mom-Mom's kitchen, he ate three in the park; contemplating the things he might have done with the father denied him while compiling inventories of the things found, given away, and sold.

Though one room in his grandmother's house was dedicated to the few things he couldn't let go of—a museum without visitors—Junie didn't hold onto much.

Among the items coughed up by the park:

A shovel used to bury a man who was not his father. Junie put his weight on it for a month before it broke.

One hundred and twelve baseballs and three dozen footballs. He threw each of them as far as he could into the woods and eventually found them all again.

A small arsenal of pistols, which he rendered moot with a hammer before taking them to a scrapyard for a few bucks.

A tin lunchbox from the 1960s embossed with characters from the "Gunsmoke" television program. The pail belonged to Reginald Vernon Oates, a still-on-death-row janitor who lured young boys into the park to play cowboys and Indians. Who in this world plays cowboys and Indians anymore?

The body of an alcoholic Jewish housewife from the suburbs, a taxpayer who took a ride with the wrong guy after her sixth glass of wine. The disappearance of Mitzi Glick was news, trumping equally violent but more mundane mayhem.

$613 in loose change complemented by a brown paper bag with several hundred dollars of small bills held together with rubber bands that had rotted into the currency. He used the money to pay the taxes on his grandmother's house.

The skull of a plumber's apprentice who liked dope more than he liked paying for dope. Junie held on to it for a while. In weak moments, he thought it might be his father. In weaker moments, he believed it would speak to him.

"This is my beloved son with whom I am well pleased . . ."

It didn't. He gave the skull to a guy he knew—one of his few neighborhood peers to survive the corner—who taught high school science.

A strong box, empty, with a rusty but workable key in the lock. Junie kept the box in the map room at Mom-Mom's. Inside the box he preserved a copy of the police report of his father's disappearance.

Although Tilghman Reed was most likely dead, he was presumed so on circumstantial evidence and bad police work.

Someone said they had seen Reed take a bullet outside a sandwich shop near his girlfriend's house. Someone else said the wounded man— "It was Tillie, sure as I know Tillie it was Tillie"—was thrown in the back of a car headed west.

Fresh blood was soon found near the entrance to Leakin Park. A block away a car matching the one from the sandwich shop was set on fire. Two hours later, detectives were at Mom-Mom's house.

Junie Bug found everything in Leakin Park—sunshine on a rainy day, the devil beating his wife—but not someone to call his own.

"A one-sided love would break my heart," sang his great-uncle on the Orioles' big hit in the twilight before Elvis. "It's too soon to know . . ."

-o-

Junie knew his father wasn't alive. But he imagined, now and again— less so when digging than when he strolled the woods at magic hour—that he was.

"What," repeated Junie, kneeling down to scratch the soggy earth with his hands, "have we here?"

The harvest is rich, the workers are few and the native Susquehannock, who used the Dead Run to fish and bathe and trapped beaver in the woods, believed that midsummer's eve is the best night for gathering magical herbs.

Legend holds that on this night—which some years shadowed Junie's birthday and other years hit it on the head—a distant relative of the dew of the sea blooms. The person who tastes the dew becomes fluent in the language of the trees. If sprinkled across the forehead, future lovers come to visit in dreams.

And Junie always spent his birthday in the park.

"What is it?"

The woman had startled Junie as he poked around the area that had set off the loud, rapid beeps; on his hands and knees in a section of the park near the 19th century mansion that served as headquarters for the Friends of Leakin Park.

Junie had been lulled into a brown study by the silence, the dusk and his concentration on the somewhat enormous size of what lay beneath him.

"Well," he said, getting up slowly to meet the stranger. "Don't know yet."

"Well let's find out, Junie," said the woman.

He lingered on her face. Junie wasn't surprised that she knew his name; he was known in circles that frequented the park for charity races and the annual orchid festival. His blue-ribbon honey brought a measure of notoriety. Kids called him "The Shovel Man" and more than once he used the tool to defend himself.

Junie was given pause by the woman's light brown forehead, the curve of her lips and the set of her eyes. They reminded Junie of Gladys Knight and Gladys Knight reminded Junie of his mother when she was young.

Mama was easily found. Head south to the city line and turn off of Baltimore & Annapolis Boulevard through the stone gates of Mount Auburn cemetery, a neglected tangle every bit as stubborn as Leakin Park.

Push beyond the graves of world champion boxer Joe Gans, civil rights pioneer Lillie Mae Carroll Jackson, a gifted athlete named Tony Brown—stabbed by his girlfriend at nineteen, his plot marked by whitewashed piece of lumber lettered in black marker—and scores of runaway slaves.

Her headstone read: "April Lange Reed—Daughter / Mother / Friend—1949 to 1991."

April Reed died of a stroke—hypertension complicated by diabetes, depression and cigarettes; no need for Junie to look for his mother because he had buried her, paying for the funeral and a granite tombstone topped by an angel and the labor needed to clear away a path to her family's plot with money generated from the thing that generated everything in his life.

Junie hesitated and smiled, his mother come to life.

"Let's find out?"

The woman held Junie's gaze.

"Let's find out what's down there."

It would take a month of Junie Reed and Shirley Jackson working together to unearth the 1973 Ford Pinto Squire station wagon—fake wood paneling along the sides, 8-track tape player in the dash—that a cuckolded city worker had buried with a back hoe the same day his boss drove it from the dealership to the park.

The Pinto rolled out of the showroom just days before Junie's father disappeared, but a gold cross around the neck of Tillie Reed's skeleton was not in it.

The car was empty, packed by the God of things unseen with every misfortune spared Junie in the years he searched for his father.

JUDE THE IMPALER

A PERPETUAL NOVENA—every Wednesday—to the Patron Saint of Hopeless Causes.

Acts of faith in the City of Baltimore a few years after the King assassination riots; devotion and sacrifice and Ma Tazza dragging the kid she'd raised as a son to the St. Jude Shrine on the other side of town.

Sometimes Cherry wanted to go and sometimes he didn't. It all depended on what kind of trouble appealed to him when Novena night rolled around.

"Don't give me a hard time," barked Ma, three broken rosaries in the pocket of her raincoat, no way of knowing that what was hopeless today was a bowl of ice cream compared to what was coming.

"Get in the car, Cherry . . . last time I let you stay by yourself it cost me a fortune. Maybe I'll drop you at the game on the way home if it don't rain."

The Baltimore Orioles were playing the Detroit Tigers that night in a ballpark consecrated to America's war dead, one of whom had long been a bead on Ma's rosaries; baseball behind a wall of steel letters promising that TIME WILL NOT DIM THE GLORY OF THEIR DEEDS.

Cherry loved playing ball, music, girls, and taking things that belonged to other people and he was very good at all of them.

He'd taught himself to play piano by breaking into Protestant churches at night and on Sunday playing the organ at Our Lady of Pompei, where a woman with a baby grand in her living room gave him lessons until her husband complained that there was no milk for his coffee in the morning.

Ma pulled the old Chrysler away from the curb and Cherry punched the radio until something came out of the dashboard that moved.

"When you believe in things that you don't understand, then you suffer . . ."

-o-

Ma never told anyone but Jude what she prayed for, confusing perpetual with perennial, like a Lily of the Nile.

"Don't get lost," she said, going inside the shrine, where she would stay for at least an hour.

Cherry grabbed his baseball glove and a screwdriver from the back seat, knowing that a thirteen year-old strolling with a baseball glove was not likely to be taken for a car thief, and walked across the street to the Lexington Market.

Cruising the stalls of pork and fresh vegetables, the grilled sausage stand and soft shell crabs on beds of ice, Cherry pocketed five Chincoteague oysters and went back to the shrine and a drone of petitions muffled by wooden doors.

He'd enjoy an appetizer, pop an ignition with the screwdriver, take one of the girls he was seeing for a ride and be back at the shrine by the time Ma was walking out.

Squeezing the leather mitt around the biggest oyster, Cherry worked the shell with the screwdriver. It opened easily and he sucked it down. Same with number two. The third resisted, oyster juice making it hard to hold the shell in the mitt.

Gripping the mollusk in his bare hand, Cherry used the strength in his shoulders to force the screwdriver into the shell, where the wide, flat head of the tool slipped and ran clear through his palm.

Blood everywhere and nothing ever the same again.

His taste for oysters and knack for popping locks. Catching a fastball and the things Ma prayed for. Which hand he slipped beneath a woman's dress.

And the way he played piano, from this moment on unlike anyone who'd played it before.

-o-

Cherry stole the Apicella's still-smells-like-new Ford Granada a couple hours after the bars closed on Thanksgiving. It wasn't exactly theft. Mrs. Apicella left the keys on the seat and told the delinquent what time her husband would be stuffed with mashed potatoes and snoring like a cow. Cherry and Pete Kanaras threw their guitars in the back and aimed for Los Angeles.

So long East Baltimore.

Look out Tinseltown!

The car—milk white with a Landau roof of powder blue vinyl—was a lemon the moment it left Detroit. Instead of reporting it stolen—American flag decal on windshield, LIVE BETTER/WORK UNION bumper sticker, Maryland plates RMA 060—Mr. Apicella hit his wife so hard she cracked her head on the piano where the twelve year-old Cherry Triplett took his first formal music lessons.

"Man, Cherry," said Kanaras, lighting a joint before they were out of the neighborhood, a Johnny Winter 8-track into the ersatz wood grain of the dash. "You are *too* wild."

"Wild enough to meet Frank when we get there?"

"Maybe."

"Wild enough to try out for the Mothers?"

"Easy, superstar," said Kanaras, passing the joint to Cherry and staring out the window as they passed the pink and orange glow above the Bethlehem Steel plant in Sparrows Point.

Both of their fathers had worked the mills at one time or another. Kanaras's old man sat him down in high school and told him to "shit-can that colored music" and start working his way up the seniority ladder like a man. Mr. Kanaras would live to see his pension gutted before he died of mesothelioma.

Cherry, who could count the times he'd been with his father on one hand, took a deep hit of the reefer—white lung, black lung, green lung—and handed it back to Kanaras, who took it without looking.

"Easy does it, chief . . . it's a long road from the basement to the cut-out bin."

-o-

Kanaras, just on the other side of thirty, had paid his dues in band vans with many a psychotic drummer and narcissistic guitar player who never made a dent in the soundtrack to the universe. Not to mention lead singers who believed themselves the natural offspring of Sinbad the Sailor and an especially good looking Avon lady.

He'd been to L.A. a handful of times before Cherry and his talent barged into his life; had learned a few things, made a few friends and enjoyed himself.

Cherry, too cute to be a minute over seventeen, had never been west of Hagerstown or south of Annapolis. California was the long-held dream—he'd seen clips on TV, just a month or two ago, when Elton John sold out Dodger Stadium two nights in a row—the Golden State a verdant bowl as yearned-for as if his name were Joad, tear-ducts caked with dust.

"You never read *The Grapes of Wrath*?" said Kanaras, whose education was made up of never-returned library books and ear plugs.

"Christ, Cherry. Lester Bangs isn't the only motherfucker who ever had a thought."

Cherry threw another tape in the dash—he only relinquished the wheel after drifting into the other lane and sometimes not then—the idea of crossing state lines in the Apicella's new car nearly as exciting as fucking her in the middle of the day while other kids sat in class pretending they understood Steinbeck.

"Class is a pleasure when Jerome is not in it," the nuns at Pompei wrote to Cherry's grandmother, the rosary-rattling mother of his never-present-long-enough-to-be-missing father.

Kanaras shepherded the Gemini capsule from turn to turn (if Cherry didn't know McGuinn he sure wasn't going to know Gene Clark; what the prodigy's metal head could not fathom his fingers knew beyond thought) across the continent.

In this way, the unlikely friends (Kanaras rode shotgun because Cherry was the ticket, though Pete knew better than to say it aloud) made it from Baltimore to Bristol, Tennessee and from Bristol to Nashville, where Cherry couldn't give a shit about the Opry but insisted they drive by the 16th avenue Quonset Hut where Johnny Winter recorded "Second Winter," the fabled three-sided double album in which one side of the second LP was blank, more or less like Cherry's conscience.

Some two hundred miles west of Nashville they pulled up to the Music Gates on Highway 51.

Cherry made the trip to Memphis reluctantly, even bitched about it like a pussy until Kanaras said they would either pay their proper respects or the kid could make the rest of the trip by himself.

It was 1975 and the world had not yet come to an end.

Two short years and a dozen cross country trips later—trying to feed himself with a weekend gig at a strip mall ballet studio for ten year-olds—Cherry sat at an upright in an empty room and played "How Great Thou Art" for the soul of Judy Apicella just a few days after her husband hit her for the last time.

Armand Apicella went to jail and Cherry played the hymn in silence, remembering how Kanaras had to force him to rest his palms upon the scarred stone wall of the mansion, how Judy made him fried salami and cheese in the middle of day and how stupid he was.

Stupid—even innocent if you can call a born thief who learned to play music the way Cherry did innocent—with Congo Square in the rearview mirror and Los Angeles just a bee-line beyond the setting sun.

"Frank recorded his last album at the Roxy . . . let's go there first," said Cherry over scrambled eggs and pie at Chiriaco Summit, the Granada filthy and beginning to rattle, spider cracks in the windshield from stones flying from the back of a gravel truck.

"Nope," said Kanaras, who had no expectations beyond making it home in one piece while Cherry wanted everything, wanted it all.

"No?" said Cherry, all hopped up on Judy's diet pills, bits of egg on his cheeks and chin. "Penguins in Bondage! Pygmy Twilight!"

"Nope," said Kanaras, wiping his mouth with a napkin, wondering if he might toss the obnoxious goof into the desert before they made the last one hundred fifty miles. "We're going to Babe and Ricky's.

Cherry made a face, bit the inside of his mouth so hard it bled onto his lips.

"Who the fuck are Bay-bay and Ricky?"

-o-

The bottom dropped out of Cherry's mania somewhere outside of San Bernardino and he was dead asleep when Kanaras pulled up to 5259 Central Avenue, just off of East 53rd in South L.A., the sun white at noon like a thin slice of unsalted butter.

It was Christmas Eve and it was sixty-five degrees,

Pete punched Cherry in the arm—"wake up Jerry Lee"—shook out the cobwebs and went to see if anyone was inside the club at the ungodly hour of 12:20 p.m. on the day before Christmas. He peered in—all dark—and walked around to the back where Miss Laura Mae might be doing something in the kitchen.

"Wait here," said Kanaras. "We're gonna sleep in a bed tonight."

Cherry leaned against the Granada—in L.A. at last—and rubbed his eyes, the smog less oxides and volatile organics than a haze of desperation shot through with false hope and calorie-heavy promises.

Clouds of petitions—novenas to the gods of lucky breaks, if you can bounce high, bounce for her too; Fitzgerald haunting used bookshops not five miles from here in search of his own pulp before his death—a drone of petitions hovering between the sunshine and the most beautiful people Cherry had ever seen.

The warmth of the sun and even the poor people taking Christmas Eve naps on the sidewalk around Babe and Ricky's looked good.

[Every Christmas, Victoria Spivey used to tell Kanaras and the other white boys who grew up on lasagna and the Glimmer Twins—kids trying to soak up blues more profound than having the air conditioner in the car break down in August: "You gonna be cold and hungry when the hawk come down and the gigs dry up . . . best stock up on them canned goods."]

This year, instead of laying in stores, Kanaras took a chance on a neurotic piano player that women found irresistible, scraping his knuckles against the splintered wood of Babe and Ricky's back door while Cherry turned his face to the sky.

As they left Baltimore, Kanaras told him: "If you're a four in L.A., you're a nine in Baltimore."

Groovy, thought Cherry, tired of waiting for Kanaras to come back to the car, but what if you're already a nine in Baltimore?

And then hopped behind the wheel and drove off because if you're a thief in Baltimore—even if it's an honest mistake that all of your friend's belongings, including the way he makes his living, are in the car when you abandon him—you're a thief in Los Angeles.

-o-

Cherry fiddled around with the radio. When old man Apicella sprung for the 8-track, they threw in the FM, a tub of Jerry Vale and Al Martino tapes scattered in the back, a blanket of hamburger wrappers, dirty clothes and empty beer cans over their guitars. He manipulated the knob like he worked Judy Apicella's clitoris—"A Little Bit of Heaven, Ninety-Four Point Seven—KMET—Tweedle-Dee!"—until Neil Young's voice warbled out of the cheap dashboard speaker.

Young had just released Zuma—a guitar album, big chords—and as an elliptical solo spooled and unspooled and like neon suds circling a copper drain, Cherry pointed the Granada toward the ocean on the notion that he hadn't gone all the way if he didn't wade into the surf.

"And they built up with their bare hands," sang Neil as Cherry found the last of Judy's diet pills, washing them down with warm cola. "What we still can't do today . . ."

It was a straight shot down Slauson from South Central to Venice Beach, about fifteen miles (Cherry had a good sense of direction even if he didn't have much sense), and Zappa—can you fucking believe it, he shouted to the palm trees—FRANK!—following Neil on the radio, the smartest asshole in rock and roll working out seven minutes of intergalactic neon of his own.

The music sounded better out here—Frank and Neil not just on the radio but in the next canyon—and Cherry followed the only prescription he'd known since birth: If one is good, six is better.

He parked the car as close to the beach as possible, thought about taking his guitar but figured he'd wait until he made some friends before breaking it out. He took off his shoes and dove into the water in his ripped jeans and pink Robin Trower t-shirt.

SWIMMING ON CHRISTMAS EVE!

He spent more than an hour in the water—*"singing to an ocean, I can hear the ocean's roar . . ."*—his mind racing ten times faster than his heart as Laura Mae sat Kanaras down with a bowl of chili and put him on that night's bill.

"Help me get this raggedly-ass tree out the closet," she said, promising the guitarist that his no-good friend would surely show up in time. "We'll decorate it right on the stage."

Nine hours later, just before the birth of the Messiah in a manger— "What happened to all those Johnny Winter fans?" the Mad Albino would ask one day, "Did they die?"—Kanaras played rhythm on a borrowed guitar behind Don Preston and Bunk Gardner while Cherry stumbled around Venice Beach wondering if he should report a stolen car stolen.

Round and round in his brain, the last of the diet pills missing along with everything else: *"It serves me right to suffer . . . serves me right to be alone . . ."*

By looking for what didn't exist, he missed the prize twice: neither present for the past or the present; too young to have been at the Fillmore with Frank, too sick to enjoy what danced beyond his nose.

Staring at the black waves from the boardwalk, the night coming down with a chill that reminded him of home—nary a Rhonda or a Caroline in sight—Cherry cried into the darkness.

"You fucked me up Judy . . . you really fucked me up."

APR · 57 ·

THE KING OF A RAINY KINGDOM

EARLY THIS MORNING, some fifteen hours ago, Pio Talle was an unhappy man. And now, near the end of a long and rainy Valentine's Day in East Baltimore—idling in his pretty car at a pocked curb across from St. Wenceslaus Roman Catholic Church—he is something else.

Not happy, but no longer unhappy.

Engaged, occupied.

Focused.

Before dawn, Pio couldn't sleep. Every standing hour of his sixty-two years throbbed in his legs and he had to urinate, again. Getting up a third time, he stayed up, sitting at his kitchen table with a glass of water, making pro-and-con lists that went in circles.

What the hell am I going to do?

A few months earlier, he had succumbed to a Christmastime "take-it-easy, Pop—you've-earned-it" campaign by his wife and kids—and retired; persuaded against his wishes and instincts to close his watch repair and jewelry shop on Eastern Avenue, a cramped storefront haunted by the tolling of the Great Bolewicki Depression Clock.

[Few know that Pio's grandfather built that clock on commission back in 1931, the way the great bluesmen were given cab fare for a song. Nilo Talle? Never heard of him. It's Bolewicki they remember, the icebox king who put his name on it after Nilo bolted the clock to the front of his appliance store.]

Pio's reward for closing up shop felt like a bribe but it drove like a dream: a spanking new, 1992 Lincoln Town Car; a floating sofa in midnight blue with crushed velvet upholstery and all the extras that make up a "lifetime achievement award."

As though a life could be measured in sixty-two years, a little more than twelve months longer than his grandfather had lived with less to show for it. But he played along and tried not to let the family know how much he resented it; taking it easy ever since the bull and oyster roast where the car was driven right up to Pio's table inside the old fire hall.

"SURPRISE!"

The sucker-punch had been eating at him for months and now he had to find a Valentine for a woman he'd known since the tenth grade, the former Mary Theresa Driscoll from long-gone St. John the Evangelist way the hell across town where the bars were once covered with shamrocks and now sold you beer from behind bulletproof glass; a roller of pennies who for years could only talk about how she was going to Hawaii once her husband retired.

Treesey and all four of their kids—professionals long removed from the city, their tuitions paid one broken watch at a time—were on Pio's shit list.

Warm behind the wheel with a hot cup of coffee and the defroster blowing, Pio cruised Fleet Street on his way downtown. At the corner of an alley called Port Street, he saw a light on at Bonnie's Bar and stopped to get the breakfast he didn't have the stomach for at home.

"Christ, I'm glad to see you," said Bonnie, unlocking the door and then locking it again once he was in. "I was just thinking about you."

"No you weren't."

"The hell I wasn't. You ain't working no more, right?"

"That's what they tell me," said Pio, taking a stool and trading his empty paper cup for a fresh mug of coffee.

Not yet 7 a.m. and Bonnie was in high gear, all worked up about something she'd seen on television, Pio losing bits of what she was saying as she walked back and forth between the bar and a coal stove in her living quarters behind a curtain in the back.

"Miniature boxes . . ." she said. "Don't seem right to call 'em boxes, though . . . more like worlds behind glass. Guy named Puptent or Skipjack or something built 'em for a rich lady in Chicago. Bedrooms from palaces and big shot offices in skyscrapers. Kinda look like fish tanks."

"But without water," smiled Pio.

"Or fish, smartass," said Bonnie, returning from the kitchen with a fried egg sandwich on toast and a limp that Pio hadn't noticed before. "I was thinking that we should have something like that."

"Where?"

"Where the hell do you think? You're the only guy I know could do it."

"Never done anything like that before, Bon."

"And people said I'd never get to Graceland so I got in the car and drove myself," said Bonnie. "I got the nickels to pay for it and this is how I want to spend them."

Pio took a sip of coffee and closed his eyes for the split-second "thank you" he whispered over each meal, even Treesey's meatloaf, the weekly penance he paid for marrying an Irish woman.

And then he kept them closed a moment longer, seeing himself beneath his Nanootz's great clock, a marvel with crystal hands of water that bubbled pink and blue, telling the time with the encouragement that "it's not too late . . ."

Pio had never been able to grasp that inspiration, forever a little kid shrinking below the clock and now, out of work, no longer able to deny that he'd sat in the store longer than he ever expected or wanted to in order to ignore the small mountain of potential he'd been carrying around since grade school.

Pio opened his eyes.

"*We* ought to have one?"

Bonnie slapped the bar: "Right here!"

Pio grabbed his sandwich and took a bite before she could slap the bar again, about to tell her to take it easy when he remembered that he didn't say that to anyone anymore. Bonnie walked over to a canvas tarp hanging where a wall used to be, the one that separated the bar from the house next door before the old lady there croaked and Bonnie bought the place from her kids.

Lifting the tarp as Pio swiveled on his stool to watch, she said: "Here's where you come in."

Pio wiped his mouth with a napkin—"Good sandwich, Bon"—threw it on the bar with a couple of bucks and got up to leave.

"Hear me out," she said, rain beading across the diamond shaped window in the door. "Where the hell you going anyway? It's rainin' cats."

She started explaining what she wanted—a full wall of glass boxes that would run ceiling-to-floor, the first phase of her plan to turn Miss Bonnie's Elvis Grotto, just a neighborhood gin mill with pictures of the King instead of Johnny Unitas, into a museum she'd decided would survive her.

In the boxes, Bonnie wanted a neighborhood guy named Albert, who dyed his sideburns black, called himself "Al-Vis," and danced on her bar for money before he got religion and went to nursing school; Alvarez, the long-haired reporter who put her name in the paper more times than the local councilman got ink; the legendary Virginia Baker, queen of the

49

playgrounds who warned generations of grimy-faced hoodles that if something wasn't decent and it wasn't right they should stay the hell away from it.

And how putting the making-ends-meet history of the corner of Fleet and Port behind glass—from the days of clipper ships on through her grandmother's split pea and ham soup for can factory workers to that very morning—wasn't only right, it was necessary.

"Just as important as anything that ever went on anywhere," she said, dropping the tarp and walking back to Pio, who was about to file her yakety-yak in the same cabinet he'd assigned her when they were kids and his grandfather stopped in for a beer while sharpening the knife that carved the ever-present ham.

Under N for nonsense.

Pio sore at the people he loved most, unable to answer the simplest of questions.

"Where the hell am I going?" he thought, seeing Bonnie wave her arms around but no longer hearing her, attuned to the cracks in the sidewalk where her absurdities grew like weeds, pilgrim seed strong enough to splinter concrete.

"Okay," he said.

"Okay?"

"I'll do it."

"Good," said Bonnie, hiding her surprise and going for her purse. "How much you gonna need to get started?"

"I'll let you know," said Pio.

"You do that," she said, walking him out to his car with an oversized mortician's umbrella, the kind they used to cover families at graveside downpours, a left-behind from a regular who liked to get half-a-load-on between funerals.

"Let's show'em," said Bonnie. "Let's knock'em dead."

-o-

A floating sofa
Cushions behind moving glass
Baltimore a noir

-o-

Pio drove from Bonnie's to the Pratt library downtown and was first in line when it opened. He walked past displays of "Love Story" and tributes to St. Valentine—beaten with clubs in the Third Century and beheaded—and found a small shelf of books devoted to the work of

50

Eugene Kupjack, reading that the master was a jeweler's son who'd started making miniature rooms right about the time Pio was walking the streets with his grandfather.

[None of Pio's kids cared about keeping the family store running. He'd still be there if one of them had wanted to stand with him at the bench. And surely they owed him the privilege of seeing if any of the grandchildren wanted to learn once they were old enough.]

Pio paged through a lush book of Kupjack's work and paused at a gatefold of royal bedchambers. Staring into folds of pleated silk, he remembered how his Nanootz would slow down at certain alleys on certain days. If there was a lone housedress hanging on the right clothesline on the right day, the wily *arrotino* knew the coast was clear and Pio would get a treat to watch the grinding wheel and tell anyone who asked to come back in a little while.

[Why an entire lifetime to connect those dots? Pio had never been unfaithful to Treesey, though he'd wanted to choke her a few times. How many snowballs and candy apples and sometimes a bouncing ball to keep him content on the curb—"Junior, watch'a da wheel for a kupple mih-nootz" while Nanootz ducked around a corner to sharpen something behind a window shade?]

Kupjack, the book said, had found greatness by combining uncommon craftsmanship with theatrical suggestion.

On his way out of the library—rain hard against the plate glass windows, hard in the face of the Basilica of the Assumption across the street—Pio passed the gift shop and bought Treesey a canvas tote bag for the picture books she brought home about Hawaii and Cancun and, once, an illustrated, five-volume encyclopedia about the history and culture of the Fiji islanders.

Back home, warm and dry in clean clothes, he tried to share his excitement about the project over dinner with his wife, only to find himself alone when Treesey put down her napkin and went to bed, an uneaten pork chop up against still warm mashed potatoes on her plate.

-o-

The rain did not let up. Pio cleared the table, did the dishes, waited for Treesey to fall asleep and tried to watch a little television to calm himself down before heading out again, the weather just as nasty as it had been all day as he guided the Lincoln along the exact route his grandfather walked to make a pocketful of change and a meat cleaver sing.

In a short two miles, the not quite happy but no longer unhappy Pio Talle drove from a neighborhood struggling to hold on to one in a free fall; his belly full, as the car idled at the corner of North Collington and Ashland streets, with his pork chop and Treesey's pork chop and the one she'd set aside for the day after tomorrow; not a half hour left in February 14, 1992.

Rain started to freeze in the shadows of St. Wenceslaus Church, whose chipped cornerstone said it had been built in 1904 but not that the corner had been the kingdom of Robert the Shoeshine Boy back when just being Catholic was not enough to attend St. Wenceslaus school. You had to be Bohemian and Catholic.

Pio's blood ran quick as he surveyed the slum; hot and effervescent in a way it hadn't for years, the Great Bolewicki Depression Clock pushing toward midnight in the bleeding heart of the Holy Land.

In another day, from a bed at Johns Hopkins Hospital just a couple blocks away, Pio would swear that he'd heard a sundial chime on a rainy day: "It's not too late to do something great . . ."

Ill winds blew through rows of houses without windows as Pio inspected the ruins of Oktavec's grocery, its front door covered with gray, splintered plywood stenciled with a number to call if an animal were trapped inside; his gaze narrowing to a set of filthy marble steps in front of the abandoned store.

Theatrical suggestion?

Sometimes art is the lie that tells the truth. And sometimes it's just a lie.

Tiny window screens painted with white swans and blue ponds in miniature houses as the horror trickled toward the block where you'd lived all your life; the result, and not the cause though people smarter than Pio were too mean to accept it and most people in Baltimore were not as smart as him.

"The world," his grandfather liked to say, "she's a run right on time."

Not a timepiece in the universe to contradict it and nothing wrong with old man Oktavec's steps that a hammer and chisel and a bushel-and-a-peck of make-believe couldn't fix, Pio determined to whittle the marble whale down to a row of gleaming pearls in front of cared-for rowhouses of orange and red brick.

It would be 1936 and he would be six years-old again, shielding his eyes against the July sun as he sat on this very corner with a grape snowball, Nanootz belting back schnapps with one of his few equals:

William Oktavec, the man who invented the painted window screens of Baltimore; Pio right here when war broke out that summer in Spain—war all corpses and latrines—with everybody blaming everybody else, just like they always do.

From a window in the old Wenceslaus convent, Pio saw a nun in a white smock and even in the dark, he knew it was trimmed in blue; East Baltimore gone to shit so bad that Mother Teresa declared it enough of a Calcutta to start an AIDS hospice with the Sisters of Mercy. The nun closed the window and drew the blinds closed.

A few of the old families were still around; widows mostly, women some twenty years older than Pio who'd once given his grandfather many a knife to sharpen and maybe something else, maybe not; pensioners hemmed in not so much by poverty as hearts broken in ways that paralyzed them. You might call it love.

Mary Livanec had long outlived her police detective husband, a man assigned to guard the Beatles at the Holiday Inn when they played the Civic Center in 1964. A decade after Detective Livanec's death (forty years of honorable service and all you're remembered for is telling Ringo which door to use), a reporter called on Mrs. Livanec after a particularly mundane atrocity and asked her if she was going to stay.

"Only way I'm leaving," she barked, "is down the front steps of St. Wenceslaus in a box."

How to harness such loyalty in a country where the only static population is in the boneyard and every new subdivision of farmland has a street called New Cut Boulevard?

Pio took a long sip of coffee, watched a rat run across the frozen street and put in a Billie Holiday tape, an old favorite he'd found in a drawer of tweezers and loupes while cleaning out the shop. His musician friends had turned him onto Billie when everybody else was listening to Jerry Vale.

Turning up the volume, Pio listened to snatches of conversations from concerts spliced between the songs, Billie telling the audience how she lugged buckets of water all over Baltimore to scrub marble steps for nickels, how she had to bring every penny home to her mother or risk a beating, how she "hated those goddamn steps . . ."

It made him think of a woman whose obituary he'd just read in the paper: eighty-four year-old Agnes Jaskowski, a retired stringbean snipper from the waterfront packing houses who remembered when Monument Street was a dirt road.

The New World Order had swept Aggie's block a couple of years ago and no doubt hastened her death, neighbors hugging each other and crying as they packed up to leave but not pissed-off Jaskowski, who'd lost two fingers in the snipping machine and, smoking on a break with the other cannery ladies a half-century ago, had jumped in the harbor at the foot of Fell Street to save a kid from drowning.

Not long before Pio retired, Agnes brought in a silver pocket watch—her grandfather's, inscribed in Polish—to be fixed. Nobody in her family wanted it; her kids were too busy planning an intervention to force her out of the house she'd been born in to care about a watch. Agnes was betting that if she had it repaired, it would keep time long after she was gone and she was right.

Bending Pio's ear—he didn't have the nerve to tell her he was closing up for good, didn't want to hear her accuse him of running like everybody else—Agnes banged her cane against the floor and raised hell about a neighborhood gone to hell in a single lifetime.

Sometimes she'd claim that she'd seen it coming for years—"What do you expect after you give'em their rights?"—and other days she'd blame the politicians and say money changed hands and the fix was in going all the way back to Truman. And here she was talking about how some goddamn drunk had crashed into her immaculate marble steps and ruined them.

"Just going to leave 'em busted up. Won't be running them animals off the steps all day long anymore," she said. "Won't be spending half the goddamn day sweeping up their trash."

Pio put down the piece he'd been working on and was glad he didn't have any other customers, recalling the humiliations his grandfather had suffered on the street (the old man carried a pistol, but Pio never knew it) and how once, after a bad scene with a man named Smith ranting about wops and guineas putting their greasy hands where they didn't belong, his grandfather told him that there was clean anger and dirty anger and one you were supposed to let out like steam from a boiler and the other you didn't want to know because it stuck to your insides like roofing tar.

Sorry the moment the words left his mouth, Pio baited the old Polack.

"What happened to Monument Street, Ag?"

And Aggie Jaskowski, who might be taken for anyone's kindly, eight-fingered grandmother on the street, looked at him like he was an idiot and said: "Niggers."

-o-

The hole that Bonnie had paid a couple of stevedores to make in the wall was big enough for a hundred fish tanks.

But if she wanted one of that goof Al-Vis shaking his fat ass in a white suit on top of the bar while busted onions put dollars in his drawers, she'd have to find somebody else.

The box Pio would build—from the stained glass of broken transoms and steps that had waited fifty-five years for his return—would make sense.

The canvas library bag that Treesey had thrown across the room on her way to bed was filled with tools and Pio stepped into the freezing night with them like an assassin. He grabbed a loading dock dolly from the trunk; nary a pigeon to peck French fries crushed and frozen to the asphalt, the night dark and cold with muffled screams, cackles—was that a television or someone's evil stepmother?—as a police helicopter flew by, its spotlight dark.

"Jesus," said Pio approaching Oktavec's, his fist just below the head of a sledge hammer, words flat against the cold as he shuffled on a thin sheet of ice, strands of light seeping out from the few houses not yet falling in upon themselves.

"Jesus Christ," he said, swinging the hammer against the top step, aiming for a chip made by a long-ago bullet; rearing back to strike again, and then again, the third smash cracking the step into unequal thirds like a rotted tooth.

Pio knelt down for the biggest chunk, about one hundred twenty pounds worth; his breath coming hard and his nose running raw, grunting as he shoved and shimmied the slab toward the rusting dolly.

[As a boy walking through Locust Point with his grandfather, he'd once watched a German stevedore lift an entire block of marble from a set of steps to win a drinking bet. No one gambled on men who pried the backs off of wristwatches.]

Pio rolled the slab onto the dolly and began inching it toward the curb, hoping that the wheels didn't snap. Across the street, a cop in a cruiser with his lights off watched Pio the way a kid might watch dogs fuck in the middle of the day.

He bent down to lift the marble into the trunk; lips cracked and bleeding as he stood with the slab, sinews stretching from his shoulders to the small of his back, straining the distance between hubris and stupidity and . . .

"HOLD IT POPS!"

Pio jerked and fell backward, dropping the marble against the lip of the trunk , which would never close properly again. The heavy stone broke a taillight, hit the bumper and landed on his left foot, breaking three toes. Pio doubled over in agony, his intestines pushing through tears in his stomach, fire spreading from his gut down through his groin like 10,000 shards of hot glass, down from his scrotum to his knees and into his calves; a double, inguinal hernia popping just above his testicles.

Officer U. Lima, six years in the United States and four months on the force, jogged across the street and knelt beside Pio, the older man slumped and moaning against the Lincoln, knees knocking in the cold.

"What the fuck, mister?"

This the fuck: had Pio asked anyone who knew what they were doing, he'd have learned that the way to depict masonry in miniature was to paint heavy paper to look like stone.

Lima clicked on his radio to call for an ambulance and Pio begged him not to.

"No," he said between gasps. "Please, no."

Shining a light across Pio's ashen face, Lima asked, for himself and not anyone else, hoping to understand something he'd never seen before: "What are you doing?"

Delirious with pain, Pio thought he was telling the cop about Nanootz and the clock that had shamed him every hour on the hour for as long as he could remember; how his grandfather used to preach that every man was born to "do somethin' they ain't never got'em in this world," how it was already the bottom of the eighth and he had to get a hit before the game was over.

"I'm saving it," he said.

"Saving it?"

Pio nodded and asked the cop to help him get the slab in the trunk.

"I'd be taking care of this car if I were you," said Lima, picking up the hunk of marble and dropping it in the trunk. "Do you know where you are?"

Pio was silent.

About to call again for a medic, the cop demanded: "Can you tell me where you are?"

"I think so," said Pio.

A report of a shooting on the next block hit Lima's radio and by the time he'd gotten Pio behind the wheel, a police chopper was lighting up the area like a night game at Camden Yards, the noise deafening as Pio tried to thank the cop, who was already squealing off in a swirl of blue.

As Pio pulled away from the curb, running over the dolly and puncturing a tire, a bottle sailed down and hit the Lincoln in the center of the windshield, cracks spreading across the length of it like crystal veins.

GRANADA IN THE DRINK

PIO TALLE WAS walking fast through Patterson Park, trying to get home before swift, dark clouds delivered a summer thunderstorm. He spotted Falooch in a crowd by the boat lake and walked faster.

"Pio . . . hey Pee."

The city had drained the lake for repairs and found a car on the bottom. When the car was pulled up, the trunk popped open. In the trunk: a body, both pretzel and raisin.

Pio nodded without breaking stride and Falooch grabbed his arm.

"You're not going to believe this one, Pee."

For Christ's sake, thought Pio.

Falooch Rosario was a bore on mundane subjects like the weather: "Cats and dogs, pal, gonna come down cats and dogs . . ."

Baseball: "Those bums might never win another game . . ."

And the time of day: "Later than you think . . ."

When there was real news—like the discovery of a brand new Ford Granada sunk in the muck of the Patterson Park boat lake with a body in the trunk—*il vecchio barbiere* was insufferable.

The lakebed was foul in the August heat and the winds of the coming storm carried the stench into open windows of rowhouses ringing the park, windows closing one by one as black clouds rolled in from the harbor.

Falooch leaned in, his breath atrocious: "It's my sister's car. Missing since the day she drove it home. Remember?"

Antoinette Tukulski had driven her 1977, powder blue Granada with power windows and 8-track stereo—the salesman threw in an Al Martino tape to close the deal—home from the dealer fifteen years ago. She'd bought it with money her husband didn't know about and it disappeared that very night.

And while the police looked for it, they didn't look too hard. It wouldn't have mattered if they did.

"... 'member Pee?"

Pio didn't. But he'd never forget how Antoinette would disappear when they were playing tin can and red line and stickball in the street and some of the boys would follow; how she let them touch her in Chink Alley for loose change.

The alley was a short stretch of cobblestone off the corner of East Pratt and Chapel streets, not far from where Falooch now had Pio trapped.

Its spooky legends prompted all manner of dares and childish bravery simply because a Chinese family—the only one in a neighborhood of Italians and Poles, Germans and hillbillies, a clan seemingly comprised entirely of old people—lived at the end of the narrow lane.

They sat in the front window and emptied stew pots of boiling water into the gutter. Big kids told little kids that the oldest of the old was "way more than a hundred" and kept a meat cleaver up her sleeve.

Everybody ran through that alley as fast as they could, some with their eyes shut and some collecting nickel bets. But Antoinette and her full and getting fuller twelve year-old stood still and made dimes—quarters if you wanted to go below the equator, quarters.

Pio had followed her into the alley more than once, the memories both thrilling and shameful enough that fifty years later he went out of his way to attend her funeral.

"Long time ago," said Pio, staring beyond Falooch to a man perspiring in a brown suit. He looked like a failed salesman; sweat dripping from his brow to a notebook, shaking his pen and wiping the page.

"Police," said Falooch. "They're looking for my nephew."

"Which one?"

Like most everyone who dealt with Falooch—from his dead wife, to whom he spoke every morning to three generations of men who'd sat in his barber chair—Pio wasn't listening.

[Back when they were both working and business was slow, Pio would see Falooch crossing Eastern Avenue toward his watch repair shop and groan; praying that a customer or the mailman or even a loser hustling broken vacuum cleaners would come by so he could excuse himself.]

"The son of my sister who owned the car," said Falooch, perturbed. "Tookie."

"The one on dope?"

"He straightened himself out."

Pio turned to go and Falooch grabbed his arm. He was always touching people—hand on the shoulder, holding a shake too long—as though he couldn't speak unless his hands were on you.

"Want to know who was in the trunk?"

"Sure."

"They don't know."

And that was why Pio Talle—grandson of the man who built the Great Bolewicki Depression Clock, a timepiece that reminded people not that it was later than they thought but there was still time if you hurried—ignored his old friend.

Falooch was a goof.

Yet today, the gods had ordained that the Orioles would lose another game; Falooch's nephew would not escape before the cops showed up; and cats and dogs would fall from the sky in numbers not seen in a century.

"Gotta go," said Pio, pushing past and sure to be late for dinner, his wife hurrying a half-mile away to bring in wash from the line, talking to herself with a clothespin between her lips.

"What the hell does he do all day?" she said, forgetting to turn down the flame beneath the skillet before running out to grab the clothes, the first drop of rain splashing her forehead. "Running the streets all day like a kid."

Before Falooch could grab Pio again, a reporter shoved a microphone in the barber's face and the watchmaker escaped, jogging past a stone wall carved with the head of a bull, water spouting from its flared snout.

Falooch spoke first.

"They got water ballet up the pool later on."

"What?"

"Might be a good story for you."

"The police are saying you know who the car belongs to."

"It's my sister's."

"What's her name?"

"She's dead."

"Did you recognize the body in the trunk?"

"Nothing left to recognize."

Two more TV trucks pulled up in time to film the coroner's staff shake the body into a plastic bag and then—KA-BOOM!—cameramen hit the ground and turned their lenses on Eastern Avenue. The street had exploded with a water main break.

A sinkhole opened in the asphalt. Cars parked on both sides began floating away. Pio saw an old woman with a shopping bag in each hand swept down the gutter.

Water shot thirty feet in the air—a geyser in the city—and the sky split open.

Screams and sirens; roofs leaking, basements flooding, kids laughing.

Water went up and water came down in equal measure at the corner of Eastern and Montford on a late summer day deep in the bleeding heart of the Holy Land.

"Thar she blows!" cried Falooch.

Half the crowd ran away from the gushing main and the other ran toward it, the Granada crime scene abandoned in the chaos. Falooch corralled Pio one last time.

The coroner's crew hurried the gurney over the soggy lawn, their shoes sinking into mud to the ankle. Police blocked off the Avenue, directing traffic into the neighborhood, cars backed up at every stop sign, windshield wipers useless.

It would take the Orioles an extra three hours to lose that night because of the rain delay. And because the storm had bypassed the counties south of town, Tookie didn't need an umbrella to slide into the back of a police cruiser.

A few blocks up the Avenue, the Great Bolewicki Depression Clock tolled: "It's not too late to play your ace . . ."

Falooch asked: "Do you think I'm a good person?"

Rain spilled off the old barber's Roman nose like a water slide.

"Are you a good person?"

"Yeah."

Grabbing a cop's gun and shooting Falooch would be too easy. Pio wanted to get his hands around his throat. Stunned—rain soaking them as surely as the poor soul in the Granada was drenched to the bone—Pio stared into the simpleton's eyes.

He remembered that Falooch knew what his sister was up to in the alley when they were kids. And he knew that she gave the money to Falooch, who gave it to his father, saying he'd earned it doing odd jobs.

In the dark circles beneath Falooch's eyes he saw Antoinette beyond the alley, graduating from quarters to dollars—many hundreds of dollars downtown on the Block—until a stevedore named Tukulski proposed and they moved way out to Elkridge where no one knew them.

Soaked to his balls, Pio screamed into the roar of the storm: "WHAT KIND OF STUPID FUCKING QUESTION IS THAT, FRANCIS?"

Falooch looked Pio in the eye.

"I know who was in the trunk," he said. "I know everything."

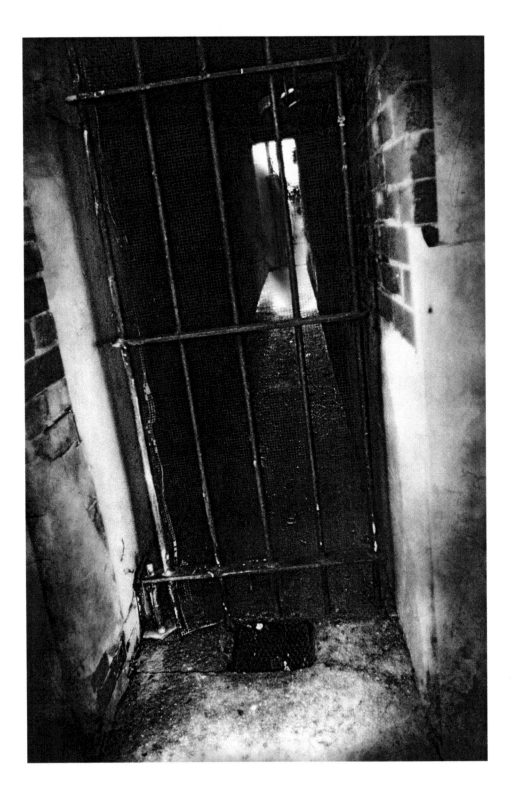

AN ALLEY MOST NARROW

THE WATERMAN'S WIDOW sat on a milk crate sizing crabs by hand, bushel baskets by her brown and purple knees as she talked about a Baltimore childhood during the Second World War, more money to be made at Sparrows Point than working the waters of Crisfield.

"Back around the other way now," she said, waiting for the truck that took the day's catch to the city that left its mark on her decades earlier.

It was her mother, she said, who had the good wartime job as a tin flopper at Bethlehem Steel; her mother who stitched new outfits for the same baby doll every year; her mother who only asked that her husband get a tree for the rowhouse they rented where Decker Avenue hit Boston Street, the block torn down years later for a highway that was never built.

"Mom did it all," said the woman. "You couldn't depend on my father for anything."

-o-

Only a drunk would wander from one end of town to the other for a Christmas tree when you could buy a hundred of them right around the corner.

When the whistle blew at the Baylis Street broom factory, the boss called everyone to the loading dock for the traditional turkey, a fifth of Maryland Rye, thanks for a job well done and have yourself a very merry.

Walter Waddell walked away with the $16 weekly pay he got for painting broom handles, the frozen bird under his left arm and his fist tight around the bottle.

"Who's bringing home the bacon tonight?" laughed Walter as he passed Whitey Stefan's saloon. "The kid is gonna call me Sanny Claus."

Beyond the neon and fake snow, Walter spied an old friend and ducked in for a quick one, two at the most. He took a stool by the door, set the bird and his bottle on the bar and ordered beer for himself and Willie Jones, a neighborhood saloon singer with a soft spot for Jolson.

"By the time the old lady gets off the streetcar, I'll have the tree up, turkey coming out of the oven and the girl cleaned up for dinner," said Walter as a toy train emerged from a cardboard tunnel, blew its whistle and snaked through rows of sparkling bottles.

"Then you better get moving," said Willie, finishing his beer. "I'm headed over Silks to do a couple numbers."

"One more and I'll walk you down," said Walter, motioning for the barmaid to set them up. "Aggie Silk makes a good pea soup."

On the other side of the world, Allied troops trudged across the Marshall Islands. Across the harbor in Fairfield, Bethlehem Steel launched its 300th Liberty Ship of the year, the Arunah S. Abell.

Walter quaffed a quick one and followed Willie outside, uncorking the rye on the sidewalk to share a belt with his caroling friend and leaning against a stack of tires in front of Tolan's garage to watch the red-headed Welshman amble down the street singing, "God rest ye merry gentlemen . . ."

-o-

By the time the sun was down, the temperature had dropped to fifteen degrees and Walter was headed over Edison Highway on a streetcar, offering his bottle to anyone who crossed his path.

Back at Stefan's, no one could remember who'd left a turkey at the end of the bar so Whitey's wife threw it in the oven and made sandwiches for everyone who didn't have anything better to do on Christmas Eve than sit in a gin mill.

One went to a nine year-old girl who popped in to ask, after scanning the crowd, if Walter Waddell had been there. No one was sure, but hey kid, take a bag of chips and some sodie pop to go with that sandwich.

By the time the girl lay in bed hoping there'd be a new dress for the doll sitting where the tree was supposed to be—wondering how a sugar plum was different from a regular plum to keep from wondering whether her father would show up before Santa did—Walter was arguing with an elderly black man selling trees outside the 29th street tinderbox known as Oriole Park.

"Three dollars," said the man, switching off a string of lights.

"It's after midnight," said Walter, knowing the time but unable to account for its passage between the last drop of rye and a boilermaker a moment ago at a tavern across the street. "You ain't gonna sell it now."

"Ain't gonna give it away neither," said the man, locking the gate. "Why'd you wait so long?"

"You know," said Walter, fishing out his last dollar and pushing it through chicken wire with frozen fingers. "It sneaks up on you."

The man grabbed the closest tree and with a strength that made Walter glad he hadn't pushed his luck, heaved it over the fence.

"Now go on home, mister."

-o-

A sharp wind blew off the harbor, across empty streets and through Walter's pants in the hours it took him to walk from 29th and Greenmount to 1214 South Decker Avenue with a six-foot Scotch pine over his shoulder.

Sweat froze across his brow and pine needles stabbed his back and neck, sobering Walter up enough to realize that he'd done it again.

"She's gonna mop the floor with me," he mumbled, hoping to sneak in the back door without waking anyone.

Reaching the long, narrow "airy-way" that divided his house from the one next to it, Walter made for the nickel gray light of Christmas morning.

Unlatching the gate, he dropped the tree and slumped against the cinderblock wall, hoping, just before passing out, that his wife hadn't locked the storm door.

She stood in the window above his head, having walked the floors all night after borrowing an artificial tree from a neighbor, their daughter gripping the sill with her nose against the cold glass.

"Okay," she said, pulling her housecoat around her. "Go down and let him in."

ROOM 829

"Wolfe unearthed the Earth . . ."
—John Mason Rudolph, schizophrenic poet

IT WAS STANLEY Bard who told me that Thomas Wolfe lived in Room 829 of the Chelsea Hotel.

Bard was the manager of the Chelsea at the time, about a decade ago, before a corporation pushed him out. Stanley's father—David Bard [1905-to-1964]—had been part owner of the Chelsea and had known Wolfe.

The great writer, who died before turning 40 while undergoing brain surgery in 1938 at Johns Hopkins, lived at the Manhattan landmark while working on "The Web and the Rock," his follow-up to the immortal "Look Homeward, Angel."

"We had a bellhop here back then named Pernell Kennedy, a confidante of the guests who took care of them personally," said Bard. "After Wolfe died, there was still a pair of his shoes left in the room. Pernell put them in the basement and forgot about them."

-o-

In the first Spring of this new century, I rented Room 829 for an assignation with a woman I hadn't seen for a long time. It was not Wolfe that attracted us; the mojo magnet is never literature but the stuff that makes it possible. A shared love of Tom and his kin through the age— Twain, Richard Yates, Tom Nugent—connected us.

Before the meticulously planned rendezvous at the Chelsea, I'd only touched her twice: Once underwater at a surprise 30th birthday thrown by her husband; a quick squeeze of her foot as she swam by.

And once in the vestibule of St. Alphonsus church at the corner of Saratoga and Park, around the corner from what long ago had been Baltimore's Chinatown.

She stood just outside the sanctuary—built in 1845 and Oz-like in its vaulted columns; a shrine where old school Communicants regularly participate in the Latin Mass—as pregnant as a woman can be without giving birth.

The church was a stop on one of our chaste strolls around Baltimore, early afternoons where we'd find a bench on the street and I'd read her early drafts of my fledgling fiction. For some reason, she had a Magic 8 Ball in her bag, the classic kiddie oracle the size and shape of a duckpin bowling bowl.

You ask the ball a question, turn it over and through a small window, an answer appears upon which you can chart your fate.

I held the toy in my left hand with my right on the pulsing globe spinning inside her belly and asked a question unspoken. As she smiled, I turned the ball over and received this answer:

You may rely on it.

-o-

After that, except for a quick glance at the funeral of a friend, we did not see one another for nearly a decade. Her life took her away from Crabtown while mine burrowed deeper into all the zip codes east of President Street.

One day, a letter arrived on Macon Street—21224—saying how often she had thought of the stories I'd read to her way back when; tales of an artist who cuts a hole in his grandfather's roof, the Virgin Ruthie arguing with an angel in a hot air balloon above Patterson Park, Orlo and Leini living in Eden.

The letter said she was happy to discover that the stories had found their way to print and that she was finally taking a chance with her own.

I wrote back. She wrote back. Valentine's Day came and went. Then Easter. Early May arrived with a plan: meet me at the corner of Prince and Mott in lower Manhattan, outside of Old St. Patrick's church.

She appeared with the last light of day and—against the walls of New York's original Catholic cathedral—we kissed for the first time. I broke free and hailed a cab: "Take us to 23rd street and 7th avenue."

More incredulous kissing in the cab and then—at 223 West 23rd—up the ancient elevator that the young Stanley Bard used to ride with Pernell the bellboy. We got off on the 8th floor.

"Tom's room," I said as we crossed the threshold and fell into bed.

The first time was gentle before turning wild. The second time was riotous from the start—she called it a "violent passion," the kind of sex, she believed to be rare in a marriage of considerable years—before rippling back toward gentle.

We confirmed all of the mutual, not-acted-upon hunches from years ago (Remember that time in the alley next to the church, remember that other time?) before settling down enough to open presents.

There were books from me and books from her; stories by and about Tom, whose centennial had been commemorated the years before with a United States postage stamp.

"He'd leave this room in the middle of the night with a new manuscript in his hand, narrative hot from the typewriter," I said. "And then go walking the streets, sharing a bottle with bums and telling anyone who'd listen: 'I WROTE TEN THOUSAND WORDS TODAY!'"

She said that she'd wanted to be a writer since she was eight years-old—two perfect circles set atop on another. After referencing more incidents from Wolfe's chaotic life—his pain and his doubt and the bodies left in the wake—I asked: "Do you want it that bad?"

To which she answered: "I don't know. This is the wildest thing I've ever done."

We played some more and, just before her return to real life—one Wolfe never experienced, not as a child or an adult—I pulled a brand new Magic 8 Ball from the satchel of presents.

I don't remember what we asked this time around, but I can tell you this.

The question I'd posed years earlier at St. Alphonsus has yet to come true.

Johnny Winter Dream Sequence
[Sparrows Point Visitation]

"Days and nights succeed each other in oppressive heat that both descends from the sky and rises from the Earth . . ."

—Saramago

THE COFFEE SHOP used to be a downtown dive. I played there once upon a time with Pete Kanaras for drinks and cab fare. Before that it was a fortune teller's parlor and the neon hand was still in the window, the juice dried up.

Back in the 1930s, when Orlo was dismantling the Velvet Room in the wake of Leini's ultimatum, 1821 North Charles Street had been a lunch room with high-backed wooden booths, liver and onions and a rack of Bromo Seltzer on the wall.

Now it's the summer of 2011: mid-July with temperatures hitting 100, 103, 105. Heat with a life of its own.

"It's so goddamn hot," said an old-timer sitting on a milk crate outside the door, "the chickens are standing in line to get plucked."

No one had been plucking chickens in Baltimore for more than forty years when I walked into the Too Kool for Skool Café the other day, stopping in for a quick double-espresso on ice only to be enveloped by the voice of God's own bluesman: the Reverend Blind Gary Davis.

Death don't have no mercy in this land
He'll come to your house and he won't stay long
You'll look in the bed and somebody will be gone

A dozen city dwellers—most of them elderly, all sickly and trapped in rowhouse ovens—would die before the heat wave of 2011 broke.

People were predicting the end of the world and, more than ever, people believed it.

Yet today—in the eleventh hour—good things were happening in

Baltimore, proven by the fact that the voice of Blind Gary Davis was caulking every crevice in a neo-Bohemian coffee house where two decades earlier pissing-in-their-pants-drunks had tortured me and Kanaras for "Danny Boy."

Thirty years later: Gary Davis barking through a pig-nosed amp cabled to a laptop computer.

The barista had moved here for the same reason ten thousand other End of the Empire hipsters had done: The ride is cheap and if you can manage not to get shot, it's possible to live as you please.

The kid knew next-to-nothing about the building where she worked and had never heard of Orlo and Leini. But she knew her blues—knew that the best Robert Johnson in recent memory came courtesy of Dion— and she loved Gary Davis.

We bonded over a disdain for Clapton, which naturally led to a discussion of Johnny Winter which led to a disc being fished out of my backpack and placed in her dirty palm.

I left her on her knees, sobbing as Johnny roared: *"Listen to me baby, try to understand, you can never keep me so you better use me while you can . . ."*

Over and over she asked how she could have made it to the ripe age of twenty-three without having heard of the Mad Albino from Beaumont.

-o-

The girl waved off my money as she stood to hit the Johnny replay button, one warm to my touch since the days when he was a rock star selling out baseball stadiums.

"What happened to all those Johnny Winter fans?" he *once asked.* "Did they die?"

[They did. I played at many of their funerals.]

I dropped a buck in the tip jar and walked out with a hankering for a swimming hole. Leaving the heat and dust of North and Charles, I'd have traded Bohemian Barbie a suitcase of Johnny albums for a backyard tub and three trays of ice.

When Kanaras and I were on the road with the All-Stars, stuck in the van from Maine to Florida, we'd take turns reading aloud from a beat-up copy of Orlo and Leini stories. The Greek was good with the translations.

"Ivy reaching for a Star of David from a claw-footed, cast-iron tub filled with dirt . . . Leini stands on the lip while reaching for the Star,

74

her dress riding up on her hips, discovering the six points of Light were made from broken diner china, smooth here and jagged there . . ."

Turning off of President Street onto Aliceanna, the harbor was dead in the haze but still not hot enough—not then and not now—for me to jump off the piers at the end of Clinton Street like the Garayoa and Zientek boys used to do.

Passing the Sip & Bite where Aliceanna dead-ends at Boston Street, a kid spraying their dog with a hose, the answer came to me: Sparrows Point.

She wasn't young and if she was pretty, it was only in pictures. But she was cool. And she knew things you didn't need a fortune teller to know.

"If it ain't decent and it ain't right . . . stay the hell away from it . . ."

I met her last summer when young Porterfield—whose camera never met an above-ground pool it didn't like—shot a movie at her house. I traded work on the soundtrack for dinner at Ikaros and—after the crew had packed up—leaned over the side of the pool and dunked my head before heading home.

The woman called after me before I shoved off and said anyone who could play the pie-anna like me could drop by for a swim anytime, anytime at all.

And anytime is today.

Traveling out North Point Road from the city is a trip through the Deep South, lots of green and open fields, V.F.W. halls and volunteer fire departments with signs for crab feasts, barbecues and carnivals.

There weren't any cars in the driveway and I didn't see anyone in the yard. I parked on the side of the white clapboard house and walked around to the pool, a blue saucer shaded by great oaks, silver maples, Scotch pines and a weeping willow, my oasis in the Mississippi of Crabtown.

Down I stripped and in I went, the water like a warm bath but the air at least ten degrees cooler than the city, a hint of a breeze coming off of the upper Bay.

Floating, I started playing a game I learned from a drummer who got religion. He said that when he wanted to divine the presence of something bigger than himself he would stand in front of a tree or a flower that was absolutely still. Then he would begin praying and if the leaves or branches swayed, even the tiniest bit, he knew that his petition had been heard. Maybe not answered, but heard.

I stayed in for an hour, staring at the trees as a song took shape in my head, worried when the words came—"I will meet you in the interim ..."—that I might be going the way of Blind Gary and the drummer for the Lord.

A storm rolling across the bay and the sky went dark. With the crack of thunder, I got out of the pool and grabbed my shorts and shoes as lightning struck, racing for the screened in porch.

Inside, I dried off with my t-shirt and saw an old cot in a corner. Lying down with my shirt balled up under my head, I stared through the screen—nothing was still, the wait for the sway proof of God not applicable—and watched the deluge make the water in the pool look like it was boiling.

As the rain hit heavy on the plywood roof of the porch, I drifted off.

-o-

I dreamt that I was walking through a carnival on a supermarket parking lot. More than a carnival; it was a low-rent circus rolling from the ruins of one highway shopping center to another circus.

The circus had landed along a desolate stretch of Baltimore. It was dusk and as I approached one of the canvas tents, an acrobat walked toward me like a ballerina on asphalt.

It was Polly Jean looking severe and beautiful at the same time; Polly Jean a trapeze artist followed by a troupe of pinheads dressed in gingham. As she drew near, paying me no mind, I called out to her.

"Who is Johnny Winter?"

Polly looked me in the eye and answered as though talking to a child: "Johnny Winter is one of the greatest guitarists the world has ever known ..."

And then she walked away, the pinheads in her wake chanting: "Johnny Winter! Johnny Winter! Johnny Winter!"

The dream evaporated on the hem of Polly's faded costume and I opened my eyes to darkness and crickets.

THE SACRED HEART OF RUTHIE

I WAS DAYDREAMING in the Confession line Saturday night as the Catholics gathered for Mass in the squalor of my old neighborhood, pondering the great things I would accomplish . . . when my pager went off.

Emergency.

Code Four.

Obstetrics.

It's not a good thing when a cardiac surgeon is summoned to the delivery room. It is something I have only read about in books.

"Bless me, Father," I whispered before bolting out a side door of St. John the Evangelist. "For I have sinned."

-o-

I hit Eager Street in my loafers and began running toward downtown, my childhood in the shadows between the Church and Mercy Hospital, the neighborhood where my life began and ended and began again within hours of my birth in April of 1968.

Martin Luther King Jr. fell in Memphis on a Thursday and Baltimore was ablaze a day later. My mother was hit while getting out of a cab as she brought me home from the hospital.

Here.

Right here.

Armed with pea-shooters a post-modern homeboy wouldn't use to scare a cat, a couple of opportunists took my mother's purse and her wristwatch and her shoes, shot her three times and left me squawking in the street.

Dodging the gunfire, an Oblate Sister of Providence—a member of the black order that took over St. John's when all the others left—grabbed me from my dead mother's arms and raced inside the convent.

The first African-American order of Catholic nuns, the Oblates got their start with the help of a French priest running from the massacre of believers in South America. Their stated mission: "The education of colored children."

That was one hundred eighty years ago.

Because my survival was in doubt, they named me Thomas and believed that finding an infant on the sidewalk outside their chapel the day after Martin's martyrdom akin to finding Christ in the manger.

This is no small part of the freight I carry, running toward fresh tragedy more quickly than an ambulance could twist through these Baltimore streets.

For all of my success and all the good fortune my success has brought them, the Oblates never forgave me for refusing to be Catholic. Their crumbling convent is now home to an AIDS hospice run by disciples of Mother Teresa, a new sisterhood come to Crabtown from Calcutta to serve the Lord at the corner of Valley and Eager.

The Archdiocese cut St. John's loose a year after the riots. Old-timers who hadn't lived in the neighborhood for decades threatened to burn down what was left of the parish before they'd see it turned into a gym or a car wash, just some of the suggestions floated when the City moved to acquire the property.

And then the Catholic Workers stepped up and filled the void with whole wheat Eucharist and songs of pacifism and labor.

Sunlight that once made halos glow and wounds bleed now splinters across scarred and largely empty pews, benches greased with the stink of people grateful for a place to sit down. Renegade priests drop in to say Mass as they bounce between Belfast and Bolivia, offering Communion to folks that any fool can tell are not Catholic.

But I am not so easily fooled.

Running past touts and fiends and whores—their stout hearts pumping blood to brains paralyzed by incessant strategies—I glimpse a handful of cared-for homes where good people live trapped behind locked doors: men building model airplanes, women peeling potatoes; girls doing up their little sister's hair and nerds who'd rather watch the Nature Channel than Scarface.

Each block of rubble holds one or two houses owned by an aging factory pensioner or the widow of a pensioner; folks who thought they'd made it into the middle-class and didn't think they had to follow the middle-class out of the City to keep what they'd earned.

The pager burns a hole in my pocket.

I am fast and I am good and I have devoted my life to slaying the

Monster that Ate Baltimore City, running faster than I am able through piles of trash in the alleys, people lined up on one corner for dope, the other for Chinese.

All of Daddy Wong's kids went to college except the one killed when he came out from behind the glass to talk sense to a neighborhood boy he'd known all his life; a gaggle raised without English in the same neighborhood as the rest of us. All of them went to college and nobody paid their tuition but their father and nobody told them they had to believe this or that to escape where they were born.

All they had to do was study and help their parents work one hundred twenty hours a week in their bulletproof shit-hole.

I remember seeing one of the Wong girls on a stool in the back of the carry-out, the rear door open to the alley, when I'd come home from school. She had a skinny leg on each side of a bucket as she peeled carrots, a math book open on the floor.

All they had to do was work without bitching and maybe believe in something bigger than work.

The houses blur, blocks of scorched and de-mortared brick that people once called home, and I remember, with every feces-and-needle littered house, all the kids I used to play with who are dead.

I see faces from the days of peanut butter and jelly and multiplication tables and Fat Albert and wonder how many people could be saved with the pristine valves that rot in the slums of Valley and Eager.

The world despairs for the rhino, its horn ground into aphrodisiac, carcasses left to rot on the plains. What of barely used gall bladders and perfect livers? The corneas of kids who couldn't see past the corner?

If my mother had lived to raise me, would I be planted alongside of Dink-Dink and Boo?

Why did I survive?

At what price have I prospered?

Has so much changed in nearly forty years that nuns can't run out of the convent to scoop up three-strikes against them babies the way they did me? Their mothers are just as dead as mine, dead in their slippers as they wait for the new package to hit the street.

There is no convent. There are no nuns.

But the harvest is as rich as ever in the Third Fucking World of Baltimore.

I run past the old Irish graveyard where my mother is buried, her plot donated by a Church benefactor who felt sorry for us. High above the cemetery, on the other side of the street is the corrugated pyramid of the Maryland Penitentiary where the man said to be my father faces east three times a day while serving a life sentence for killing a Polish man who made his living baking pies.

The dead baker's son summed it up in the papers: "We knew it was a colored section, a little rough, but the Jews who sold us the business said you could make good money there."

Shit.

This neighborhood was desperate when I was born.

What is the next rung down from there?

The old 10th ward is a penal colony now, an ever sprawling complex of prisons and super prisons that grew as the vibrancy of St. John's—its ten thousand parishioners, eight grades of school and twenty-two stained glass windows—shattered one pane at a time.

-o-

The city rushes past and I feel like I am being carried.

The way the Oblates carried me in from the sidewalk when I was less than a day old and gave me a name and a home; the way, a dozen years later, the Oblates carried me and my straight A report cards to Transfiguration High School in Southwest Baltimore to arrange four years of study with their Xaverian compatriots.

The way, four years after that, the Xaverians handed me off to the Jesuits and the big boys at Georgetown told me to forget about everything but what they put in front of me and I'd wake up in the middle of the night screaming and run through the streets because my potential was eating me alive.

"Why can't I be a dermatologist?" I once screamed at a Jesuit scientist researching the roots of addiction. "Why save someone's life if they can't stand to be in their own skin?"

They told me: "The heart is the seat of love in the body . . ."

They told me: "You were born for greatness . . ."

They told me: "Shut up and do what you're told."

On like this from birth through my first residency, the priests and nuns playing pawnbroker with my un-payable debt while I searched in vain for a single Catholic among my kin.

My father's story didn't go any further than a fat file at the Maryland Department of Corrections. Holy Rollers from Carolina on my mother's side.

After my mother was murdered, the Oblates sought out my

grandmother and persuaded her that I would be better off with them and the old woman went to her grave believing it was best for all concerned.

-o-

I began torturing my saviors in the second grade.

"Thomas," said the priest from the other side of the Confessional screen. "You've been in this box three times today. How much sin can one boy commit in an afternoon?"

"I don't know, Father."

"What is it, son?"

Silence.

"You're the smartest kid in school, so I know you haven't been cheating. And I've never known you to lie. What is it, son? Looking up Tonya's skirt again? That's no sin."

"Worse."

"How bad can it be?"

"I don't want to become a Catholic, Father."

"Thomas, I Baptized you myself."

"No one asked me."

"Asked you what?"

"No one asked me if I wanted to be Catholic."

"I see."

"My class is getting ready to make our First Communion."

"I'll be there."

"But if you take Communion, you're Catholic."

"And why is that, Thomas?"

"Because it's real. Other churches say it's just a symbol, but Catholics believe it's real."

"You've studied well."

"And I don't want to be Catholic."

"Because you don't believe?"

"My mother wasn't Catholic. My father isn't Catholic. I wasn't supposed to be Catholic."

The priest came out of his box and around to mine. Parting the ragged velvet curtain, he said, "Not supposed to be is a religion unto itself, Thomas."

"I don't want it."

"Then say no."

"Can I?"

"The Sacrament of Refusal springs from absolute free will."

"Will it make trouble?"

"Bet on it."

"But I can say no?"

"All the great believers have."

"For real?"

"For good," said the priest.

"Wow."

"All right, Thomas," said the priest, going back to his side of the screen. "Proceed."

"Bless me Father, for I have sinned . . . It has been forty-five minutes since my last confession . . ."

-o-

Even at seven, fingering the white handkerchiefs the nuns tacked to the sinner's side of the box, I knew what I was confessing.

My life was saved by Catholic charity and it has prospered through Catholic education and I have never gotten over it. I am a success because of my mother's death, my guilt as thick and humid as that carried by any man whose mother died giving birth to him.

Faster, smart guy.

Run faster.

Time to do penance.

I sprint across the Fallsway where men huddle around fire barrels and turn south on Guilford toward the harbor, wondering if a cop might jack me up on a profile, costing precious moments. In my work, any difference is all the difference. I was more likely to get shot for my shoes.

At Guilford and Saratoga, I hit the House of Welsh, down where the rag factories used to be. I veered from the boarded-up restaurant and raced up the steep hill of Saratoga to Mercy, dodging medic wagons and cabbies as I burst into the emergency room.

January 8, 2000.

A cold and bitter night in the Holy Land.

-o-

"What is it?"

"Premature labor and heart failure."

"Who?"

"A kid," said a nurse, hurrying with me to the elevator. "Kid with a bum heart."

"Age?"

"Sixteen, tops."

"What's been done?"

"Oxygen. Monitors."

"Echo-cardiogram?"

"Done."

"Fever?"

"One-o-one. One-o-one and a half."

The elevator doors opened on the intensive care ward and as the nurse handed me a portable video monitor, a nun in full black habit—the kind that were rare even when I was a kid—ran toward the operating room.

I watched a film of the girl's heart and saw dye injected into the aorta was rushing back into the left ventricle. No way to tell what was torn or if the whole valve would have to come out, but you didn't have to be Christian Barnard to see it was a mess.

Babies having babies hadn't been news in Baltimore since before I was born but this little mother had blood leaking back into her heart by the cupful. An infection—probably from an abscessed tooth, common among junkies, the homeless and runaways—had sent a pathological dose of endocarditis through her veins. It hit her heart like bleach on hamburger.

I'd have to cut it out and put in a new one—from plastic or a pig or some poor soul—or the girl would die before the night was out. I couldn't be sure about the baby.

The elevator opened on the top floor of the hospital with a more complete view of Baltimore than I have given you: the harbor aglitter, a pair of modern sports stadiums paid for with taxpayer money, the cranes of the working port and the Key Bridge beyond them.

A winter moon above the charred metal pyramid atop the Penitentiary.

In my face: torn leaflets, endocarditis, wild fluctuations in arterial pressure, fluid retention and steady leakage.

I ordered both operations and ducked into the scrub room to change out of my street clothes.

"Baby first?" asked the nurse.

"Both."

She stared—"At the same time?"—and I stared her down.

Don't let the nuns take credit for saving my life. Don't let the Archdiocese tell you about diversity when they use my black face to solicit money for minority scholarships.

I stand before you because *my* heart can take it.

-o-

Blood pressure dropping.

Patient failing.

They wheeled her in on a gurney, began running lines, moved her to the table and began draping off as my A-team lined up on both sides: savants and geniuses and craftsmen from every discipline.

In the middle: Albert with his long table of instruments.

Albert the head scrub.

Albert my right hand.

Albert my polar opposite: a big, tough Polish kid from the South Broadway waterfront, unlike anyone I'd ever met growing up in the same city; pork chop sideburns and heavy eyelids, a dead-ringer for the King of you-know-what.

"I know this girl," he whispered in a choking voice.

"Who is she?"

"Little Ruthie Wonder."

"Who?"

And Albert leaned back in to tell the whopper that the girl had told her parents, the whys and wherefores of how she found herself with child, the reason they cut her loose, the truth that trumped all the believable lies she could have told.

"Her name is Ruth."

The infection was stimulating contractions. I had a few quick moments before making the sternal split and wanted a few words with this beautiful girl, this lost in a world of trouble girl getting swabbed with Betadine, wide swaths of foaming bronze antiseptic along her chest, the curve of her abdomen, her groin; thick ribbons of orange and brown outlining where we would cut.

I spoke softly as the anesthesiologist turned his knobs.

"Ruth, can you hear me?"

"Yes."

"I like your name."

"You do?"

"Do you know what we're going to do?"

"Yes."

"You do."

Her eyes began to drop.

"What?"

As I oversimplified a miracle I had yet to perform, Ruthie's violet lids came down over the golden light in her eyes and if she heard another word I said, she would not remember it.

-o-

It only takes three short weeks for endocarditis to destroy the aortic valve, half that time in the heart of a pregnant teenager more concerned with finding a meal than brushing her teeth.

Just the blink of a golden eye for the angel to appear as Ruthie sank below the waves.

She let him have it, both barrels.

"You abandoned me. Just like everybody else. You do this to me and then you disappear?"

"Just because . . . "

"Spare me," said Ruthie. "Let me die."

"Watch your mouth."

"You put me in this cartoon and can't even get it right:"

"The Master of the Universe was not going to leave the throne to brush your teeth."

"I could have used a manicure while He was at it."

"He, She, Them, It . . ."

"Why does everything have to be so hard?"

"Because it's a million times more difficult to push the clock back than forward."

"Just leave me alone."

"Way, way, way back."

"Fuck you."

"Before the house, before the cars, before the servants . . ."

And before Ruthie could speak again, the angel's trumpet melded into a dented stew pot and his head became a mop of gray curls below the *kipah* of a bent old man at the corner of Baltimore Street and Central Avenue, his crooked finger brushing hair from the fever of Ruthie's brow.

"Old Zadie."

The peddler nodded.

"Way back, bubelah."

"How far?"

"Do you remember Hendler's ice cream?"

Ruthie smiled, smacked her lips.

"Back before the money came."

"All the way?"

"Whee! Whee! Whee!"

"All the way . . ."

"Home."

-o-

"I knew something like this was going to happen," said Albert. "Poor little rich girl. Used to think it was hip to hang down the waterfront. Never wanted to go home."

I parted her lips, exposing rotted gums.

"Rich kid couldn't afford a toothbrush?"

"Miss Bonnie would pretend to be mad. 'Get outta here,' she'd say and Ruthie would bite her lip trying not to cry. How can a kid like that not have anywhere to go? She'd dawdle and Miss Bonnie would show her the door: 'Get the hell outta here before you get in trouble.'"

"She's got trouble now."

The perfusion crew assembled the heart-lung machine as the OB team prepared for a swift C-section. The tracheal tube was in and she couldn't talk or breathe on her own.

Word had gotten out that something that never happens was about to happen and there were too many people in the room: students and researchers and groupies; cardiologists and a couple of guys from internal medicine and Jesus, Mary and Joseph, tonight, of all nights, the goddamn director of development walks in with a camera around her neck.

My anger tasted like green pennies. A girl and her baby dying on the table and I had a vision of a documentary that would never be made of my accomplishments.

"How did they treat you, Thomas?"

"Like a butterfly."

"And how is that?"

"They loved me like a butterfly."

I snapped out of it and ordered everyone out of the room except those who had to be there. I nodded to Albert, who announced: "Gentlemen, start your engines . . ."

A great and translucent globe of unblemished flesh vibrated before us with a new planet about to spin out into the world. They cut and found the head—steady as she goes—and were about to bring out the fetus when . . .

"WHAT THE FUCK?"

"DROWN IT!"

"SHE'S KNOTTING THE CORD!"

"BURN IT!"

An RN, a convert, twice-divorced and childless, a nurse who'd entered the convent in middle-age, was ranting and raving with a loop of umbilical cord in her hands.

"STONE IT!"

An obstetrician threw an elbow at the nurse's throat to rescue the infant. The mother's diastolic had been near zero from the moment they brought her in. Pulse rate: forty. Arterial pulse: sixty and dropping.

"WE'RE LOSING HER!"

Did it occur to me to pray?

Or remember a single sin from the short list—variations on pride—I was about to confess an hour ago?

The difference between a good surgeon and a great one is a fine line. The prize goes to the one that works faster, with fewer wasted motions; who can sew like Betsy Ross with the British at the door.

I nudged Albert and he leapt. Putting the saboteur in a headlock, the muscle of his bare and meaty forearm flexed the image of a thorn-choked heart emblazoned with the Agony of the King.

I love Albert but I hate that tattoo and have asked him to keep it covered when we're working. What kind of Catholic puts a crown of thorns around the head of a mere singer?

As he tightened the headlock on the nun and dragged her out, she tried to kick the operating table and screamed: "THIS WON'T CHANGE A GODDAMN THING!"

I knew she was right.

And did not think to pray.

-o-

Infants in utero do not tolerate pulmonary bypass very well, although they tend to do better than infants out of utero do on the street.

In the midst of this insanity, I no longer regretted that the Church had kept me from choosing my own way. I was graced for a moment not to think of myself at all.

Working fast to reach the baby before the anesthesia did, the OB team brought the child out quickly: female, caramel, no bigger than my fist with a full head of curly black hair. They suctioned mucus from its tiny beak and—holding the prize high in the air—raced her to pediatric ICU.

Out in the hall, as nurse raced by with the infant, a security guard held the nun for the cops and Albert spotted Ruthie's old patron in a corner, chewing her fingernails and five wads of nicotine-gum.

"Miss Bonnie, how'd you get up here?"

"I took the elevator. Jesus Christ, Albert, I'm going koo-koo out here. I'm on pins and needles. How's my Ruthie? Did she have the baby?"

"Can't talk, Miss Bon."

"Can't talk? To ME? Shit on you, Albert. What the hell's going on?"

"Fatigue, Miss Bon," he said before disappearing into the operating room. "Chronic heart fatigue."

"How much goddamn fatigue can she have for Christ's sake?" said Miss Bonnie to the door as it closed in her face. "She's only fifteen years-old."

-o-

Albert returned and I went to work.

Dropping a small, vibrating saw into the girl's sternum—a flat, dagger-shaped bone without which the ribs would not form a perfect cage—I opened her in a single swoop.

Steel retractor blades held the chest open like a half-read book and when I ordered "bypass" the perfusionists began siphoning her blood through $100,000 worth of machinery for the hour or so it would take to do the job.

I snipped through the pericardial sac, a thin, protective membrane, and peeled it back to reveal the stark and stunning beauty of a beating human heart.

The throne of love.

A ruby, pumping like a piston until I stopped it with 1000 ccs of potassium chloride so cold it nears freezing; ice-cold saline squirted from a turkey baster over red muscle and yellow fat; as cold, according to Albert, as it was on the school day afternoon when Ruthie told him he could have kissed her until he asked.

-o-

I cut out the bad valve as easy as coring a brown spot from a potato and Albert passed me a ring of sizers to measure it, the sizers always reminding me of the summer as a shoe clerk on Howard Street.

I was in high school, kneeling down in front of women all day and bringing my pay back to the convent where it was dispersed to those less fortunate than me. They crossed and uncrossed their legs and I measured their feet and brought out boxes from the back in sizes that were not always as perfect as this new valve had to be.

90

I examined the diseased root and within it, the feathery leaflets that open and close some forty million times a year in a normal heart.

In a healthy valve, the folds are spectacularly beautiful, a trinity of virtually transparent ventricles as fragile as the skin of a pear. Not only was this girl born with two leaflets instead of three—creating irregular vibrations, the geometry less pleasing to the eye—but they were shredded, shriveled and ripe with moss.

There weren't more than a hundred beats left.

How this kid got here, I don't know.

But she made it just in time.

Surfing the unswerving punctuality of chance to meet me.

I am the corrective.

To substitute good for bad, I could have gone with a replacement valve from a pig heart, but those come with artificial sewing rings that breed bacteria. Synthetic valves are problematic because they demand a lifetime of blood thinning drugs that would make future childbirth as dangerous as this one.

So I ordered up a selection of cadaver valves, which pose the least risk of infection.

"Nobody ever got this close," whispered Albert, passing me instruments as I stitched, close to clamping off the aorta and bring her blood back to flush out the potassium.

"What?"

"At Miss Bonnie's," said Albert. "The sad boys and stupid men stood five and six deep to carve their initials on Ruthie's heart."

And I had my hands around it, a gurgle of warm water running through my fingers and onto the crippled Communion as I massaged it back to life after an hour of repair. I could have set the paddles on it to finish more quickly but it was responding well enough to my touch.

As I squeezed—gentle but firm, the way I'd been raised, the way this girl should have been brought up—the blood returned, the heart began to hum . . .

Holy Mother of God!

Tiny marks began appearing like lines slicing through the mercury of an Etch-A-Sketch, symbols pulsing bright as this patched-up ticker began beating to the rhythm of my hard lesson.

I have seen hundreds of living human hearts but I'd never seen anything like this. No one else in the room seemed to sense anything out of the ordinary so I kept quiet and tipped the heart just above the ribs to better read its hieroglyphics, rubbing my thumbs across it the way you clear a peep hole in a fogged window.

The broken organ of a little girl who was about to drop dead out on the sidewalk just a few hours ago was preaching to me like a Joe Frazier uppercut.

"No one asked you to suffer along with your greatness, Thomas . . . it was your idea . . . this has *never* been about you . . ."

Imagine that.

My life—all that I have done and intend to do—not about me.

The operations had gone perfectly. Mother stable and going to make it. Baby alive and kicking. The seal between my work and the mistakes of nature imperceptible.

"Come on," murmured Albert, impatient for me to close up.

Would my guardians have balked if I'd wanted to become a priest?

Within the cracked-open temple of the Holy Ghost before me, I marveled at a bloody Eucharist scrawled with Stars and sheet music and thousands of tiny crosses and strained to hear it whisper: "Eat me . . ."

All my life—lo, these past thirty-odd years—I've been told what to want and why I should want it, a pawn pushed through the battlefield to serve a Queen, some knocked-up runaway who'll go on welfare the morning her breasts run dry.

My life . . .

Not about me.

A miracle no more than a curiosity to my Maker.

In one of the required theology classes at Georgetown, the priest closed the door one day to depart from a text he'd written himself, to say that when we die—as best he could fathom—Judgment Day is nothing more than a two question quiz.

The first is worth one hundred percent of the grade.

And the second is just for fun.

How did you love?

And what did you learn?

Nothing I'd ever done or could have done would have changed this moment; all my effort reduced to winding the springs of a world that runs right on time; the great I Am humbled in the moment of his greatest glory.

I held the heart as high as it would go to read what had been scrivened.

A constellation of Hebrew stars: "Man plans and God laughs . . ."

A hymnal of hillbilly spirituals: "When I in awesome wonder cry . . ."
And a mansion made from a million splinters of the Cross we bear.
Good work, Thomas, it said.
You are free to go . . .

THE AMBASSADOR STRICTURES

WHEN GIBBY WAS little, his father worked on ships and it was just the kid and Mom at home on Chapel Street in Baltimore.

Gibby is telling the story a day after his negligence killed a man on a container ship in Long Beach. He is stoned, drunk and running his mouth, not shutting up long enough to hear the advice he'd asked for.

"I remember walking into her bedroom when I was about three and finding her face down in a pillow, sobbing. I asked what was wrong and she said, 'Nothing . . . go play.'"

The three year-old—"I mighta been four"—wandered off to dump everything out of his toy chest and lay down in it.

"I brought the lid over my head and there in the dark I knew that whatever *was* wrong, it was my fault. Up to me to make it better. Not old enough to write my name."

On the nights I didn't go into Mom's room with my blanket, I slept with a transistor radio under the covers and somehow, not old enough to say my name properly, knew what the groups were singing about.

Mom was twenty-four, less than half the age I am today.

Twenty-four.

She was sad and she was beautiful and I never found out why she was crying on that sunny morning in Baltimore except that sometimes she cried more when the old man was home than when he was at sea. And then my little brother was born and the old man was away more than he was home.

-o-

"The grimy light; the congealing smell of cigarettes that had been smoked long ago and of liquor that had been drunk long ago; the boasting, cursing, wheedling, cringing voices, and the greasy feel of the bar . . ."

—Tillie Olsen

-o-

95

Gibby, his seaman's papers revoked by the Coast Guard, a trial pending in the death of his shipmate, paces a priest's office high above the City of Angels, a Catholic boy with a heavy load.

On the advice of a guy at the union hall, Gibby has come to Archdiocese headquarters to talk about the death of his friend, a fellow stoner (they'd smoked a joint at the rail just before the accident) crushed between two shipping containers when a guy-wire got away from him.

["Fuck the Church," said the captain as he held Gibby for the Coast Guard. "Get off the goddamn dope Lukowski and get yourself a good Jew lawyer."]

But Gibby winds up talking about love and lust, telling the priest "it doesn't make any difference anymore" why his mother was sobbing all those years ago.

What he wants to know is why—why, since he lost his virginity thirty-five years ago in the galley of a wooden tugboat—he'd only known the ginger of set-yourself-on-fire love when the woman was married with young children."

Abiding adultery, a sin the sages put on a par with murder (neither can be undone) from the time Gibby was a teenager to his life as a brazen man battling the devil *and* the deep blue sea.

"You think that's the thing we should talk about?"

"Yes."

"Well Gilbert . . . they say our deepest truths are in our earliest memories."

All tangled up in the weak links of other people's anchor chains.

Gibby, never even close to engaged, knew more about knots in a marriage than those in the seaman's manual.

A rolling hitch: glimpses of the struggle stolen through a knothole in the fence, the play-by-play—honest error compounded by flagrant foul—relayed by the most partisan of correspondents: the wounded wife.

"They show up with pie or half of a baked chicken," he said. "You wouldn't believe the stuff I've got back home in the china closet. Dishtowels and rosaries and recipes."

And chapter and verse about the monotonous ways that men can be jerks.

"They all have names," said Gibby, pacing the office, picking up gospel geegaws from Latin America and setting them down. "Fuck Head or Dumb Ass. Jerk Off."

The priest laughed and wondered what the husbands called Gibby.

"Serious Father, not making it up. One woman called the asshole she'd married at seventeen *Bob*. That wasn't his name but it fit."

So direct, so terse—*BOB*—rinse and spit. He was some kind of assistant bank manager and insisted, with two little kids and a new car payment (a Jetta for him, a junker for her) that they couldn't afford a vegetable garden. And then went out and bought a set of golf clubs.

The clubs were a crucial family investment, allowing Bob entrée with heavy hitters so busy chasing little white balls of status it claims their peripheral vision.

"I walked over to her house one day with a tomato seedling in a milk carton," said Gibby. "By the end of summer we were eating tomato sandwiches on her porch."

Gibby's married girlfriends told truths they hadn't the courage to broach at home: how long they'd hung in, why they stayed, how much more they could take.

"They talk," he said, "and I listen."

As the priest listened now, somewhat impressed at the nuance of this merchant marine who might soon be going to jail if things didn't break the right way, wondering if the sailor had had a Catholic education back home in the Premier See.

Gibby talked about getting high with his married lovers in the middle of the afternoon, dancing away the short hours of the assignation (but not all of them) in their underwear.

He described the cracker-box on Chapel Street, the alley house he'd inherited after his mother passed away.

"It's my house, where I eat," he said. "Not some stupid fucking motel. Christ—sorry Father. I mean, damn . . . they jump and clap and laugh like they haven't laughed in a hundred years."

Gibby the errant dairyman, spared the bloody nose and the bullet's sting by hopping the next slow boat to China. A lucky man, up to the moment the container slipped, skimming the cream: food and sex and music, sea stories and laughter.

"Sometimes, once we've had our fun," said Gibby. "They look in the mirror and say they don't recognize their life anymore."

-o-

The priest was a Jesuit, trained in psychology (beloved by his mixed-up students across town, respected by the Archdiocese, for thirty years a member in good standing of Alcoholics Anonymous) and to him the mystery of faith was all pretty obvious.

"You're not here to confess the accident?"

"No. It was an accident."

"You want to confess the adultery?"

"It's like I'm George Jetson on the moving sidewalk," said Gibby, pretending to run in place in front of the priest's desk. "Jane! Jane! Stop this crazy thing."

But Jane can't help Gibby.

Nor Mary Lou, Peggy Sue or Barbara Ann.

Not today.

And so he'd puzzled out that a priest might be more helpful before he met his fate than a lawyer; high above Tinseltown and a continent from home. Perhaps a fellow traveler, an unmarried appraiser of forbidden fruit and vows that could not be kept.

"Bless me father, for I don't want to live this way anymore . . ."

"How long since your last confession, Gilbert?"

"I don't know. Eighth grade mabye?"

The priest speaks softly and says he knows just how Gibby feels; that in his work broken, attractive women come to him all the time—"just like you." That young mothers are always the most compelling and it's probably bound up with the promises they struggle to fulfill.

"These promises," he tells Gibby, finally getting up from his desk. "Were not made to you or me."

Gibby nods, remembering some of the promises he and his lovers had made to one another, all of them genuine and fleeting: this corner on this day, a restaurant in an alley, out on the street in bright summer sunshine.

The penance he receives is sweet—*"Deus, Pater misericordiarum, qui per mortem et resurrectionem. Filii sui mundum sibi reconciliavit . . ."*— and feels more like a blessing than debt:

"Do you think you can do that, Gilbert?"

"I do," says Gibby as the priest leads him to a wall of windows and points down some twenty stories to a demolition site where a wrecking crew is razing an ugly brown compound that looks like a reform school.

"See that building the ball is banging into right now? That's the kitchen where Bobby Kennedy was shot."

How is it that our oldest memories fade in clarity at the same time they increase in intensity? As the ball swings back for another assault on the ruins of the Ambassador Hotel, Gibby feels something move inside of him and remembers the day after the shooting and his 5th grade class going to Mass at St. Stan's on a weekday with the neighborhood Polish ladies, all of them in black. A saloon across from the church was giving out buttons that said PRAY FOR BOBBY.

He heard the buzz from the transistor radio he kept by his bed to listen to ballgames, one of a thousand things in the warehouse of stolen goods that was the four room house on Chapel Street; record players and Krakow hams and cases of Tang that followed his father home from a long night of unloading ships

An echo of the broken heart of the genius of Southern California: *"We could be married . . . and then we'd be happy . . ."*

As Gibby took the elevator down to the street, he almost believed it.

THE
BASILIO
STORIES

I KNOW WHY I WAS BORN
[1964]

WIGMANN CAME TO a few hours before dawn on Christmas Eve, face down on the sofa of a rowhouse saloon in the Holy Land. The old beer garden had been in his family since the turn-of-the-century and passed down to him with the recent death of his father.

Wigmann rubbed the back of his neck.

"What am I going to do, Pop?"

The photograph stared back at him, mute alongside a bowl of ginger snaps soaking in sweet vinegar on the bar. The woman who'd promised to transform the cookies into sour rabbit and dumplings—a girl named Barbara he would introduce to the family tonight at dinner, the one who'd grown weary of apology—should have arrived hours ago.

A toy train emerged from a tunnel behind the wall with a shrill whistle and bubble lights percolated against the silvery sheen of a tin ceiling, reflecting in mirrors advertising "The Land of Pleasant Living," the destination Wigmann had sought while waiting for his sweetheart.

She'd many miles to cover and Wigmann had bided his time with one more beer.

Just one more.

Standing, he killed the train and walked to the front door, a draft frosting his toes as he turned the locks, the door bumping against something heavy.

Slipping outside, feet freezing against tiles that spelled out "645 Newkirk Street," Wigmann beheld a heart breaking bounty.

A pile of presents, ribbons fluttering in the wind, were arranged around a roasting pan. Bending to lift the lid, Wigmann set his fingertips against the frozen skin of a cooked goose and began mourning the loss of his private Christmas: a German chapel crumbling inside an Italian cathedral.

Wigmann rifled through the gifts, but his beloved—who'd banged on the door with the heel of her shoe and let the phone ring a hundred times—had not left a note.

-o-

Tradition, Basilio's grandfather often said, is nothing more than hard work and planning.

The calendar is not a line, but a loop and you could not trust something as important as tradition—Christmas Eve the richest of all—to chance.

As Wigmann wept into his pillow, Basilio's grandfather stood at a basement workbench alongside a stone tub where eel would soon soak in milk. The Spaniard was hammering together a gift for his namesake grandson, an easel made from grape crates.

[The wine had turned out especially good that year, fruity and crude, the white better than the red and the words "Boullosa & Sons" written across clay jugs before gifts of it were made to friends and relatives who lived along the alley that separated Macon Street from Newkirk: an extra bottle delivered to Wigmann's Beer Garden to help ease the loss there.

As sad as it was, the dead man's son was supposed to bring a new face to the table and in this way, girdered by hard work and new blood, tradition rolled with the calendar.]

Driving the last screw and oiling the hinges, Basilio's grandfather brought the easel from the back of the basement into the long kitchen where the feast would take place, where his Italian wife sat separating anchovies to be deep fried in dough.

"It's finished Mom," he said.

Weak-sighted, the woman wiped her hands on her apron and used her fingertips to make out the easel's form beneath a ring of florescent light on the ceiling.

"It's good."

"I think so," said Grandpop, putting away his tools.

Two floors above, Little Basilio slept with dreams coursing through his brain in the shape of his age: a pair of perfect circles, one set atop the other.

Inside the endless eight, the boy raced through the games he would play that night, felt the long wait ahead and realized why he was born.

[Born to paint the pictures in his head, to sketch the kitchen in the basement, to capture the clouds as the wind drove them past the bottle cap factory down by the railroad tracks, to capture the air that swirled across the tarred rooftops.]

The night before, Basilio had gone to bed knowing that he liked to draw.

Today, he would wake up with the knowledge that he was an artist the way his father was a tugboat man and his grandfather was a machinist at the shipyard.

A skylight above Basilio's head—hexagon panes embedded with diamonds of twisted wire—brought the breaking day into his room on a rolling bank of low, nickel-gray clouds, the kind that tease children with the promise of snow.

The boy opened his eyes and inside the skylight glass, the boy saw himself as a grown man living with his aged grandfather, painting the day-by-day story of their life together.

Basilio's father—at home with the rest of his family on a cul-de-sac where no one baked eel for Christmas—had slept below the same skylight thirty years before and told the boy over and over of the sacrifices made for a better life among the lawns outside the city.

Yet every weekend, summer vacation and Christmas Eve, Basilio's parents dropped him off on Macon Street.

To walk to the corner for wheels of fresh bread.

Wake up to the scent of smelts frying in olive oil.

And measure the universe by the width of a narrow rowhouse in the Holy Land.

Basilio heard his grandfather's feet coming up the stairs and knew it was time to go to the fish market.

Today was the day.

-o-

Wigmann took the gifts that had been left on his doorstep and packed them in his old man's car. He piled the packages on the backseat and set the roasting pan on the floor, thinking, as he walked back and forth between the house and the car, of the Christmas Eves of his childhood.

There was no place for goose at his family's feast. The tables pushed together in the basement of his aunt's house down the alley would be crowded with thirteen kinds of seafood in honor of the Savior of the World and the twelve who had followed Him.

Every year, Wigmann's father would lead all of the children from the crowded table to the beer garden to watch trains run through a sawdust village of 19th century Germany.

With the big meal a dozen hours away—his father dead and his sweetheart gone—Wigmann wasn't sure if he could stomach it this year.

The singing. The hugs. The love.

A basement filled with his mother's family: the bombastic Bombaccis.

Wigmann's mother and Lola were the youngest and oldest of five first-generation sisters who lived up and down the alley.

Tonight's feast would take place in the middle of the block, at the home of Francesca Boullosa, the middle sister and grandmother of an eight year-old boy who had just awoken with the knowledge that he was born to draw everything he saw.

-o-

Basilio gathered nickels and dimes and quarters from the top of the bedroom dresser, slipped them into his pockets with a few colored pencils and ran downstairs.

Next to the boy's place at the table—years later, the artist would stand in the basement and recite his family's seating arrangement for visitors—stood an easel Basilio would use long after the sidewalks had cracked on Macon Street.

"Sit," said his grandmother, touching the boy's head, buttered toast and hot Cream of Wheat on the table.

"When can I try it?" said Basilio.

"Eat," said Grandpop. "Then wash up."

In the car, as Basilio drew on the inside of the windows with his fingertips, Grandpop told the boy why the day was so special: "So you won't forget. The empanada, my mother made it with chopped nuts. Your grandmother uses raisins. Who knows what your mama will use. One day, if you marry the right girl, she will make it and I'll be gone."

"You're funny, Grandpop."

Together, they walked through the aisles of Broadway Market, and, as Basilio stared at pictures of his heroes hanging in a record store across the street, Grandpop pulled him toward the crushed ice of the fish stalls—do this in memory of me spiced with five pounds of shrimp—and told him again why this day was important.

But Basilio was thinking the thoughts of an eight year-old who wakes up one day knowing why he was born: of listening to Beatles records with his cousin Donna and which new albums they might get as presents; of how long would it be before she walked through the front door of their grandparents' house with her red plastic record player.

"Today, we eat like kings," said Grandpop, preaching to a boy who had no idea what kings ate.

[Anyone who was blessed to eat their fill wore a crown. Enough potatoes. Plenty of fruit. And a sea of fish across three tables pushed together and covered with white cloth.]

The black eel—his wife's tradition, Bombacci and Boullosa mixed together in the restless boy like pigment on a palette—was a once a year treat: its sweet, firm length divided by the inch, breaded, baked and piled on pastel china.

"You nail the head to a piece of wood and pull the skin back with pliers because she is too slippery to hold," said Grandpop as the fish man coiled three feet of eel into the bottom of a sack.

Basilio reached out and touched the creature just before it disappeared.

"Grandpop," he said, "can we stop at the record store on the way home?"

-o-

Wigmann sped east on Eastern Avenue with the roasted goose rocking gently near his feet.

Seeking absolution—the God of Second Chances was here Wigmann, right here in the Holy Land while you were passed out—he turned south onto Clinton Street and raised a cold cloud of dust, rumbling toward the water's edge, praying that a third chance would be the charm, a fat wad of inherited cash in his pocket.

Halfway down the gravel road, the mansion at the old Pound shipworks began rising before Wigmann, higher than the tongue of flame above the Standard Oil refinery, an ornate, 19th century structure known as the Salvage House.

It looked worse for wear against the nickel gray skies over Fort McHenry as Wigmann pulled his old man's Volkswagen into the yard; the gutters sagging, paint peeling from the upper floors and a quartet of gargoyle pigs sneering down from the four corners of the roof.

Wigmann growled at them as he got out of the VW with the roasting pan in his hands, drawing the attention of a gray-haired man slashing the thick skin of pig feet with an oyster knife before tossing the trotters into a black kettle over a backyard fire.

Orlo Pound was pickling enough Christmas pig feet to give to all of the people who had helped keep his secret and still have some left over to share with his lover, tending the pot in a small circle of peach trees at the edge of the Patapsco on a cold December morn; chuckling as he stirred it with a broom handle, a trio of Retrievers trying to stick their snouts in the bubbling vat of and an empty cask waiting to receive layers of pork upon layers of kosher salt, onions and spices upon layers of pork.

Wigmann remembers coming down to the Salvage House when he was a kid with his father and how Orlo would give him gadgets from his great store of them; pocket watches without hands and port holes without glass that a kid could stick their head through and pretend to be Popeye the Sailor Man.

So many more thoughts of his old man in death than before; Christmas the time for remembering a wind-up toy the junkman called a "Dinky Doll," a monkey that hung from pipes on the ceiling while raising a tiny beer can to his lips; remembering how he'd lost Dinky before he could show it to anybody and how hard, being a big boy of eight or nine, he'd tried not to cry in front of his father.

"I don't want to cry," he'd sobbed on the ride home from the Salvage House. "But my body does."

Back when Orlo had nothing but youth and conflict and yearning in his life—wanting Leini to be his and his alone, not caring to share her with her children much less her drunkard husband—the junkman had kept the mansion in perfect shape.

Now he was too content to get up on a ladder for minor repairs.

Laying churning stick aside as Wigmann approached, Orlo let out a belly laugh that smothered the sad and beautiful world of pain he'd survived, recognizing in the disappointed face of the saloon keeper's son the little boy he used to know.

"Junior!" cried the junkman. "I thought that was you."

And in that moment—the boy gone but the dark hair, curved brow and coal black eyes remaining in a man who looked nothing like his father—Orlo remembered that young Wigmann was the nephew of his lover's best friend.

Francesca Bombacci Boullosa and Eleini Leftafkis Papageorgiou had been close as sisters since attending P.S. 228 together on Rappolla Street.

When the pretty girl from Greece enrolled in the fourth grade without knowing five words of English, the feeble-sighted Francesca helped with her homework and invited her to big family dinners along the alley separating Macon and Newkirk streets.

All these years later, Francesca remained the newly widowed woman's best friend.

"Hi Mr. Orlo," said Wigmann, taking a seat in a metal folding chair near the fire, freezing his ass off as the junkman par-boiled a cauldron of trotters.

"What brings you down here after all these years? Doing some last minute Christmas shopping like your old man used to do?"

Once Wigmann hit puberty, he didn't want to hang out with his father or tag along on the annual holiday visit to the Salvage House for last minute gifts you couldn't get in stores.

One Christmas Eve, Wigmann told his father he didn't feel like going to Mr. Orlo's, the same way—staring at a pile of gifts on his freezing stoop that morning—he didn't want to sit around and wait for Jesus to be born in Aunt Francie's basement.

The next year, the boy begged off again and after that Mr. Wigmann didn't ask his son to go anywhere with him anymore.

"Dad's gone," said Wigmann, taking the lid from the roasting pan and ripping off a leg from the goose, the dogs jumping on his lap.

"I know, I was at his funeral."

"How old are you now, Mr. Orlo?"

"Sixty-seven last summer."

"Dad was only fifty-two," said Wigmann, gnawing on the drum stick, picking off pieces of the carcass and teasing the dogs with it. "It's our first Christmas without him."

The bird was delicious and Wigmann wondered how it might have tasted to share it with Barbara, warm from the oven, a white tablecloth spread across the family bar. He threw a bone to the dogs and started on a wing.

"Save me the wishbone?" said Orlo.

"What's your wish?"

"I'm building a star out of them."

Wigmann pointed to the kettle.

"What's that?"

"My holiday ritual," said Orlo. "Pickled pigs feet with fig jam."

"For you and your friend? She used to give us Hershey bars wrapped in red and green cellophane when we were little. She still gives them to the little kids wrapped in five dollar bills."

"How can I help you, Junior?"

Wigmann lifted the goose from the pan like a football and tossed it into the middle of the yard. He watched the dogs rip the bird to shreds and then he startled himself.

"I need an engagement ring."

"Ah," said Orlo, covering the pot. "I got plenty of those."

Although Wigmann's vision was smaller now, Orlo's kitchen looked almost exactly the same as it did when he was little, when his father and the junkman would eat bowls of pig knuckles and *spaetzle*, washing it down with bottles of beer.

The junkman moved toward a stove near the hallway, bending over the oven and fiddling with the knobs as Wigmann inspected a china cabinet filled with records and buttons and school lunch boxes and pictures of three young men with long hair and guitars and one goofy looking guy with long hair and a drum set.

"What's this?" asked Wigmann.

Orlo turned the knob 350 degrees to the left, char-broil to the right and 200 degrees to the left. Wigmann heard a loud click and the oven door popped open.

"What's what?" said Orlo, pulling out a large tray of rings.

Wigmann tapped the cabinet glass.

"What are you doing with this kiddie stuff?"

"I've always collected fun things, Junior. You know that."

"But why this?"

"Because they're going to be huge and I like the way they cut-up," said Orlo. "This kid Frankie Lidinsky over near St. Wenceslaus gets everything the minute it hits the street and tells me what to look for."

"People are already throwing it away?"

"No," said Orlo. "There's just a ton of it out there."

"What's that hairy thing?"

"Hair."

"Whose?"

"John's."

"No."

"Yeah."

"I don't believe it."

"Don't."

"Where'd you get it?"

"From a friend whose old lady makes up beds at the Holiday Inn. She worked their rooms when they were here in March. Already been offered a grand for it."

"Gimme Frankie and Dino," said Wigmann. "I can't stand that screaming."

"Some of it's nice," said Orlo, walking the rings to the kitchen table, the tray alive—a chest of pirate's jewels—in the sunshine streaming through the window above the sink.

Wigmann picked up the rings one at a time, slipping them on all of his fingers as far as they would go—"Okay, Ringo!" laughed Orlo—and began separating them into piles: diamonds, emeralds, rubies, ornate antique settings and sleek modern ones; sapphires, opals and pearls.

"No prices on these," said Wigmann.

Orlo brought a cutting board to the table and began mashing cloves and grinding allspice across from Wigmann; a large bowl of kosher salt waiting, the room scented with the fragrance of nutmeg and cinnamon as a pot of figs boiled on the stove.

"Let me tell you about your father."

Wigmann stopped fiddling with the rings.

"Your old man was a character," said Orlo. "He'd come down here on afternoons when he couldn't stand being behind that bar a moment longer."

I know that feeling, thought Wigmann.

"And of course he loved everything German. He *loved* that Babe Ruth was German. That Mencken was German. These great Americans from Baltimore. I'd open up my Germanica room, he'd put on lederhosen and we'd drink out of steins shaped like Bavarian castles."

"Can I see the room?"

"All doorknobs now," said Orlo. "Floor to ceiling doorknobs from around the world. After he had a few, he'd get very serious, almost grave, and start talking about how he envied me because I was a real American, free like other people aren't."

"He envied you?"

"He did and he didn't," said Orlo. "He envied how I could go anywhere at any time for any reason without having to explain. Still could if I didn't ache so much. He envied my freedom and I envied him his son."

"Me?"

"Your father missed you coming down here with him. It upset him that you didn't want to come down here anymore."

"Ain't that I didn't want to."

"Only time I saw him cry."

"Is that true?"

"You'll hear it said that people love lies," said Orlo. "All I know about it is sitting on this table and out back in the pickling tub. Never been married."

"But I thought . . ."

"Nope."

"I've been messing up," Wigmann said. "I was expecting my girl last night and instead I got drunk and missed her. We were going to have an old-fashioned German Christmas, candles on the tree, just the two of us."

"Every year somebody burns their house down trying to have an old-fashioned Christmas," said Orlo.

"This is the big night, *the* night you wait all year for," said Wigmann. "And there's nothing I want to do less than sit around that table."

[I'd like to be there, thought Orlo, chuck this swine and enjoy a nice plate of fish. Wouldn't I love to hold her hand next to a cup of coffee and a plate of cookies.]

"Because your girl won't be there?"

"She might show up," said Wigmann, separating the rings into three piles: maybe, forget it, and gotta have it; his father's money tingling in his pocket as he played eenie-meenie-miney with an emerald and a ruby. "There's nothing I was looking forward to more than her knock on the door. It's Christmas and I feel bad about my father. Did he really say that about me?"

"Come on Junior. You come down here for the first time in a dozen years to ask questions there ain't no answers to and then you don't believe what I tell you."

"I wish he would have told me himself," said Wigmann. "I feel bad because I miss my girl more than I miss him."

"Of course you do," said Orlo.

"I want to chuck it all. Hop in Dad's car, find her and keep driving."

"I've ridden that train," laughed Orlo.

"You think it's funny?"

"I didn't then," said the junkman. "But I do now."

Jolly old Saint Orlo at the laughing stage after years of working himself to death to make Leini happy; the peace and wisdom of old age making him smile no matter how much his knees hurt, his back permanently wrenched after carting bathtubs from one end of the city to the other for his secret bride. In bad weather, his teeth hurt.

A year ago, in inexplicable sympathy with his adopted nation, Leini's husband had taken his life and Orlo hadn't stopped laughing since, not a whit of guilt.

"When was this?" asked Wigmann.

"Back in '55," said Orlo, chopping an onion. "Took the 2:12 Oriole

Wing to New York City to see a Chinese witch doctor what was gonna cure what ailed us."

"I didn't say I was sick," said Wigmann.

Orlo remembered when he was Wigmann's age, it was the year Leini got married, a year into their affair. He'd sat brooding on the roof of the Salvage House as his lover's wedding guests danced in a circle behind Ralph's Diner across the lunch.

Then, inexplicably, a softball game broke out, Leini at the plate in her wedding gown and then, less curious, Ralph's burned to the ground, Orlo watching from his roof across the way, harbor winds fanning the flames toward downtown.

As youth fades, the world beats acceptance into you or kicks the life out of you.

"All I want to know is where the train is going and when it's gonna get there," said Wigmann.

"That's all?"

"I wish you'd stop making fun of me," said Wigmann, who couldn't remember his father laughing much, even when something was funny. When his mother wasn't laughing or crying, she was yelling or preaching or asking her husband how in the goddamn world he could sit for hours without changing the look on his face.

"What makes you think I can answer these questions, Junior?"

"You're still making the pigs feet aren't you?" said Wigmann, who'd only tried the trotters that sweetened his mother's spaghetti sauce but once.

"That I am," said Orlo. "You know what that goofy Chinaman wanted me to do?"

"What?"

"Drink the gallbladder of a bear crushed inside a milkshake."

"And?"

"That or go home empty-handed."

[I'm ain't going home empty-handed, thought Wigmann.]

"He said it would give us energy." said Orlo.

"We want children too."

"Save your money on gall bladders," said Orlo. "It's cheaper just to love somebody."

"Didn't work?"

"There's a lot you could do with your time besides wait around for someone to see things your way," said Orlo.

"Did you know the city wants to put an expressway through this neighborhood? Already taking people's homes on Boston Street. Half the Polacks in Canton are dying of broken hearts. Crooks offered me $6,000, take it or leave it. They want to come right across the harbor with a double-decker highway to block out the sun.

"A mile the other way and they'd be coming for your father's bar. We could use somebody like you to help us fight the bastards."

Wigmann nudged the ruby to the side. Orlo turned down the flame under the figs on the stove and gathered up the salt and spices and onion to take outside.

"Did you hear what I said?" asked the junkman.

Wigmann held up an emerald in a half century old basket setting.

"This one," he said.

"For that much you could have the Beatle hair," said Orlo. "It'll be worth ten times as much long after that ring is gone."

"How much?"

"Emeralds crack easy," said Orlo as Wigmann stood up to follow him outside. "Be careful with it."

Wigmann, took out his cash.

"Listen to me, Junior," said the junkman. "If they screw this part of town, Baltimore City is finished."

-o-

For all the stands of anticipation being braided in Little Basilio's imagination—his very pulse directed to the moment when guests would stream through the front door of his grandparents' house—that's how determined Wigmann was to avoid the evening.

Wigmann had been Basilio once. He'd walked through his Aunt Francie's door with his parents and a warm dish and expectations, stuffing himself with treats while waiting for the clock to move.

But Wigmann wasn't a little boy anymore and he knew it as he drove away from the Salvage House in a light snow, a backseat full of presents and an emerald ring in his pocket.

At the Broadway Market, Basilio and his grandfather carried a hundred dollars worth of seafood out into the snow: Scallops and a bushel of oysters. The snapper and the eel. Clams. A fat rockfish. Shrimp, squid and mussels.

It was cold enough for the fish to sit in the back of the car while Grandpop indulged Basilio in a visit to Kramer's, the candy store on Eastern Avenue where corn popped in the front window and a fan pushed the scent of hot caramel out onto the sidewalk. The scent was the only advertising Kramer's ever did; caramel and fresh popped corn mixed with the clean, brisk wind and the snow as Basilio walked inside with his grandfather.

The youngster would do all of his shopping here and go home with a dozen paper bags of sweets across which he would letter the names of the people he loved and draw pictures of birds and guitars and narrow houses along Macon Street.

Wigmann watched the boy and his grandfather from a pay phone across the street from Kramer's, rattling change in his hand, wondering what to do.

Above his head, the Great Bolewicki Depression Clock goaded him: "It's not too late to start a new tradition."

Sucking on a candy cane, Wigmann gave away three of the gifts left on his stoop to the first three people who walked by: A blind man drumming his fingernails against a metal pan rattling with change; a kid with a runny nose being dragged down the street by his mother; and a not-fat-enough man in a Santa suit ringing a bell in front of Epstein's department store.

"Thanks," said the old buzzard. "Nobody ever thinks to give a gift to Santa."

With one eye watching Basilio and his grandfather browse the candy store, Wigmann dropped a dime into the phone and called home.

"Hi Ma."

"How early did you leave this morning?"

"Did I get any calls?"

"No."

"You sure?"

"What's the matter, hon?"

Wigmann paused to search for his father's cool resolve but that was half-a-pause too long.

"I need a favor, Junior."

"What Ma?"

"It's really your Aunt Francesca that needs the favor."

"What is it?"

"I don't know how my sister does it every year. All those people for a sit-down dinner. I hope you can be on time . . ."

"Ma, what do you WANT?"

"Watch yourself, young man."

"What, Ma?"

"Can you go down Pratt Street and pick up a Spanish man off a ship?"

"It never ends," muttered Wigmann.

"What's that?"

"Is the ship in yet, Ma?"

"I don't know. What's wrong, hon? I know you miss your father, we all do. But we've got to make the best of it and you know how good your Aunt Francie has been to us."

"What's the name of the ship?"

"Hold on, I got it right here."

Wigmann's mother put down the phone and he could hear her rummaging through her apartment upstairs from the saloon, picturing her in house coat and slippers. By the time she was back on the phone, Wigmann was munching on a bag of Kramer's caramel corn.

"What are you eating?"

"Nothing."

"Junk? You're going to ruin your dinner."

"It is ruined," whispered Wigmann.

"What?"

"The name of the ship, Ma. What's the name of the ship?"

"The Galicia."

"What pier?"

"I told you, Pratt Street."

"What's the man's name?"

"Mr. Steve. You remember Mr. Steve. He always brings goodies you can't get anywhere. Mr. Steve."

"I remember."

Wigmann hung up and leaned back in the booth to watch Basilio and his grandfather pull away from the candy store, munching a handful of caramel popcorn and wondering, in a swirl of flurries on Eastern Avenue, if he should go down to Pier Five or leave Mr. Steve to find his own way to Macon Street.

-o-

A letter from Spain was wedged between the storm door and the front door of 627 South Macon Street when Grandpop and Little Basilio returned from their errands. Grandpop shoved it into his back pocket and carried the food in from the car.

Basilio ran upstairs to arrange his bags of candy on the bureau beneath the skylight and draw a name on each one, but before he could smear the letters with glue and dust them with sparkles, he was called downstairs.

On the way down, he noticed his easel alongside the Christmas tree in the front window. Basilio's father and uncle had arrived while he was out, both were in aprons. Oil bubbled in a deep fryer and knives were sharpened against whetstones, the better to scale the fish and slice their bellies. Dough for empanada had been rolled out. It was time to work.

Little Basilio was assigned the tricky task of helping with the little stuff and staying out of the way. Up and down the steps they marched him for the right spoon, a certain bowl and the colander. A thousand times, up and down, a thousand passes by the idle easel.

Walk, they said, don't run.

Amuse yourself.

Be a good boy.

The preparations took most of the morning and all of the afternoon. Christmas linen folded and waiting. A pyramid of fruit sat in the center of the table as the snapper baked in the oven. Basilio's father took off his apron, sent his son upstairs for a nap with a kiss on the head and went home to clean up before returning with the rest of the family.

-o-

Like the screw of a great ship laboring against the current, Wigmann found himself on the parking lot of Connolly's, a green, ramshackle seafood house on Pratt Street to sit and wait and do what he was told.

Wigmann brought a few presents in from the car, the pile now reduced to a single package on the back seat as he walked through a stiff wind into the fish house, sitting down at a wobbly wooden table. Tortoise shells and seaman's knots hung on pale green walls.

Wigmann set the gifts on the table and looked for a waitress. Aside from a few folks getting carry-out and a man shouldering a half-bushel of oysters to his car, the place was empty. A bus boy mopping the concrete floor began setting chairs on top of the tables.

"I'll start with a beer," Wigmann said to the waitress, unwrapping one of the presents when she left and finding a paperback of *The Diary of a Young Girl.*

The oddity of the gift—a kid's book about by a Jewish girl to celebrate Christmas made Wigmann wonder what else Barbara had left that he'd given away. She inscribed it: "Anne just wasn't some kid who happened to keep a diary. She was a natural."

117

Flipping through the book as the waitress arrived with his beer, Wigmann found entries for late December and began reading.

"The Secret Annex has heard the joyful news that each person will receive an extra quarter of a pound of butter for Christmas. It says half a pound in the newspapers . . . but not for Jews who have gone into hiding."

"The oysters are good," said the waitress. "And the pan fried rock."

Wigmann put the book aside to read the menu, his headache fading with each sip of beer.

"Something heavy," said Wigmann, "Liver and onions with mashed potatoes and gravy, a side order of baked beans, the coleslaw, and apple pie. And another beer."

The waitress left with the order and Wigmann turned to Anne's second Christmas in hiding as three red tugboats with white dots on their stacks pulled a freighter—"GALICIA" on her bow—into a slip one rotting pier away.

"I couldn't help feeling a great longing to laugh until my tummy ached," read Wigmann. *"Especially at this time of the year with all the holidays . . . and we are stuck here like outcasts . . . when someone comes in from outside, with the wind in their clothes and the cold on their faces, then I could bury my head in the blankets to stop myself thinking: 'When will we be granted the privilege of smelling fresh air?'"*

Outside, as the tugboats bumped and wedged the Galicia into her berth, the air was turning colder with the setting sun; a gray December cold that moved through the floor and into the soles of Wigmann's shoes as his food arrived.

Wigmann ate fast, searched for comforting passages in the diary, ordered another beer and stuffed himself until he was nearly sick, aware that a blessing over the meal on Macon Street would be said before the hawser lines were made fast between the Galicia and the cleats of pier 5.

How many sins could you commit in one day and still tell yourself that you were a good man?

Wigmann paid the bill, scribbled the waitress's name across another present he'd brought to the table, shoved the diary in his back pocket and ambled out into the glorious fresh air of Pratt Street to watch the Galicia tie up and wait for Mr. Steve to come down the gangway.

On the way, the liver and potatoes sitting heavy in his gut, Wigmann passed a phone and dumped a pocketful of quarters into it.

"Thank you for the present," he said, jingling the ring in his pocket.

"I'm glad you liked them."

"I'll leave right now," he said.

"No." said Barbara. "Don't."

Wigmann stood at the foot of the gangway making small talk with the man on watch while waiting for Mr. Steve. It was dark and the watchman looked up at the sky as he talked about a family he hadn't seen in half a year, at peace with a seaman's knowledge that he would see Christmas arrive from a folding chair on a foreign pier.

"Yep," said Wigmann, "I'm going to drop him off, drive straight to New York and ask her to marry me."

"Good luck," said the watchman.

Wigmann took Anne's diary from his back pocket—the rising moon and a cross of white lights on the ship's stack glowing in the dark circles under the author's eyes—and handed it to the watchman as Mr. Steve appeared with a large duffel bag on his shoulder.

Wigmann drove Mr. Steve east on Lombard Street, past smoke hounds passing a jug around a fire in a barrel at the Fallsway; east toward the orange brick rowhouses of Highlandtown where Basilio was being told he must taste a bit of every dish on the table.

"How many children?" asked Steve.

"Where?"

"Tonight. How many children waiting?"

"At least three," said Wigmann. "But there could be a house full of them."

"Good," laughed Mr. Steve, his pockets jingling with silver coins. "Fill the house."

By the time Wigmann passed the Baker Whitely tugboats on Thames Street and made it around the harbor to the canning factories in Canton, the dishes from the first course had been cleared off and the three waiting children—Basilio, Donna and Jose Pepper—had been excused from the table. They were joined at the record player upstairs by a neighborhood girl named Trudy.

Jose Pepper sat next to the portable stereo, more interested in how it worked than the music coming out of it; Basilio and Donna taking turns putting on their favorite songs, the curtains parted in the front window, the tiny tree shining out onto the street as Wigmann pulled to the curb, deciding, that he at least had to help Mr. Steve in with his heavy bag and say hello to his mother.

Kneeling down outside of the basement window to glimpse the

119

celebration on the other side of the glass, Wigmann watched the meal begin anew with each fresh face that came down the steps. He imagined his old man and Barbara at the table, himself between them, explaining the different foods to her as the plates passed by, his father approving.

Wigmann's seat was empty, his plate unsoiled and his father's spot occupied by a heavy-set man from the Canary Islands peeling chestnuts with a penknife, his mother sitting close to her sisters and turning toward the steps every other moment to see if it was her son's footsteps coming down.

Wigmann belched—the invigorating cold not strong enough to make him hungry again—stood up with Mr. Steve's bag under one arm and the last present from Barbara in the other and went inside.

The house warm with familiar smells, memories overwhelming a big baby who'd spent all day stuffing himself with distractions.

"Here," said Wigmann, handing the last package—obviously a record—to Donna.

"The Beatles!" she cried, ripping the paper.

[Why them? Wigmann wondered. The Fab Four owned the world, Mr. Orlo was proof positive, but they hadn't played a part in his crumbling courtship anymore than Anne's suffering.]

"Put it on!" said Basilio, hoping Santa would be as good to him before the night was out.

Donna spun the record—*Beatles '65*—and Wigmann took her by the hand for a quick dance, gliding the girl around the room on the top of his shoes. Trudy jumped up and down with Jose Pepper and Basilio not understanding that what he was felt was jealousy.

Downstairs, Mr. Steve took a ring of dried figs from a pocket of his suit and spread them out. A three year-old circled the table, chased by a five year-old. Glasses were refilled, dishes washed and dried and used again.

Catching the Mersey beat as it pulsed through the floorboards, Mr. Steve lit a long cigar and called for the children and his bag. The kids raced down the steps—strange guests to the house were always giving children something—and Wigmann followed with the seaman's bag.

"There you are!" cried Wigmann's mother. "Sit down. Eat."

Wigmann grabbed a beer out of the refrigerator, kissed his mother on the cheek, and stood near the children and Mr. Steve. After giving the youngest kids at the table silver coins from his pocket, the Spanish seaman dug deep in his bag and brought out a box of cigars, a bottle of

Fundador cognac, a handful of unwrapped baubles, and then, one after another to squeals of delight, dolls of four young men with mop-top haircuts.

Made in Japan, no store or kid in America had the treasure being handed out on Macon Street.

"One for you," said Mr. Steve, handing the Paul doll to Donna, "And you," he said, giving Ringo to Jose Pepper, "and for you," as Trudy embraced George.

"And," he said, extending John Lennon to Basilio, "for you."

"Dolls for a boy," scoffed Grandpop.

"They're kids," said Francesca.

"You should eat a little something and take the children over to see the trains," said Wigmann's mother.

Taking the doll from his son, Basilio's father ran his hands over John's head and disparaged it in Spanish. Wigmann caught the hurt on Basilio's face as the kid grabbed the doll back from his father.

Lifelike down to McCartney's dimple, there was something odd about the dolls. Instead of arms holding guitars, the toys had wings—thin, holographic webbing of translucent plastic shaped like maple seedlings.

"They fly," said Mr. Steve, showing the kids how they worked.

"They fly!" cried Jose Pepper, jumping up and down.

"Like angels," said Mr. Steve.

Inside the boxes were launching pistols with zip cords. The feet fit into the pistols and when you pulled the cord, the doll twirled into the air. The harder you pulled, the higher they flew.

"A flying Beatle," marveled a guest as Ringo helicoptered from one end of the table to the other.

In a moment, nearly all of the adults were taking turns zipping the dolls around the basement.

Watching the dolls fly, Leini imagined the sex she would enjoy when the other women walked to Midnight Mass with their children and grandchildren. She picked at a fried tentacle of squid while savoring the prospect of sharing her secret delicacy in a few hours with Orlo.

But couldn't keep images of her husband, a suicide, dead almost a full year now, from jarring her thoughts, and worse, what would she and the junkman do if the Salvage House was razed for the expressway. No guilt, not a whit of regret as she reached out and caught a George sailing by.

While others clamored to be the next to play—the kids jumping up and down for a turn, pulling at the hem of her black dress—Leini stared into the sweet face of the quiet one and felt an odd, wistful peace.

"Do you want to know a secret?" she hummed. "Do you promise not to tell?"

Leini gave the doll back to Trudy and asked Mr. Steve where she could get a set.

"Hell," said Basilio's other grandmother, a Lithuanian cannery worker. "By Easter they'll have shelves of 'em up Epstein's."

Mr. Steve leaned toward Leini with the self-assured smile that the Greek—still a beauty at fifty-five—only saw in the faces of certain Europeans. He offered her a peeled chestnut.

"Not only did somebody figure out how to make them fly, but made sure they flew beautifully," said Trudy's father, a mechanic at Crown, Cork & Seal. "That's about as close to intangible as you can get."

Beautifully they flew until the Jewel Tea sugar bowl fell to the floor, a glass of wine tipped over, a baby who wanted a turn started to cry and Grandpop slapped his palm against the table.

"What are we?" he demanded. "Americans?"

"Okay kids," said Basilio's mother, getting up to make coffee. "Take them upstairs,"

Wigmann grabbed another beer from the refrigerator, told his mother he wasn't hungry, and followed the children up the steps. As the kids ran outside with the dolls, Wigmann picked up the receiver on the black wall phone in the kitchen to try Barbara again.

When no one answered, he trooped out into the cold with his beer to join the children.

Trudy and Donna and Jose Pepper were tentative pulling their strings; Paul, George and Ringo barely rising higher than the wire fence before falling near their feet.

They turned to Basilio: "Your turn."

And for some reason—a vague feeling akin to the one he felt watching Donna dance with Wigmann, something close to the burn he felt when his father called the Beatles sissies—Basilio yanked the cord with all his might and John shot through the night sky as if fired from a gun.

Their heads tilted back, the children watched as the doll cleared the trees, and then the rooftops, soared beyond the chimneys and into the clouds and then—as though the stars reached down to receive him—John Lennon was assumed into the heavens over Highlandtown.

"Wow!" said Donna.

"Geezy," said Jose Pepper.

Wigmann whistled and Basilio began to cry.

"It's lost!"

"It's okay," said Wigmann, grateful for the most beautiful thing he'd seen all day. "We'll find it."

"I'm cold," said Trudy, picking up her doll and going inside.

"Me too," said Jose Pepper.

"Basilio," said Donna, rushing in the house and running back out. "Take your coat."

Basilio wiped his nose, put on his coat and followed Wigmann into the alley.

"Don't worry," said Wigmann. "I knew a girl once just as talented as you, but her family was in such a bad way at Christmas that Santa brought just enough butter to make a few biscuits."

"I don't want biscuits," said Basilio.

[We *are* Americans, thought Wigmann.]

"I know," said Wigmann, scouring the backyards and trees for the doll. "I'm just telling you how it is sometimes."

At the end of the alley, Wigmann got an idea. He sat Basilio down on a set of cold marble steps across the street from the beer garden, told the boy to stay put and slipped into the saloon. Inside, he ran to the top floor, opened a small hatch in the ceiling and squeezed his way onto the roof.

Inconsolable, his teeth chattering in the cold, Basilio watched Wigmann's silhouette zig-zag across the rooftops as he checked inside the rain gutters and bumped up against chimneys. After searching from one end of the block to the other, Wigmann appeared before the shivering boy and said he was sorry.

Taking Basilio by the hand, Wigmann walked into the bar, hit the lights, poured the kid a Coca-Cola and punched up "She Loves You" on the jukebox before tossing the soggy ginger snaps in the trash.

Pulling down an 8-foot by 8-foot wooden garden from the wall—five trains circling three platforms through secret passageways; farm houses; a town square with a water fountain and miniature Ferris wheel— Wigmann turned the bar into a carnival.

"Maybe the Beatles are just for girls," said Basilio.

"The grown-ups are wrong on this one," said Wigmann. "Just like some people will tell you that nobody eats sauerkraut on Thanksgiving, but I do."

"You're a grown-up," said Basilio.

"Only because I'm older than you."

Leaving the boy alone with the trains, Wigmann walked behind the bar and into his bedroom. A moment later, he approached Basilio with open palms; a lock of brown hair in one hand and a swatch of bed sheet in the other.

"Merry Christmas!"

"What is it?"

"Stuff that's going to be worth a million dollars because of ten million kids like you."

"Hair?"

"John's."

Basilio's heart jumped.

"No."

"Yes."

"Where'd you get it?"

"When they were here." said Wigmann. "I know somebody."

Wondering how you could know anyone that important, Basilio pointed to Wigmann's other hand.

"A piece of the sheets they slept on at the Holiday Inn, the one with the revolving restaurant on top, right there on Lombard Street. Suite 1013," said Wigmann. "Open your hands."

Wigmann set the hair and the linen in Basilio's palms and gently closed the boy's fingers around them. Over on Oldham Street, the bells of Holy Redeemer Chapel began ringing for midnight Mass.

"Yours."

"All mine?"

"To keep."

"Can I tell?"

"They won't believe you."

Walking Basilio out to the alley, Wigmann handed the boy over to a parade of women and children making their way to church.

"Just showing him the trains," he said as Basilio skipped into line with Donna and Jose Pepper, hands tight in his pockets around the frankincense and myrrh.

"Say a few prayers for me, Ma," said Wigmann, giving his mother a hug before going inside to drink a beer and watch the trains run, twinkling lights glinting off a cracked emerald ring and a pair of scissors laying open on his bed.

TOO ROLLING TOOKIE
[JANUARY 15, 1976]

FIVE CARVING KNIVES and a brown paper bag of plastic straws. Two ice picks, a wooden handled corkscrew, one large barbecue fork and a 1950's Hamilton Beach Milk Shake mixer, a wedding gift to my parents.

I'm limping from tile-to-tile, yeah, man, me and Jimmy Page, we're "out on the tiles . . ."

No double-neck Gibson and a violin bow, just me and this broken leg, a clipboard and a retractable pen that says Tukulski Pet Food Supply.

They're running stock cars on the dirt track in the woods across the road: *"Saturday! Saturday! Saturday! See the Fabulous Funny Cars at Diabolical Dorsey Drag Raceway!"*

Even in the snow they gun those wrecks. And it's snowing pretty good now, good enough to cancel school. I'd give anything to be done with this stupid inventory and get out of the house.

Uncle Falooch pays me $20 a week to catalog every last spoon and No. 2 pencil in the house. They just passed the minimum wage, $2.30 an hour, so a twenty ain't bad, depending on how fast I go. Falooch has got plenty money but he spends half of it on old radios and stuffs the rest under the mattress. He lives here for free, he's Mom's mother's brother, so he makes up stupid chores for me to do and slips me a couple bucks so he don't feel like a freeloader.

Mom says I waste the money on "worthless crap." She should know.

A pair of mounted butterflies, a large, porcelain wine decanter shaped like a poodle (poodle bites, baby, poodle chews it); more than a hundred "bingo daubers," in all colors of watery ink to mark bingo cards; a pair of burned pizza pans, and, above the stove, a saloon clock that reminds us at every meal that we are fortunate to be residing in "The Land of Pleasant Living."

Mom went batshit when I told her what I was doing and ordered me not to "come near any of me and your father's personal stuff. Why the hell does he have to know what we got in the house?

"Ain't it enough *he's* in the goddamn house?"

In the foyer: a pair of antique barber chairs; a ceramic knick-knack of a rooster chasing a white girl paired with one of a black boy chasing a hen; a broken Montgomery Ward organ, more of a toy than an instrument, just another flat surface for my mother's knick-knack paddywhacked nightmare of frogs and lily pads and toadstools.

The closet: two tennis rackets, one wooden, one aluminum; nineteen assorted coats, including one with a moth-eaten fox head, and a canister vacuum cleaner: EUREKA!

I wish Basilio would come by and get me. That asshole never calls. He either shows up or he doesn't.

Above the kitchen sink, a gem Falooch has coveted since he got too old to live by himself, an Emerson my mother got when she made her Confirmation at St. Augustine's over in Elkridge. They call it a portable but it weighs a ton, like a car battery with a couple of knobs and a dial in see-through, salmon-colored Bakelite.

"Knock, knock . . ."

"Who's there?"

"Emerson."

"Emerson who?"

"Emerson big titties you got there, sister!"

I got it turned to WAYE-AM and "Time Was" by Wishbone Ash from Argus. Got it up as loud as it'll go. My parents are out trying to make all of the day's deliveries before the roads get too bad and Falooch is half deaf.

Man, it's really coming down. I can hardly see past the statue of the Blessed . . . well, whaddaya know! Here comes the Rock Star, banging up the drive in his mother's space station Pacer—Montrose, Space Station No. 5!—wearing state trooper mirror shades in a fucking blizzard!

Yee-haw!

I keep trying to talk him into running the Pacer over at the dirt track across the street. "Right, Tookie," he says, dark brown Beatle hair down past the collar of his Quadrophenia army jacket.

"Get in the fucking car."

What a car! "Mellow Yellow" paint job; brown vinyl bucket seats, fake wood paneling on the dash—Adjust-O-Tilt steering column!—and black vinyl roof. Factory-installed 8-track built into the console and a born-again bumper sticker on the ass.

"God Gave Rock & Roll To You."

My folks are gonna kill me when they find out I split, like they almost broke my other leg after I fell off the roof when I was up there drinking beer instead of cleaning out the gutters. I'm supposed to start up the Crock Pot for dinner. What'd they expect me to do? Stay home?

Fucking Basilio. Everybody in school tried to lay a nickname on him but nothing stuck. We're seniors at Transfiguration High, best friends. Rock and roll has never let us down and I ain't gonna let him down.

If Basilio's crazy enough to come get me in a blizzard, I'm crazy enough to go. Stove off, lights off, a quick shout up to Falooch—he's either dead or sleeping—door locked and I'm gone.

First thing when I open the door, a thick cloud of pot smoke billows out into the bite of January (not November winter, not December winter, not New Year's Day winter. January winter. JOHNNY WINTER!)

He doesn't help me with the door, doesn't help me with my crutches, he just sits there swiveling his head as Captain Beefheart howls along with Zappa's guitar, Frank bending strings the way Einstein bent light.

(Beefheart's thirty-five today. Last week, Zappa told Dick Cavett: "The disgusting stink of a too loud electric guitar. Now that's my idea of a good time.")

Basilio's got a paper cup of Dunkin Donuts coffee on the dash and a half-smoked joint in the ashtray. The new *Rolling Stone* is face-up on the passenger seat, Bob Dylan and Joan Baez on the cover all bundled up like they're on a fucking ski trip.

"What a pile of shit," I said, fishing the joint out of the ashtray as Basilio turns around in the driveway. "Keith Moon could eat Joan Baez for breakfast."

"Yeah, but Bob might give him a run for his money," said Basilio, putting his nose close the windshield to see, snow coming down harder than ever, heading for the place he was always headed: the City of Baltimore.

Rock and Roll.

II
[AUGUST, 16, 1977]

Dear Tookie—

Hey, Crazy Motherfucker. Greetings from the poop deck!

The sun is going down over the Gulf and I'm hiding between containers topside, getting stoned with a couple beers I hid in the galley ice box.

The sunsets are stunning, breathtaking even before you catch the heavy-heavy, so you can imagine how sweet they are with a nice buzz. I started sketching the stern of the ship. I think I'm facing Haiti.

We're headed for New Orleans again, New Orleans every twelve days, coming in empty and going out with everything from frozen chickens to Kodak film. I'm too fried to draw so I thought I'd drop a line. Been too long.

I think my work is getting better. I've been drawing the men who work in the steward department, their big faces poking into pots of boiling water. Most of them are Puerto Rican on this run, back and forth between San Juan and New Orleans, sometimes Beaumont, Texas.

When the rest of the crew headed for the whorehouse I looked up Johnny's parents in the white pages and there was his old man: John Dawson Winter, Jr. I grabbed a cab on the dock and rode by the house, but I didn't knock.

The chief cook sweats right on through the paper of his cigarette and every ten seconds wipes his face with a filthy rag and says, "It's a hot tamale today!"

He looks like Ernest Borgnine, only not as handsome!

I guess you know that Elvis died today. I was sitting in the galley waiting for chow and we were getting fuzzy reception out of Miami and there was Dave Marsh—I READ IT IN *ROLLING STONE*, IT MUST BE TRUE!—preaching on TV with news anchors like it was Dallas or something.

A black messman looked up at the TV—it hangs on chains screwed into the ceiling—and laughed, hard and ugly.

He really put effort into it. HA! HA! HA!

I wanted to knock his teeth out. I used to catch a buzz with him in his focsle and listen to Parliament-Funkadelic and Sly. Didn't even know I gave a shit. I always thought the Beatles gave birth to themselves.

I was already cranky 'cause I was coming down from tripping, couple hits of windowpane last night, didn't get a wink. You know how when the flashes are over and that Morse code runs up and down your spine for hours? Reefer buzz I got going now is taking some of the edge off and I'm hoping to sleep before the 4-to-8 rolls around again.

I dropped about an hour before sunset, washed it down with a beer, tied my ankles to the legs of the steel desk that's bolted to the deck in my room and hung myself upside down out the porthole.

They're big and rectangular now, not the round kind like on the *Titanic*. Secured my ass with a Baltimore knot. Know what a Baltimore knot is, Took? The bosun named it after me. It's a knot that's never tied the same way twice!

Tripping my nuts off, hanging out the port hole, my head just a foot above the waterline as the ship pushed through the ocean, spray soaking my head as I stared up at the stack and the stars, everything twirling like flying lamp shades. Black night, a million diamonds and I'm seeing the moon wash purple and pink and popsicle green.

When the guy from the 12-to-4 came to get me to relieve him, he had to haul me back in. The Baltimore knots held fast, though. Wouldn't be writing to you now if they didn't.

You know how I found out Elvis was important, Took? I mean *really* important? Scratch that mop, wrack that boiled noodle between your ears.

Howie Wyeth.

Remember the blizzard in our senior year when we went down the waterfront to see Mr. Orlo and bought that old Meershaum? I almost pissed myself laughing when you called your parents after we got stuck down on Clinton Street. "Hi Pop, me and Basilio went to the library . . ."

Hey Took—YOU FORGOT ALL ABOUT THE LIBRARY LIKE YOU TOLD YOUR OLD MAN NOW!

We were making fun of *Rolling Stone* for putting Dylan and Joan Baez on the cover. That magazine got mixed in with all the shit I threw in my bag when I shipped out the day after we graduated. Finally got around to reading it.

Howie played piano on that Rolling Thunder tour—me and you asking our parents for money to go see Foghat at the Civic Center while Dylan's putting on Ziggy make-up and rocking out with Mick Ronson and Roger McGuinn and a gorgeous fiddle player named Scarlet.

Holy Jumboly, she's hot! Like this crazy third mate on my watch likes to say: "I'd marry her brother just to get in the family!"

Here's the line that stayed with me from that article. Somebody was talking about Elvis and then somebody pointed across the dressing room to Howie and said he played a piano that was "ancient, holy and American."

Man, I even like the way those words look on paper: ancient—holy—American.

I wanted to find him right away—in New Orleans you can find anything; maybe ask him about his grandfather, see if I could pick up a couple of tricks, but the closest I've gotten so far is a new album by a guy out of D.C. named Robert Gordon and Link "Rumble" Wray!

Rockabilly, Tookie: Elvis, holy American piano, amphetamines and the Killer!

I bought it on vinyl and one of the engineers (one of the guys who took the Elvis news hard, told the messman to shut his goddamn mouth) has a turntable in his room and copied it onto a cassette for me before we shoved off.

Then I was looking through some other magazine, some newsprint rag they were giving away in a record store on Decatur, and some New York guitar player named Robert Ross said Howie used to play drums for him.

"If you ain't at your best," said Ross, "Howie's gonna bury you in a barrage of brilliance on a yard sale kit made out of trash can lids and spaghetti pots . . . very rare."

When I find him, Took, I'm going to ask him for both of us: What the fuck was Mick

Ronson doing on tour with Bob Dylan?

Musicians are different from me and you. I'm not sure how, but they are.

You think Robin Trower wrote "Rock Me Baby"? Start reading the publishing credits and you'll find out who the real cats are. Everybody wrote that song, even some goof named Johnny Cymbal.

JOHNNY CYMBAL!

I'm learning so much stuff out here, Took (not about being a seaman, I kind of fake my way through that). My old man was the real thing. He left Macon Street when he was sixteen for his first run to Venezuela on a Beth Steel ore ship. I'm just playing.

But I like it and I don't think I'm coming back to go to college like my folks wanted me to do after we got out of Transfiguration.

Remember the day we got our diplomas? Me and you and Flannery racing up CharlesStreet in Mom's Pacer, passing a fat one and listening to Trower kick the shit out of "Too Rolling Stoned"?

132

Takers get the honey, Tookie Took. Givers sing the blues.

I told my parents I needed a year to figure it out. Not sure how much I need now, but I know I need more. I got a cheap room near the SIU hall in New Orleans and between ships I stay in and paint. I don't even get high that much (not too much) when we're in port. Me and a hot plate, my brushes in vegetable cans.

I miss Trudy, but not enough to come home yet. She took a bus to visit once and I'm trying to get her to come again. Don't want to lose her. I'm gonna finish this beer and try to get some sleep. We hit New Orleans in a couple days and I'll drop this in the box.

Write to the return address: B.B.; Ordinary Seaman, c/o the S.S. Esmeralda, Navieras de Puerto Rico, 2700 Broening Highway, Baltimore, 21222.

Hey, Took, is it really running away from home if you're already gone but you just don't come back?

I remain, too fucking wild,

The extraordinary ordinary . . .

III
[JANUARY 7, 2006]

I buried Falooch today, just me and two or three people who knew him and weren't dead themselves yet. Fuck it was cold, the ground frozen and my bad leg acting up.

I kept turning around, thinking I'd see Basilio walking through the tombstones with that "I'm smarter than you" smile on his face. Don't know why. Haven't seen him since the day we graduated. But that's what I was thinking, my mind wandering while the priest laid the mumbo jumbo on ole Falooch.

Last I heard, Basilio and Trudy got divorced and he was living in the house where his father grew up, painting pictures of crabs and rockfish on the sides of seafood trucks. I think he's got a grown daughter, that's what his mom told my mom at the supermarket a while back. When Mom passed it was just me and Dad and Falooch and then it was just me and Falooch.

I bet that old goat has three hundred radios stuffed in here. I'll find out soon enough. I'm gonna inventory every stationary bike and Kewpie doll from attic to basement; even the nail the Sacred Heart is hanging on. And then I'm gonna sell all of it on eBay, air the whole joint out and sell it to the first asshole who shows up with cash.

What did Mom always say? The whole kit and kaboodle.

I got the old A&P clipboard here on my lap, rolling a fat one—Basilio used to call them "Fidel Burgers"—4:30 in the afternoon and it's dark already, all by myself in this house, really alone, for the first time in my life.

This shit costs $100 for an eighth. You get about five skinny joints out of it. Me and Basilio used to buy a pound of tumbleweed Mexican for $140 in high school, sell three-quarters and keep the rest for our trouble.

Sometimes the only buzz you got was a vicious headache. A couple of tokes of this hydra-ponic shit—man, it's got colors I haven't seen since I played with crayons; half-a-doob of this and you're done for the day. I'll be cooked soon enough, laying on the twin bed Falooch slept in with the six-shooters carved into the headboard and ten million radios.

Falooch collected radios like other people bring home lost dogs. He'd find them in alleys and garbage cans, bring 'em home and patch 'em up. These shelves are just cinderblock and cut up plywood; rechargeable batteries and surge protectors and extension cords all over the place.

Every night he'd tune all of them to a show on the same AM station: "George Noory's Coast To Coast," nothing but flying saucers, shadow people and life on Mars. Before I started getting high and running out as soon as dinner was over, I'd come in and listen with him. Falooch said he liked the show because it proved that man doesn't know anything.

(Man, this is good dope. Fifty times stronger than it used to be and I don't enjoy it half as much.)

Falooch always had his eye on my mother's Bakelite Emerson and when she died, the first thing he did was sneak it in here with all the others like I wouldn't know. I'd rescue it and he'd steal it back and I'd come and get it again until I got tired of playing and let him keep it. He's got it in a place of honor near the window, next to a 9-volt plastic Ferris Wheel from that dumb carnival show on HBO. We don't even have cable. He must have sent away for it.

Once, when it was just me and Falooch living here, fighting over who had to do the dishes, I saw a write-up in the *Sunpapers* saying Basiio's old friend Mr. Orlo had died and the new owner was going to sell all the junk for next-to-nothing.

I told Falooch about the radios Orlo had and talked him into getting out for a change. We got lost and came home, Falooch giving me a bunch of shit about why you shouldn't go any farther from home than your feet will take you.

People think it's a long way between the 'burb and the city because it looks so different but if it ain't rush hour and you take the tunnel, you can be at Basilio's grandfather's house in fifteen minutes.

Twelve miles away and I never saw him again.

That snowy day when we drove to the junk house is one of my favorite memories of all time. Everything closed but hospitals and police stations but we went out anyway, riding around, getting high, driving up this lane of oyster shells covered with snow to a castle with SALVAGE HOUSE painted on the side in ten foot tall letters.

Basilio said Orlo used to give him a couple bucks and a six-pack to touch up the letters in the summer.

We looked through all of the junk, one room was nothing but doorknobs and another was like a hippie museum. I found an original copy of *Look at Yourself* by Uriah Heep, the one that came with reflective foil on the front so you could, you know, look at yourself. Still got it, mint condition.

Basilio asked about some busted frames in a corner and Mr. Orlo made us hot chocolate. We walked out to the end of the pier with our mugs—the real deal, milk and Hershey's syrup, none of that Swiss Piss crap—and finished off the roach, watching the tugboats go back and forth past Fort McHenry in the snow.

Basilio kept saying that if he could just get that scene to yield. I always remembered that word he used, yield. If he could paint tugboats riding past Fort McHenry in the snow the way he wanted to that he'd be a real artist.

I don't know what the fuck he was talking about. He could draw anything. Once this lady down the street from his parents' house gave him $100 and who knows what else to paint Dion DiMucci on one of her kitchen cabinets.

I was listening to "Coast to Coast" once and someone called in and told Noory that Dion was jogging down the street one day and saw God. Noory plays a lot of good music on his show when he's not talking to people who've had their appendix taken out by aliens.

Sometimes Basilio drew faces at the bottom of the letters he sent me from sea, the guys he worked with, his own mug, George and Ringo. I loved getting those letters, the stories he told. You know how people talk about something cool that they've seen but you haven't, like Niagara Falls or one of those skull mountains in Cambodia?

I never saw the things Basilio saw. After high school, I started taking care of things around here. Never saw much outside of Dorsey, but I did see an eclipse once in the backyard.

Then the letters stopped. A couple of times I thought of calling, thought he'd come to my dad's funeral and then I thought he'd come to my mom's and today I thought I'd see him walking through the graveyard to ask if I wanted to get high.

Wish I knew what happened to his mother's car. I think Mr. Boullosa paid three grand for it at the AMC dealer in Glen Burnie in '75. It'd go for almost $6,000 today in good shape.

Me and Basilio thought 1976 was so un-cool. We said we were having fun—we did have fun, a lot of fun—but bitched a lot about how we'd missed the real stuff; daydreaming about things that happened when we were nine and ten, the Stones touring with Ike and Tina, flying that flag for the first time: the Greatest Rock and Roll Band in the World.

By 1976, Evelyn "Champagne" King had taken all the chicks away, the old Lion King

Elton was on the throne and things just seemed to get worse every year, especially when Keith Moon died in '78.

There was the Ramones. God bless those glue-sniffing knuckleheads. They saved rock and roll for a couple of days but nobody was listening when they were alive. Joey dead, Johnny dead, Dee-Dee dead.

A couple years ago, they came out with Volume 5 of Dylan's Bootleg Series: *Live '75, the Rolling Thunder Revue.* I'm not sure I can hear Howie's "holy ancient American piano," but I like it, especially "The Lonesome Death Of Hattie Carroll" 'cause it's a Baltimore song.

They release everything today, all the stuff that used to be mysterious and legendary. It's all out there now; the vaults are empty and nothing's secret in the Information Age. Not even Brian's smile.

Humble Pie had this song we all listened to: "Thirty days in the hole . . ."

More like thirty years if you ask me. Whew, I'm buzzed. You can trip on this shit. Better stand up and put some music on, open the window on this witch's tit.

I'll tune 'em all to 105.7 FM, WKTK, Good Time Oldies: all Beatles, all Stones, a lot of Who, "Lola" by the Kinks at least once a day, Cream and Skynyrd, and, if you're really lucky, every now and then, some Nazareth, Mott the Hoople and "Rebel, Rebel" by Bowie.

"Helter Skelter" as loud as it will go. I'm gonna dial 'em all up to the same station the way Falooch used to.

Me and Basilo thought we were cooler than everybody else because we could name all of Zappa's albums in order, from *Freak Out* right on through *Roxy & Elsewhere.*

We'd translate "knirps for moisture" to fuck with our Spanish teacher and thought Bob Dylan was square for playing cowboy music, not hip enough to know it was hillbilly music.

Who could figure out how Mick Ronson teleported from Bowie's Spiders to helping Dylan put on make-up for the Rolling Thunder Revue?

How do you get all those guitars out of your head so you can think straight?

Mick Ronson and Steve Marriott dead . . .

Howie Wyeth dead.

Elvis dead.

Zappa pink slipped with prostate cancer, just like my old man.

How weird is that?

Beatle John and Beatle George.

First my parents and now Falooch, dead as a hammer in this bed just a couple days ago, all of his radios giving the morning's traffic report going at once.

The day we got our diplomas, the centennial class of the Transfiguration High School of Baltimore, was the last time I ever saw Basilio Boullosa.

For all I know, that crazy motherfucker's dead too.

Good God, how we loved to ride around all day and all night, getting high and listening to Johnny Winter wail.

"Every now and then I know it's kind of hard to tell . . . but I'm still alive and well."

WEDDING DAY
[1988]

SICK TO HIS stomach on the cool marble altar, Basilio Boullosa was dressed like a million bucks and dreaming of green bananas.

Bananas that rot before they ripen.

Green with envy.

Green with promise.

Green, straight to black.

From his spot on the altar of the Basilica of the Assumption of the Blessed Virgin Mary in Baltimore, the young painter could see everything.

The happy couple, the priest before them, and three hundred of their guests.

He saw his parents, his baby daughter and a tear—for him—in his mother's eye.

Opposite Basilio, at the head of a row of bridesmaids, sweet icing on a bitter cake: Roxanne.

They'd been introduced just before the curtain went up on this cold, bright afternoon in late December, their conversation limited to which way to turn and when to do so; instructions for a parade route.

(The night before, since Roxanne hadn't yet arrived from out-of-town, Basilio had rehearsed with the bride's widowed mother.)

All he had pledged was to bear witness to love's great pageant, yet the young man who made his money painting signs was more spooked today than when it had been his turn, not so long ago.

You don't get a view like this when you are in the barrel, he thought, when it would be bad form to turn around to see what's behind you.

Joseph loves Mary.

And Mary loves Joe.

They do.

They do.

They do.

Basilio's best friend was marrying the girl of his dreams before God and family in the first Roman Catholic Cathedral in the United States.

And Basilio, who had not picked up a sincere brush in more than a year, who'd moved in with his parents after his marriage had died like an infant in its crib and had tried and tried and tried again to paint his daughter and attempted a portrait of Joe and Mary for their big day only to duck flying shards and crusty glue from his shattered sugar bowl; the same shit that rained down when he tried to capture Trudy the way he remembered her back when she wanted him: riding a bicycle through her parents' neighborhood; Basilio who every week sent Trudy a small support check by drawing crabs and fish on the sides of refrigerated trucks—this young man had agreed to testify to the power of love.

High Mass incense wafted over the 90-proof shot of courage in his stomach as Basilio managed to smile for the good things before his eyes; wondering why people say things they can only hope to be true.

Paint or die, the good news and hard truth.

The altar glowed in the warmth of three hundred faces bathing Joe and Mary in beams of joy, but it was a dim bulb next to the flood lights of devotion the betrothed poured into each other.

Basilio's wedding ring tumbled through nervous fingers in his tuxedo pocket and while he wasn't sure at age twenty-six that if your search is true you will happen upon another heart of contradictions that feels as you do, he still wanted it.

He'd rid himself of the ring today.

Leave it on the altar.

Or drop it in the poor box.

When Basilio was a boy and his family drove into the Holy Land for Sunday dinner at his grandparent's house on Macon Street, he'd lead the younger kids in make-believe Mass down by the bottle cap factory, consecrating sugar wafers into Hosts; all of the children kneeling together on the sidewalk to watch him scratch—wedding cakes like flying saucers onto the sidewalk with rocks, the smart-alecks teasing him that he wanted to marry his cousin Donna and torturing him that he couldn't unless he wanted to go to jail.

In the Catholic church, matrimony is the only sacrament in which the priest is merely a witness; in truth, the man and woman marry themselves.

You make believe the way you make a painting.

The way Basilio had not for so long.

"Joseph and Mary, have you come here freely and without reservation? Will you love and honor one another until death? Will you accept children lovingly from God?"

Basilio tried to catch Roxanne's eye.

"All the days of my life," promised Mary.

"Each and every day," said Joseph.

The priest asked for the rings and Basilio had to think for a moment so he didn't pass his bad luck onto Joe.

He'd taken the dive before any of his friends.

"I love her, Dad," he told his father, arrogant in his youth. "That's why."

His parents were merciful when Basilio came back to the same kitchen table to tell of the collapse and ask for his old room back.

Taking the ring from Basilio and placing it on Mary's finger, Joe prayed that he would never take his wife for granted as his bride asked God to remind her to always give her husband encouragement.

As they exchanged rings, Basilio washed the cathedral with the busy brushes in his head, his real ones dry and brittle on a windowsill of the house he'd shared with Trudy and a red and gold umbrella behind him on the altar.

Red and gold: the colors of Spain.

Basilio's grandparents' marriage had been arranged in a basement kitchen in Highlandtown by people who knew better and it had lasted for fifty-seven years. He glimpsed his face in the golden chalice held aloft by the priest and he began whispering to his reflection: Take it easy. No big deal. You're just helping out a friend.

Not only had Joe done the same for him—best friends and best man—his old buddy from Transfiguration High spent a long evening trying to persuade Trudy to give it another try.

"What'd she say?" Basilio had pestered. "What'd she say?"

"She just said, 'Joe, I gotta go . . .'"

The bridal party was turned out in verdant shades of Eire with accents of orange in homage to Mary's dead, Protestant father; green and orange in tribute to the troubles her parents had overcome.

In Basilio's row: Emerald bowties and matching cummerbunds.

In Roxanne's: Kelly green and black velvet.

Satin sculpted and scalloped along white flesh and freckles and in each pretty head, fragrant blossoms of orchid: trellised, Dreamsicle petals of *comparettia*.

A wedding's worth of just-this-morning blooms had not come cheap, but Joe had paid the cost with the surety that it was money he'd never have to spend again. Mary hadn't need to grace her head with orange for it was a natural, coruscating copper, a crown trimmed in white lace.

The flowers took Basilio back to his childhood, back when Grandmom was living and Grandpop still slept upstairs in their bed; back to summer vacations painting flowers in their small backyard, adolescent easel built from grape crates and set beneath the clothesline, the alley behind Macon Street exploding with roses in May, tomatoes in July; sunflowers and figs as the summer wore on, the vegetable man idling through the alley in a pick-up with a scale hanging in the back.

If any of his juvenalia survived, Basilio didn't know where.

The Flowers of Highlandtown.

How to get back there?

Basilio traced Roxanne with desire dipped in paint; green satin and black velvet hugging plump curves; hair barely tamed around a pale, oval face from another country, another age; the kind of eyes that peered over golden fans at bullrings before her people were expelled from the land of Basilio's ancestors and a mouth like a baby's heart.

"I do . . ." said Joseph.

"I will," said Mary.

-o-

Two great Baltimore temples stand face-to-face on Cathedral Street: the Basilica of the Assumption of the Blessed Virgin Mary and the Enoch Pratt Free Library.

Joe and Mary strode from one to the other with the promise of Spring in their hearts, applause in their ears and the bite of December at their backs. It was dusk, a few stars and a pale moon showing as a cop held back traffic for the bridal party to cross over to the reception.

Basilio wanted to say something to Roxanne—something new—but he couldn't think of anything and now the library was in front of them, its doors dividing a dozen display windows inspired by the department store palaces of the 1920s, windows dressed with the Story of Joe and Mary.

Baby pictures side-by-side, First Communion portraits and posters of them at pastel proms.

The streetlamps came on and flurries of snow danced in their margarine glow. Basilio breathed in the winter air, close enough now to

144

dust Roxanne's every pore. Glancing down at his shoes and the thick white lines of the crosswalk, he said: "Just like Abbey Road."

In her best *scouse*, Roxanne thanked Basilio for taking her hand—"very much . . ."—as they stepped over the curb and he took it as a good sign.

The lobby of the library was crowded with long tables covered in white cloth, a ballroom walled with books, and Basilio and Roxanne stood together behind their chairs at the head table as Joe and Mary were introduced as man and wife for the first time.

Scanning the crowd for his parents and daughter, Basilio spotted a sign on a shelf above the bride and groom.

"Look," he said, touching Roxanne's elbow. "New Fiction."

What kind of good luck speech can a best man give when the thought of marriage is turning his stomach? The one he has rehearsed.

"GERONIMO!" shouted Basilio, before tossing back a glass of champagne.

Taking his bride's hand, Joe took Mary out onto the floor for the first dance of their marriage, arms around each other, whispering and laughing, eyes locked.

Roxanne scanned the shelf at her elbow and pulled down a fat book of paintings by Chagall. Flipping through the pages, she happened upon a bride in a white gown wandering through a sapphire canvas of cocks and fiddlers.

"What do you think?" she asked Basilio.

"Nice colors," he said, moving an index finger across the lavender bridal canopy. "I'm going to find my family. Want to come?"

"I'll wait," said Roxanne, squinting past Basilio for a glimpse of his daughter; beginning to ache—not again, she thought, not here—the way Basilio had ached on the altar.

At his parents' table, Basilio kissed his mother, put his hand on his father's shoulder and knelt down before India.

"Hey baby," he said. "Hey pretty girl."

"Da-da!"

"Baby doll," said Basilio, pressing his forehead against his daughter's stomach, making her laugh.

"Isn't her dress pretty, Daddy?" asked Basilio's mother, picking up the plate before her looking for her reflection in it. "Did I ever tell you about our wedding? The reception was downstairs on Macon Street. Those old Spaniards drank and sang for three days and the Polacks half-killed themselves trying to keep up."

She ran her finger around the gold leaf along the edge of the plate.

"We ate off of your grandmother's wedding china. It's still down there. Now that would make a nice picture."

"It's only a pretty dress on a pretty girl, Ma," said Basilio, kissing India on the top of her head and going back to his seat when the bridal party was invited to join Joe and Mary on the dance floor.

Basilio and Roxanne danced near the bride and groom; Joe winking at them over Mary's shoulder and Mary doing the same when they turned.

"Look at them," Roxanne said. "Complete happiness."

(Not that long ago, with no hope of any happiness, Roxanne had sent the father of her child-to-be away.)

"Complete?" laughed Basilio.

"Looks like it."

"Ever hear about Elvis's wedding?"

"No."

"They had a six-tiered cake—five feet tall," he said, holding his hand above the ground to show the magnificence of it. "Priscilla got pregnant on their wedding night."

"So why'd she leave him for her karate teacher?"

"Not right away she didn't," said Basilio. "Not at first."

Moving in time with the music, Basilio saw India bouncing in her chair and glimpsed a wisp of Trudy in his daughter's face.

"Have you ever painted her?" asked Roxanne.

"Priscilla?"

"Your daughter."

"Elvis took 'obey' out of the vows but only if Priscilla dyed her hair black and piled it up high in a beehive. Just like the old ladies up in Highlandtown."

"Highlandtown?"

"The Holy Land," said Basilio.

Late in the party, Mary asked the band for "Daddy's Little Girl" and walked out onto the floor to greet the melody alone. Her mother joined her after the first verse, their arms around each other's neck as Joe stood on the side and watched his bride grieve on her wedding day.

Roxanne's gaze was drawn to a far corner where Basilio danced with India in his arms.

"What are we gonna do, baby?" he whispered, running his lips over the curve of the girl's ear. "What we gonna do?"

The song faded and it was time to go. Basilio handed India to his mother—"Be good for Grandmom . . ."—and Joe grabbed his shoulder.

"Thanks a million," he said, a little drunk.

"It was all you, man," said Basilio.

"Take a walk?" said Joe

"Where's Roxanne?"

"She's still here," said Joe, pulling Basilio into a back hall, past rooms dedicated to Mencken and Poe and Maulsby, the two friends side-by-side and quiet; Basilio guessing that Joe wanted to catch a little buzz the way they used to in high school, Joe about to roll one up when they heard laughter rolling down the hall.

"Manners," said Joe.

"Manners," agreed Basilio and they crept down the hall to a reading room where Seth Manners, another mug from Transfiguration High, was pitching woo on a red leather couch with one of Mary's married cousins.

Joe and Basilio held their breath on each side of the door.

Manners had a hand up the woman's dress. She'd come to the wedding alone because her husband was working overtime to pay the mortgage on their dream house, the one they'd promised themselves, the one they deserved.

Manners was single for the same reason Mary's cousin would be one day and as he worked his way into the woman's panties, Joe inexplicably whispered: "How's Trudy?"

Basilio turned his back and headed for the reception.

"Sorry," said Joe, catching up. "Everybody misses Trudy."

"There he is!" cried Mrs. Boullosa, standing with Roxanne and India as Basilio walked into the nearly deserted lobby. "Where've you been?"

Basilio fastened the top button of his daughter's coat and hugged her until she cried. Roxanne took the orchids from her hair and set them on the baby's head.

"I'm ready," she said.

-o-

Basilio drove east with Roxanne for a rendezvous in the Shadow of the King; east into the Holy Land toward Miss Bonnie's Elvis Grotto. It was almost 11:00 p.m. when they pulled up to the corner of Fleet and Port.

"Where are we?" asked Roxanne, scooting up to a plate-glass window where a bust of the King stood in a carpet of poinsettia leaves, lights twinkling around his neck.

"We're here," said Basilio, holding the door open.

Roxanne stepped inside, her pupils opening wide in a poorly lit sanctuary for people who have nowhere to go on days when everyone is supposed to have a place to go.

Three solitary regulars looked up from their drinks to give Basilio and Roxanne the once over: a wrinkled dwarf in white face; a woman who couldn't hold her head up; and an old foreigner who needed a shave falling forward on an aluminum walker.

A cold cut buffet was set up against the wall; behind the bar, goldfish floated in and out of a white mansion sunk in a long aquarium; 45 rpm records spray painted silver and gold hung from the ceiling and Elvis crooned: "The hopes and fears of all the years are met in thee tonight . . ."

No one spoke until Miss Bonnie—deep in an easy chair at the back of the bar, savoring a voice that came to visit but not to stay—noticed her visitors.

"Why darlin," she said, putting down a movie magazine. "I was wondering if my boyfriend was gonna remember me on Christmas."

Basilio blushed and stepped over the threshold with Roxanne.

"Miss Bonnie," he said. "This is Roxanne. Roxanne, my sweetheart Miss Bonnie."

"Why hello honey," said Bonnie, giving Roxanne a hug. "Don't you two look gorgeous."

Roxanne gazed over Miss Bonnie's shoulder to a life-sized creche in the back, a manger of limbs from trees that grew along the waterfront before the piers were poured from cement trucks; tall plaster figures of beasts and blessed.

She had never been this close to one before, never one this big—not figurines behind glass, but life-size statues out in the open and she slipped Miss Bonnie's embrace to get a closer look.

She crouched for a lamb's eye view, her satin gown stretched tight across full thighs and wide hips, knees up against her chest as she peered through wooden slats to see the infant.

"She's a keeper," whispered Bonnie.

Closing her eyes, Roxanne asked the Universe for forgiveness, a clenched fist between her breasts.

Stand up, she said to herself.

You better find a way to get up.

Reaching through the slats, she plucked a stalk of hay from the manger and with swift elan, used it to gather up her great mane before returning to Basilio and saying: "You like?"

Too much.

The last straw. Basilio took Roxanne's shaking hand, stood in front of Miss Bonnie and said: "I can't keep it in anymore."

"What?" asked Roxanne.

"What, hon?" said Bonnie.

"We just came from the priest!" he shouted. "We're married!"

Roxanne flinched.

"It's true," said Basilio, pulling her hand to his lips. "By God, it's true!"

"Hallelujah!" cried Bonnie, coming in for hugs.

Roxanne smiled at Basilio over Bonnie's shoulder, mischief replacing guilt as she waved a naked ring finger before him with a look that said: "You didn't think of everything, Mr. Smarty Pants."

"Lock the front door," said Bonnie. "We got us a wedding here."

Fussing over every little thing, she smacked Basilio's fanny and said: "Honey, you shoulda gimme some notice."

"Wasn't any notice," said Roxanne.

"Oh Christ, one of them," said Bonnie. "Two of mine were like that."

And then she turned a cynical eye on Basilio.

"Catholic?"

"Of course."

"How the hell did you get a priest to say the magic words without jumpin' through all them goddamn hoops?"

Basilio rubbed his thumb and forefinger together.

"The usual way," he said.

"Well, well," laughed Bonnie. "It's good to know they didn't change everything in the church."

"Didn't all go so smooth," said Basilio.

He held Roxanne's hand in the air and said, "No time for a ring."

"Stores closed," said Roxanne.

"Wedding rings?" said Bonnie as though they'd asked her for a bag of chips.

"That's it," said Basilio.

"That's all," said Roxanne.

"Hell," said Bonnie. "Come here girl."

Roxanne walked behind the bar to the 100-gallon home of a submerged Graceland and three generations of Holy Rosary Spring Carnival goldfish floating in and out of the mansion's empty rooms, the path to the King's front door paved with bands of gold.

"Ever been fishin' honey?" said Bonnie, reaching behind the cash register for a toy rod with a paperclip hook.

Basilio hopped up on the bar, his head over Roxanne's shoulder, and the regulars followed: Ted the Clown, still in make-up from a nursing home gig; the drunken Carmen and Mr. Voliotikes, leaning in hard solitude upon his walker.

"Fish?" said Roxanne, taking the rod.

"Don't wanna stick your hand in the muck," said Bonnie, pointing to five rings nestled in slime.

"Go fish," said Basilio.

Ted scurried around the bar to stand alongside Roxanne and Carmen twirled on a barstool like a kid.

"Don't hurt the fish," said Carmen, twice divorced.

"You can't hurt them fish," said the clown.

"Don't crowd her," yelled Bonnie.

"Which one?" asked Roxanne, dropping the line into the tank.

"Any one," said Bonnie as the hook dragged gravel.

"Got one!" squealed Roxanne.

"So quick," said Carmen.

"Lickety-split!" yodeled the clown.

"Told you," Bonnie said.

Roxanne turned to Basilio with the dripping ring, but when he reached out for it, Bonnie snatched it away and wiped it clean.

"Not yet," she said, passing the rod to Basilio. "Your turn."

Oh boy, he thought, hopping down from the bar with the ring Trudy had once slipped on his finger deep in his pocket. Holding the rod over the bubbling water, Basilio asked Bonnie which ring came from which husband; if, he wondered, one was any luckier than the others.

"You see where they wound up," she said.

Basilio let the hook sway above the tank until the crowd was hypnotized, lowered the line and slipped a hand into his pocket.

"Bingo!" he said.

Turning to Roxanne, Basilio stood with a dry ring on the end of his hook, unsmiling, four others still in the drink.

Such dexterity, at turns charming and nauseating, had ultimately convinced Trudy to leave, a truth that Basilio would try to stuff into poor boxes and sewer holes for years to come.

Bonnie led the couple out from behind the bar, handed Basilio the ring Roxanne had plucked from the aquarium, gave Roxanne the ring Basilio had reeled in and ordered them to trade.

Roxanne's ring was too small, stopping at her knuckle and she slipped it on her pinky. Basilio's moved along his finger without a hitch.

"Now kiss her," said Bonnie.

"Yeah!" said Carmen.

"Right in the kisser!" said the clown.

"Show some respect," said Mr. Voliotikes.

Their lips touched and a current passed between them to light every bulb in the bar and run the ice machine.

"Love . . ." marveled Bonnie before turning for the stairs that led to her apartment above the bar. "You kids enjoy yourselves. I'll be right back."

In Bonnie's absence, Ted the Clown took over, guiding Basilio and Roxanne to a table against the wall as they stared at their rings.

"We're married," said Basilio.

"What now?" asked Roxanne.

Ted slipped behind the bar to tipple a little of this and some of that before bringing Basilio a beer and a glass of white wine for Roxanne in a goblet from which no customer had drank.

With the goo-goo eyes of the regulars bearing down upon them, the newlyweds could not enjoy themselves or leave without saying goodbye to Bonnie, whose absence had changed the room.

"This was just another neighborhood gin mill selling boiled eggs and pickled onions until Bonnie's last husband died," said Basilio. "When he dropped dead Bonnie started putting up pictures of Elvis to make herself feel better."

Roxanne shifted to take in the massive collage that was Miss Bonnie's Elvis Grotto and was particularly taken by a Graceland postcard of the tux and gown that Elvis and Priscilla had worn on their wedding day, an exhibit of empty clothes.

"And then Presley died," said Basilio. "And everybody began loading the joint up with the King, but none of it made Bonnie feel any better."

Feeling ignored, Ted leaned across the table so far that his rubber nose nearly poked Roxanne in the face, his head bobbing on a pencil neck.

"You don't think people marry clowns?" he said, smacking himself on the back of his head until the red ball popped off of his nose. "Happens every goddamn day."

Ted stuck the rubber nose on Basilio and lamented: "But all them gutter balls. Maybe that's the way it oughta be. That's the way it is."

"Dog shit!" shouted Carmen, drunk on gloom and schnapps, edging her way to the table with Baby Jesus in her arms, tripping toward Roxanne when the clown grabbed her ass.

Carmen dropped the infant and it shattered on the floor. Roxanne screamed.

"Oh my God," said Basilio, picking up the pieces. "Ted, you mental patient."

"I didn't do it," shouted the clown. "I had nothin' to do with it."

Carmen stood over Roxanne like a runaway, tangled hair in her eyes as the lights blinked on and off across the stucco paste of her face.

"Goochie-goochie goo," she warbled. "Goochie-goochie goo . . ."

"Oh Christ," said Basilio, on his knees. He hurled the rubber nose at Ted and held Roxanne's ankle as she cried. Ted polished off everyone's drink and slipped out the side door as Mr. Voliotikes lumbered toward the head of the table.

"Out of my way," he roared, kicking Carmen with his good foot.

"Why," he asked, taking Roxanne's hand. "Why you do this without your mother and father."

Roxanne wiped her eyes on the cuff of her gown and blew her nose in a napkin.

"It's my life," she said, pulling her hand away as Bonnie came down the stairs with a sheet cake in her hands. Stopping halfway down, she saw Basilio piling pieces of Jesus on the table, Roxanne in tears, Carmen passed out on the floor, the old Greek preaching and no sign of the clown.

"What the hell's goin' on here? I can't leave for five goddamn minutes without you smokehounds turning a wedding into a wake? For Christ's sake, this is the best thing that's happened here in years and you rumpots ain't gonna poison it with your goddamn war stories.

"Carmen? CARMEN! Get the hell off the floor. What's wrong with you? Somebody help her up. Mr. V, wipe your eyes and sit down. That girl don't need no Daddy. She's got a husband now."

Walking the cake over to the table, Bonnie rubbed Roxanne's shoulder and told her not to mind the others: "They ain't right."

Putting her arms around the guests of honor, she assured them, "We're making our own happiness here," and brought over a fresh pot of coffee to go with the cake.

"Okay," she said. "Mr. V, say a nice grace for us. Something for a Christmas wedding. In English."

The old man closed his eyes, bowed his head and was just starting to get warmed up—"Forgive us, Father, for the vows we could not keep"—when Bonnie shouted "Amen" and began cutting the cake.

The caffeine and sugar gave Roxanne and Basilio new strength and when Bonnie started clinking a spoon against her coffee cup for them to kiss, he put his lips next to Roxanne's ear and said: "Let's get out of here."

"Miss Bonnie . . ."

"I know, you gotta go," she said. "Let me give you something first."

From a shelf behind the bar, she took down a bust of Elvis made into a lamp and handed it to Basilio at the front door.

"Works on batteries," she said, flicking the switch on and off.

He thanked her with a kiss on the cheek and said: "You made this a special night for us."

"I didn't make it special, hon. It is special."

And the heart-shaped clock on the wall said it was time.

"Now out with you," said Bonnie. "Out you go."

-o-

The cold slapped color into Roxanne's cheeks and bit through Basilio's pants as they hurried to the car. Basilio put Elvis between them on the front seat and waited for the engine to warm up.

Stuffed with their rich lie and too full to speak, a young man and a young woman who'd never met before that day drove through the Holy Land with rings on their fingers and wedding cake in their pockets; the city as silent as the bride and groom as Roxanne stared through the darkness at rows of narrow brick houses and Basilio drove south to the water's edge at the end of Clinton Street.

The road was unpaved and the moon made silhouettes of coal piers and cranes, fuel barges and corrugated fertilizer warehouses. They drove past the hulk of the S.S. John Brown Liberty Ship and Schuefel's, the saloon where a monkey named Dinky drank beer from a can.

Gravel crunched under the tires until the road stopped at a wooden pier jutting out from the front yard of a house with "SALVAGE" painted across its side.

Basilio parked in front of a twisted guard rail as a red tugboat with a white dot on its stack pulled a barge across the harbor, the flag over Fort McHenry starched in a stiff breeze.

Engine running, heater on, he pushed the seat back and closed his eyes, fresh out of script until Roxanne opened her door and a blast of winter air accompanied her command to get out and bring the lamp.

Basilio sat up to see her walk down a warped pier beneath a feta moon, high heels steady on the splintered boards, black hair flying in a nocturne of ebony and cream. Hurrying to catch up with Elvis in his arms, he found Roxanne sitting on the edge of the pier with her legs over the side. Basilio set the lamp down and sat beside her. It was freezing.

Roxanne turning the switch on the lamp and a pink halo floated up from the pier into the night.

"Have your fun?"

"Didn't you?" said Basilio, numb fingers struggling with the ring on his hand when Roxanne kissed him with an open mouth, her saliva freezing on his chin.

"We'll die out here," said Basilio, sliding his palm across the front of Roxanne's gown to her left hand, tugging the ring free from her pinky and shaking it with his own like dice before tossing them into the harbor.

Opening her coat, Roxanne pulled the velvet gown from her chest, her breasts snug in a strapless bra.

"What are you doing?" said Basilio, laying his head against her chest, no room of his own to set up an easel, much less rattle a headboard.

Defiant against the cold, Roxanne freed her breasts one at a time, looked down at Basilio and said: "Paint my portrait."

"Nude?"

"With India on my lap."

"When?"

"Let's go," she said, and as Basilio began buttoning Roxanne's coat, he remembered the good morning light that came through the window near the sink in his grandfather's kitchen and work not yet begun that vexed him since he was a boy.

THE FOUNTAIN OF HIGHLANDTOWN
[1989]

BASILIO

I **LEARNED TO** live in the dark this year when I quit my job, sold everything I owned, and moved in with my grandfather.

This new life makes the simplest things complicated, even for a guy who decides one day to quit his job, sell everything he owns and go live in the dark.

But that's my problem.

Grandpop would tell you that.

It's a fine summer night in Baltimore and I am walking from Grandpop's house to meet Katherine, who is young and beautiful and smart and almost completely unknown to me.

I haven't told her much about myself, hardly anything except that my grandmother died in the hospital where she works, that my grandfather stopped sleeping in their bed the day she passed away and that it would be better if I met her where she lives than the other way around.

I said all this last week when I found her standing in line at the Broadway market. I was buying fresh fruit for Grandpop and she was picking up scallops and shrimp and pints of shucked oysters for a dinner party at her apartment.

Okay, she said, maybe we can do something, and borrowed a pencil to scratch her number across my bag of peaches.

And so I am walking from the little Highlandtown rowhouse where my father was born and raised, passing bakeries and record stores and coffee shops, on my way to Katherine's apartment a few miles away, up around Johns Hopkins Hospital.

It's early (I had to get out of the house) and there's still a pink wash of early evening light across the sky as I walk down Macon Street to Eastern Avenue.

The street jumps with kids on skates, Saturday shoppers coming home with carts and bundles, and heavy women squirting down the gutters.

On the Avenue, middle-aged sports with slick hair and brown shoes with white socks wait on the word; Greek men who haven't shaved for two days stand on the corners, telling lies; packs of heavy-metal kids graze for drugs and kicks and young girls walk by, dressed up for each other.

My eye swims through the center of the composition but the margins are crowded with thoughts of Katherine.

What will she wear?

What does she smell like?

What hangs on her walls?

I think: How will our time pass?

And, if things go well, will we find our way back to Macon Street?

Fat chance.

My world is ruled by Grandpop and he is driving me crazy.

Right up the wall.

I am afraid that it won't last long enough for me to get everything done.

Every morning at breakfast he says the same thing: "Why are you here?"

Like he forgets that I am living with him between the time we go to bed and the time we wake up.

All night, Grandpop tosses and turns on the sofa bed downstairs, like he's being chased, until the break of day when he asks: "Why are you here?"

And then: "It's morning, turn off that light. You think I'm a millionaire? How were you raised?"

Grandpop was so poor growing up in Spain that one summer he carved an entire bicycle out of wood, wheels and all, so he would have something to ride besides an ox-drawn plow.

It doesn't matter that he's had it good in this country for sixty years, that, in his own words, he "eats like a king" and can lock the front door to a warm home he has owned for twice as long as I've been alive.

It does not matter that he's got a good pension from the shipyard and Social Security and more money in forgotten bank accounts than I have made in twenty-eight years on Earth.

None of that means shit if you are foolish enough to leave a light on in a room you have left or care to read or draw or scratch your ass by electric lamp before the sky outside has turned to pitch.

And there is no reason to use lights at night because at night you sleep.

Electricity, says Grandpop, is money. And a poor man cannot afford to waste either of them.

Bent over and angry, pointing to an offending 15-watt bulb, he says: "You think I'm a millionaire?"

When I try to tell him not to worry, that I'll help pay for it and it's only pennies anyway—when I smile and say, "Hey Grandpop, we got it pretty good in this country"—he says I can go live with somebody else if I want to waste money.

He asks: "Why are you here?"

But he doesn't charge me a dime to sleep in his bed and eat his food and he doesn't say a word when I do what I need to do to get my work done.

Just as long as I don't turn on any lights.

God Bless America.

God Bless Grandpop.

I cross Eastern Avenue and dart between traffic into Patterson Park, where Grandpop used to play soccer way back when with other expatriates from around the world.

It's hard for me to imagine his legs strong enough to kick a ball the length of the park; he's barely able to climb the steps in the middle of the night to make sure I'm not reading under the covers with a flashlight. But up on dusty shelves near the sofa where he lays at night and talks in his sleep like he's trying to make someone understand, there are trophies to prove it.

"Grandpop," I say. "Tell me about playing soccer in the land of baseball."

The Pagoda sits on the highest hill in the park, a surreal stack of Oriental octagons in the middle of a wide, rolling lawn; a weird obelisk of Confucius bordered all around by narrow brick rowhouses, the first in Baltimore with indoor bathrooms.

When you stand atop the Pagoda you can see all of the Holy Land, all the way past Fort McHenry to freighters in the harbor and the Francis Scott Key Bridge in the mist.

I would like to take Katherine up there and present her with the view, but it's only open on Sunday mornings when the Friends of the Park are around to let you in and keep an eye on things.

159

Grandmom and Grandpop used to walk me up here when I was a kid and you could go up to the top and see the whole city. They would stay down on the ground and wave up to me and I can see them now like it was yesterday, smiling through their broken English: "Doan breaka you neck."

After awhile Grandmom couldn't make the walk anymore and as I got older other things became important and I didn't care to visit Macon Street so much.

The city let the Pagoda rot while punks and drunks and whores and glue-heads got up inside of it, doing things that made the paint peel. The city tried to tear it down a few years ago when some goof on dope fell off and killed himself but the good citizens saved it and now you can only go up on Sunday mornings.

I tried to paint the Pagoda for three years before I moved in with Grandpop and I never got it right.

I stare up at it and fix its scale in my head.

I wonder: Does Katherine know any of this stuff? Does she care? Will she want to know once she knows how much I care?

What I know about Katherine you could pour into a thimble with room to spare. She is young and beautiful and smart and puts on dinner parties with scallop and shrimp.

I don't even know if she's from Baltimore.

I leave the Pagoda and walk out of the park onto Pratt Street, passing families of Lumbees and Salvadorans and black folks as the neighborhoods change the closer I get to downtown.

I hit Broadway and turn north on a wide stretch of asphalt that rises up beyond the statue of Latrobe and the derelict housing projects named in his honor; up from the harbor a good mile or two where Broadway meets Hopkins, where my grandmother died twenty years ago, leaving Grandpop all that time and how much more to lie in the dark, conserving kilowatts to save pennies he doesn't count anymore.

Katherine's apartment is in the shadow of the hospital's great dome.

The neighborhood used to be called Swampoodle before Hopkins started gobbling it up, back when Bohemians lived there, in the days when Grandpop played soccer in Patterson Park and Grandmom sat on a bench with her girlfriends and watched.

I tried to paint the Hopkins dome too, in the last days before I moved in with Grandpop, but all I could think about was what we lost there.

160

I smeared the canvas with vinegar and vowed that I would not paint pictures of buildings anymore.

KATHERINE

I didn't know what to expect with this guy.

I haven't dated much lately because they've all been the same, but I said yes to this guy right in the market. I knew it would be different, but I didn't know how.

I certainly didn't expect to be picked up for our first date on foot.

He knocks on the door, comes in with a polite hello, and looks around.

Next thing out of his mouth: "I walked over because I sold my car when I moved in with my grandfather."

But he doesn't say what one has to do with the other.

He tells me that my dress reminds him of the sunflowers his grandmother used to grow in her backyard until the summer she passed away "right there," and he points through the window to the hospital.

"That exact same color," he says, staring just a little too long before telling me "it's gorgeous outside," and would I like to talk a walk?

He's cute, in a funny way, like a kid; younger than me and a nice change from the clever men with tasseled loafers and Jaguars, so suave and witty until they find out I'm a doctor and then they really start acting like kids.

I don't mind walking and out we go, strolling south on Broadway toward the water.

I'd bet you a lobster that we're headed for the bars in Fells Point, where every man I've dated in this town goes sooner or later, like it's the only place in Baltimore that sells beer.

But he doesn't mention Fells Point or any special restaurant or destination; he just keeps up a pleasant chatter about things you can't imagine—wooden bicycles and chestnut trees and the Rock of Gibraltar (I've seen it, he hasn't)—and now we're cutting across the side streets and through the alleys, moving east to the neighborhoods where my patients live and die.

He doesn't say what he does for a living and I wonder if it's anything at all, if maybe the good doctor is out for an evening with the unemployed. He must do something because his shoes and pants are speckled with little smudges of paint.

Maybe he's the Cartographer of Baltimore, so well he knows these cobbled paths crowded with dogs and kids and garbage cans.

"You know what I love?" he says. "I love to walk through the alleys and look in people's houses. Especially at night when the lights are on and the shades are up. You can look right in and see people eating and watching TV, talking to each other, you know, just living."

He doesn't ask me what I do and it's a relief not to have to answer all the questions, a blessing not to feel the evening turn when it finally comes out.

It seems enough for him just to know that I work in a hospital.

Our walk is slow and evening falls with a warm, clean breeze from the harbor.

How odd, I think, looking into the tiny concrete yards where kids splash in wading pools, moms watching from lawn chairs with their feet in the water, old men in their undershirts, listening to the ballgame and drinking beer; how pleasantly odd not to talk about what you do for a living.

I will extend him the same courtesy for as long as it lasts.

At the end of an alley we stop in front of a corner bar called Miss Bonnie's and he points out the red and blue and green neon floating out from behind block glass in the windows.

He talks about colors as if they are alive and in between all the loose words he talks about his grandfather.

"Grandpop won't let me turn on any lights. He sits at the kitchen table all day circling crime stories in the paper with a red pencil. Nothing bad has ever happened to him here, but he says America is going to the dogs."

A native girl on a tricycle zips between us and he talks about the shades of red and brown in her cheeks, "like autumn leaves."

He says that American Indians are the only minority his grandfather has any sympathy for because there was no New World left for them when things went bad at home.

Now we're in the park, walking quietly until we reach the Pagoda, the sun going down behind it like a tangerine, that's what he says, "a big, fat tangerine."

He shakes the gate on the iron fence around the Pagoda but you don't have to shake it to see that it's locked.

"Grandpop forgets that I'm living with him between the time we go to bed and the time I come down for breakfast. Every day we start from scratch."

"So why do you stay?"

He turns from the Pagoda and we walk east across the park toward Eastern Avenue and the Greeks.

Just beyond the railroad bridge marking the incline that gives Highlandtown its name, he spies a wooden stand on the sidewalk and says: "Wanna snowball?"

I get chocolate with marshmallow and he asks for grape, fishing out a couple of dollars from the pockets of his white jeans.

We pause at a bus stop and I wonder if maybe we're going to catch one to take us to God knows where.

Holding out his palm, he invites me to sit down and I think: This bench is the sidewalk cafe in Paris that the plastic surgeon wanted to take me to last month until he found out that a ticket to France would get me across the ocean and wouldn't get him anywhere.

We sit, the distance of five hands between us, and I look up to see that above our heads hangs one of the most bizarre landmarks in a city filled with them.

Up against the sky: the Great Bolewicki Depression Clock.

Bolted to the front of an appliance store called Bolewicki's, it has a human face and crystal hands filled with bubbling water—the little hand bubbling lavender and the big hand bubbling pink—and around it glow lights shaped into words that say: "It's not too late, it's only . . ."

And then you read the time.

Like right now, eating snowballs at a bus stop on a Saturday night in Baltimore, it's not too late for anything: It's only ten past seven.

"I've been to Germany and Switzerland a half-dozen times," I say, "and I've never seen a clock like this."

"It's something," he says. "I tried painting this clock for three months."

"How many coats did it take?"

That does it!

He starts laughing and can't stop; a wild, crazy laugh from way back in his throat and I start to laugh too because he's got such a funny, genuine laugh, like some strange bird.

Tears come to his eyes and he's spewing crystals of purple ice, trying to catch his breath.

And somewhere inside of this laugh I decide that I like this man and surrender to whatever the night may bring as the No. 10 stops to let people off beneath the Great Bolewicki Depression Clock in the middle of Eastern Avenue and my date with a guy named Basilio whose tongue is the color of a ripe plum.

He gets a hold of himself and says: "I wish old man Bolewicki would let me paint his clock. It would be the first money I've made with a brush in a long time."

He looks me in the eye.

"I tried to paint a *picture* of it."

"You're an artist?"

"I guess," he says, looking up. "This thing was so hard, Katherine. You see the water bubbling in those hands, like bubble lights at Christmas . . . did your tree have bubble lights when you were a kid? I loved those things, you don't see 'em anymore. But I couldn't get the water right, I couldn't make it look like it was really bubbling."

I watch as he loses himself in the clock, the big hand bubbling pink and the smaller one pumping lavender—"It's not too late, it's only . . ."— and he catches me looking.

"Let's go."

We walk deeper into the neighborhood and he points out things I know and things I don't.

"That's a great little place," he says as we pass Garayoa's Cafe Espanol, where, he tells me, they serve squid stuffed with their own tentacles and cooked in a sauce made with the ink.

I don't tell him that I have broken bread there with an investment banker, a screen writer and a child psychiatrist.

"The ink bubbles up in a thick dark sauce that shimmers deep green just above the surface," he says. "I tried painting with it once—thought it would be perfect for a sad night sky. But it dried ugly brown."

At the next corner, Basilio passes our empty snowball cups to a short man selling produce from the trunk of a gigantic Pontiac and in return the man hands each of us a small, brown pear.

"Lefty," says Basilio, shaking the guy's hand.

"*Senor*," says the man with a Greek accent, looking me over and winking at Basilio. "How's your old *abuelo* my friend?"

"He's good Lefty, real good," says Basilio. "I'll tell him you said hello."

"You do that, senor," he says. "Enjoy your evening."

We move away in silence, biting the fruit as the sky turns dark and pear juice runs along my mouth. Basilio pulls a spotless white handkerchief from his back pocket and wipes my chin, cleaning his own with the back of his hand and it is all so very simple and nice . . .

Until we come upon a narrow lane paved with brick and identified by stained-glass transoms as the 600 block of South Macon Street.

Basilio points down the long row of identical rowhouses, orange brick with white marble steps before each of them.

"I live down there with Grandpop," he says, pausing like someone trying to decide if they should show up unannounced at your door, making me feel like he's talking to himself and I am no longer here.

Over the next curve of the Avenue, beyond a cluster of blue and white Greek restaurants, I see the Ruth Tower rising up from the University of East Baltimore and since there seems to be no agenda and Basilio's verve faded at Macon Street, I point up to the tower where I had a blast as an undergraduate, a stone room—cool and round—with a bar and a view you can't get from two Pagodas set on top of one another.

My turn: "Up there. Let's go."

It is night now and we move through the dark campus toward a granite spiral tiled with all the great moments of the Babe's career.

It is the Bambino's only gift to the city of his birth.

Bolted to the base of the tower is a plaque quoting the slugger at the dedication: "Let the poor kids in free and name it after me."

We walk inside and start climbing, round and round, up to the sky.

I tell Basilio that when I first came to Baltimore—Good Lord, it seems like nine thousand dead teenagers ago—the top of the Ruth Tower was *thee* spot: strong Greek coffee, Delta blues, oval plates of feta and black olives, crusty bread, cheap beer and young people from around the world shouting at each other about what it's all about.

He says: "I was in the suburbs back then."

"Did you ever try to paint this?"

"Sure. Grandpop brought my old man here to see the Babe when Dad was a kid and Ruth was half-dead with termites."

We walk in and I head for the bar, reaching into the pockets of my dress for money, feeling Basilio behind me, looking around.

"So this is college," he says.

I hand him a draft beer and steer to a table with a window facing west, back toward downtown where Baltimore's money finds Baltimore's art in chic storefronts along Charles Street.

The docs I work with write big checks for paintings that probably aren't any better than the ones Basilio destroys, but I really don't know if he can paint or not. All I know is what didn't turn out: half the real estate in East Baltimore.

I sip my beer and think that maybe I can help this guy.

"Tell me about the paintings you're happy with."

He gulps beer and ignores the question, shifting east to play tour guide again: Over there is the National Brewery, home of the One-Eyed Little Man; and the Esskay slaughterhouse is there, they've got some great stainless steel letters out front; and way over there, he says, beyond the rooftops, is a graveyard where four Chinese sailors who capsized in a 1917 hailstorm are buried.

I think for a moment that he's a fraud and I will be sick.

Turning his head with an angry finger, I direct his gaze toward the Hopkins dome.

"And over there is where I fish bullets out of fourteen year-old boys on Saturday nights just like this before I have to tell their twenty-seven year-old mothers they didn't make it. Take me to your work or take me home."

And still this hard-head gives me words instead of pictures.

Grandpop skinning squirrels for dinner at the stationary tubs in the basement; Grandpop lecturing a little boy at those same tubs that a man really hasn't washed up if he hasn't washed his neck; and Grandpop making love to his bride on Macon Street, conceiving the man who would seed the artist.

"Those," he says. "are pretty good."

As we take the steps two at a time, he takes my hand.

At the front door to 627 South Macon Street, just before turning the key, Basilio tells me to take off my shoes and leads me in, dim light from a streetlamp falling across a small figure sleeping in the middle room.

"Grandpop," he whispers as we creep toward a staircase along the wall.

No one answers and as I move up the stairs, the old man stirs in his bed and my dress flutters around my knees.

Basilio keeps moving and I am right behind him, shoes in my left hand and my right against the small of his back as we climb together.

When we reach the top, he whispers in my ear, his "hallelujah!" warm and sweet.

He says: "I've never done this before."

Neither have I.

A door creaks open before us as Basilio turns the knob and I slip in behind him.

We stand still in the darkness, just inside the door, and my nose stings from the turpentine. As my eyes adjust I sense that this is the biggest room in the house, that there is only one room on this floor—as long and as wide as the house itself—and I am in it.

Basilio escorts me to a saloon table against the long side wall and sits me down on a stool before crossing to the other side of the room.

"Ready?" he asks, holding a cord.

I answer "ready" and he pulls it.

A tarp whooshes to the floor, night fills the space where the roof ought to be, the light of a nearly full moon and a sky of stars floods the room and in one clear instant I see the world this man lives in.

"There's no roof!"

My head spins as I try to take in the sky, the paintings, the smile on Basilio's face and the colors everywhere.

"I told you, Grandpop won't let me turn on any lights. I cut the roof out a little bit at a time and paint with what it gives me. I never would have thought of it if I didn't have to."

I stand, dumbfounded.

"You can't turn on the lights, but you can saw the roof out of his house?"

"He's never mentioned it. As long as I don't use electricity or bring women home, he pretty much leaves me alone."

I move close to his work, the silver light from above giving each painting a glow I've never seen in any gallery in the world and on one canvas after another I read the narrative of his grandfather's life.

Grandpop as a boy, sitting on a rocky hill, carving a pair of handlebars from the limb of a chestnut tree; Grandpop shoveling coal on the deck of a rusty freighter, Gibraltar bearing down in the background; Grandpop kicking a soccer ball, his right leg stretched out in front of him as the ball sails across Patterson Park, the Pagoda perfect in the background; Grandpop strolling down Eastern Avenue, all dressed up with his wife on a Sunday afternoon, the Great Bolewicki Depression Clock bubbling pink and lavender to beat the band.

And then, running the length of a single wall, a huge canvas of a bedroom cast in moonlight and shadows.

In the bed is a young man who looks a lot like Basilio, a white sheet draped across his back, arms strong and taut as he hovers over a dark-haired beauty with stars in her eyes.

I am transfixed and wonder if there is a cot in the room.

"What do you call this one?"

"The Fountain of Highlandtown."

GRANDPOP

* Suenos. Siempre suenos. Dulces suenos y malos suenos. Suenos de amor.*

I can feel it.

Basilio must be making a *pintura* of a woman upstairs.

I can feel it in my sleep, like she is in the house.

He must be getting good.

"Grandpop," he says at my kitchen table every morning, up before me, coffee ready for his *abuelo*, this boy is a man, doesn't he have a home?

"Grandpop," he says while I'm still trying to figure out what day it is and why he is living with me.

"Grandpop, do you remember what Grandmom looked like the first time you saw her? What did her skin look like?"

I say: "Basilio," (he was named after me, two Basilios in one house is one Basilio too many); I say: "What are you doing, writing a book?"

"Something like that," he says.

Last week it was questions about the shipyard, before that it was Patterson Park, now it's about Mama and I don't have the patience for it.

Questions and questions and questions as he makes little pencil marks on a napkin.

"Grandpop, tell me about Galicia and the corn cribs on stilts and the baskets your father made."

"Grandpop, tell me about the ox and the cart and the *cocido* your mother stewed over the fire in the black pot."

"Grandpop, tell me about the first time you saw Gibraltar."

Why does he want to live with an old man who is so mean to him? He is good company, this boy with the questions, even if he has to turn on a light to clean the kitchen in the middle of the afternoon.

"Grandpop," he says to me on his way out of the house tonight (where he was going in the shoes with the paint on them, I don't know, he should get dressed and go out with a woman before he gets old); "Grandpop," he says: "What did Grandmom's hair look like on your wedding night?"

I told him: "Turn off the light and lock the door when you go out."

This is what I didn't tell him: It was black, Basilio, black like the coal I shoveled out of ships at *la Roca*; black like a night at sea without stars and it fell down around my shoulders when she leaned over me; *que linda Francesca, que bella Francesca, que guapa Francesca para me y solamente para mi.*

He asks in the morning while we eat our bacon and eggs; eggs he makes like I made for him when he stayed with Mama and me when he was a little boy (even then he wouldn't listen); bacon fried crisp and the eggs on top, grease spooned slow over the yolk.

I say: "Basilio, what are you doing here?"

And he answers: "What did Grandmom's eyes look like when she told you she loved you?"

And after all these years, the thought of her kiss (I can feel it at night, on nights like this, Basilio you must be painting upstairs), the thought of her still makes me excited, *un caballo fuerte*, and it makes me ready, so sad and ready, and I get mad to answer this boy with skinny brushes and silly paints and goddammit, why doesn't he go and live with his father in their big house in the suburbs?

My house is small and life here is finished.

I get mad and tell him he's too much trouble, that he's wasting my money leaving the lights on.

You don't turn on lights in the daytime and a boy doesn't ask an old man so many questions.

But he doesn't get mad back at me, he just touches my arm and gets up to wash the dishes saying: "I know, Grandpop, I know."

What does he know?

By the time I was his age I spoke good English, had three kids, a new Chevrolet and seniority down the shipyard.

What does he have?

My electricity and no *trabajo*; pennies he saves for paint (where his pennies come from I don't know, maybe he finds them in the street, he takes so many walks); and a loaf of bread he puts on the table every day before supper; one loaf of bread fresh from the Avenue in the center of my table four o'clock every day without a word.

I should go easy on him.

He's the only one who really talks with me.

The only one who comes to see his old *abuelo*.

But when did he move in?

How did that happen?

That's the question you never asked, Basilio: "Grandpop, can I live with you?"

170

Suenos. Dulces Suenos.

He must be painting upstairs.

I can feel it.

I remember when his father was just a baby and I called her Mama for the first time and she became Mama for all of us; *Mama de la casa* and his father would wake up in the middle of the night and scream in his crib and nothing would make him stop, *nada*, and Mama would get so exhausted she would turn her back to me and cry in her pillow.

I would smooth her hair—it was black, Basilio, as black as an olive—and I would turn on the radio (electricity, Basilio, in the middle of the night), to maybe calm the baby and listen to something besides the screaming. Mama liked the radio, Basilio, and we listened while your father cried—*cantante negra, cantante de almas azules*—and it made us feel a little better, helped us make it through.

I had to get up early to catch the street car to the shipyard, but when the crying finally stopped sometimes the sun would be ready to pop and Mama's breathing would slow down and her shoulders would move like gentle waves, sleeping but still listening, like I can hear her now on this no good bed, and Basilio—*Mira, hombre*, I will not tell you this again—if I moved very close and kissed her shoulders, she would turn to face me and we would have to be quiet Basilio, under the music, very, very quiet . . .

So this I want to know, Basilio.

This, if you want to live on Macon Street for another minute.

Can you paint an apple baked soft in the oven, an apple filled with cinnamon and raisins?

Can you paint such a woman?

Are you good enough yet with those brushes that she will step out of your pictures to turn on the radio in the middle of the night?

Will she visit an old man on his death bed?

If you cannot do that, Basilio, there is no need for you to live here anymore.

THE LONG VIETNAM OF MY SOUL
[1989]

"Each day in Baltimore, there is a late afternoon hour—the setting sun upon the brick city like saffron butter, a moment when the abandoned bottle cap factory is on the verge of saying something . . ."

SOMEBODY ALWAYS WANTS something.

With every pass of the sugar bowl:

What's in it for me?

And when the bowl is empty (when the bottom falls out) how much ego does it take to achieve the humility of Gandhi, the loneliness of Dorothy Day or the almost comical compassion of Jimmy Carter?

Not everybody's Jesus.

On the day of the peanut farmer's inauguration, the teenaged Basilio Boullosa daubed house paint on a scroll of butcher's paper and sent it off to the White House, a kid determined to draw his way out of a split-level cul-de-sac and into the Hall of Fame.

"My pictures," he wrote, "tell the entire history of the United States."

How much humility to write to the brand-new President of the United States and ask for help with your homework?

And then lie about it?

Even before he'd abandoned the suburban comfort for which his parents had worked their asses off, Basilio's paintings rarely strayed more than a mile or two beyond the boundaries of Baltimore City.

And never would.

-o-

A dozen years and a hundred sketchbooks down the line from the Carter Administration, Basilio used his work as currency in a Baltimore that, for him—both in thought and on canvas—had contracted into five square miles he called the Holy Land.

There was trouble across the summer of '88, long weeks and longer days of fear and longing (frustration spilling to anger) through the

173

humidity and thunderstorms of June and July and August. Grandpop asking Basilio each morning at breakfast—"Why are you here?"—was nothing compared to the wringer Nieves put him through.

She'd landed on Macon Street on short notice from the family village in Spain, both kin and stranger and too cute to be a minute over twenty-three; and, from her first glass of wine in the backyard with the old man (barefoot, hem of her jeans, her only pair of pants, wet from the garden hose) turned the neighborhood upside down.

Half of Basilio's battles with Grandpop (the difficulty of two Boullosas under the same roof, one just as hard-headed as the other, the artist never asking permission to move in, simply coming for supper the day Trudy threw him out and never leaving); more than half of those problems evaporated when Basilio brought a date to the kitchen table for cake and coffee.

Some were prettier and many were smarter, but none were half as seductive as Nieves, who skipped stones across the shrinking pool of the Spaniard's life, charming an old cat that made little jokes and smiled like a young Tom.

-o-

From the time of crayons, Basilio's art was disciplined to the exclusion of everything else. After his mother died, he never made a bed, liked clean sheets but not enough to keep them on a mattress, the floor of his studio sufficient when exhausted, which in the Summer of Nieves he was most of the time.

[And broke. He'd need to ramp up his sign painting; the best advice his mother ever gave him when he began making noise about becoming an artist while still in grade school: "Learn your letters . . ."

It took a while but he'd done it; became a one-man typography shop. Not long after he'd mastered lettering, his mother was hit by a car while walking to the supermarket and killed.]

With the arrival of Nieves, Basilio's work took a sharp turn for the absurd, from the plumb and precise cornices of Hopper (the leap from Crayola to Faber took place on the front curb in 1967, the first of many Summers of Love on Macon Street, a little kid teaching himself depth and shading by trying and failing and trying to sketch the row of identical houses across the street; graduating to landscapes of the rattling bottle cap factory in its last year of making bottle caps); from a street map of Crabtown to the carnivals of Miro.

174

An absurd response to the absurdities that followed Nieves to Macon Street; awakening the ones that waited there for her.

And Basilio too self-absorbed to remember that he'd never asked Grandpop if *he* could move in. He opened the door for Nieves and paid the cab that had brought her, taking her cracked leather suitcase upstairs and throwing up in the bathroom sink.

Spanish spoken once more on Macon Street; as it only did when Grandpop had visitors (his wife Italian from Pennsylvania, his children American, and his namesake grandson claiming the neighborhood as nation, hacking up the phlegm of that morning's coffee-on-an-empty stomach in a cracked sink brown with Rothko rust.)

Upon moving in with Grandpop (barging in by degrees, one day a tube of toothpaste, the next a tube of cadmium yellow, a suitcase for his clothes and another for his paints) Basilio set out to stanch his wounds and work like he believed he could not while married to Trudy; to paint the history of Baltimore through the lens of his family.

The story was moving quickly now (Elisabeth was beautiful, Nieves funny looking in that pinched *gallego* way), Spanish in the house (over food, on canvas, linen soaking in galvanized tubs); a pot boiling too fast for the whir of a Super 8 much less Basilio's thin brushes.

Before Nieves fell from the sky, Grandpop's life in the New World was a still life, a finely arranged cart of apples.

["Can you paint such a woman, Basilio? An apple cored and filled with raisins and cinnamon and baked in the oven?]

Order upended by an urge to rifle her leather satchel (delayed, then scratched with consequence) and the mural set aside for spin-art as the narrative moved back toward the Old World a teenaged Basilio had abandoned in 1921 just to be able to eat every day.

[If you work, you can eat and Basilio No. 1 chased that promise at seventeen with a shovel, muscling coal into the boiler of a tramp steamer that stopped in Baltimore every four months and one day left the piers along Pratt Street without him.

If you study hard and don't fuck up you can be anything you want was the American promise laid before Basilio No. 2, who at seventeen was walking past those same Pratt Street piers (now empty, now rotted) waiting for a postage stamp of LSD to melt on his tongue. It was the day his grandmother, wife of Basilio No. 1, was dying up at Hopkins and the artist, just beginning to fathom that all he'd ever need to paint hugged the harbor rim of Crabtown, USA, would walk clockwise and counter-clockwise until the cheap drug wore off enough for him to face his family.]

The Old World also abandoned by Nieves (just a visit, said the letter that arrived less than 24 hours before she did, *"solamente hola y adios,"*) on the idiotic notion that there might be less heroin in Baltimore than Madrid.

A turn for the inane: Take a left on Eastern Avenue and keep walking until you see ambulatory trash with "WHITE POWER!" inked across the fat of their backs; duck into the alley behind G&A Hot Dogs and there, buy a little dope unaware that the Greek who owns the joint has hired a cop—free breakfast and a window seat on the second floor, munching chili dogs with mustard on his chin ("that's the guy," says Farantos, "the piece of shit leaning up against Miss Helen's fence"—and the cop, "Who's the girl?"); lusting and eating and photographing the Baltimore: rats, winos, mutants, Miss Helen hanging her drawers on the line and a young woman in a torn, long-sleeved work shirt that an old Spaniard used to wear at the steel mill.

"Who's the girl?"

Nieves shooting dope for the first time in *Estados Unidos.*

No one wanted the paintings that Nieves inspired and now that Basilio had bartered his inventory of Grandpop paintings to find her (save her, keep her), all that remained were paintings no one wanted.

-o-

Nieves en route to the maze of Central Booking and Grandpop asleep at the kitchen table, forehead against headlines as he dreamt of medieval Spain and a Galician childhood in the reign of Alfonso when he carved a bicycle, wheels and all, out of crooked pine.

Elisabeth crying at the sink, arms in dishwater up to the elbow. The cuckold's rage: *"What do you mean you don't know where your wedding rings are?"*

[Tears in the fading suds: "Why didn't she just ask me for the money? We could have gone to the pawn shop together."]

Pacing his studio (jittery, obsessively looking into Elisabeth's yard, her voice in the air, *"Please* find her"); Basilio inspected canvases set against the walls, two o'clock a hot Thursday afternoon in July. He yanked the tarp covering the hole in the ceiling and the room flooded with unforgiving summer light.

No review had ever been as harsh (the local writers were sympathetic, outside of Baltimore, even thirty miles away in Washington, he was unknown) and as Basilio appraised the result of hundreds of hours of work he felt stupid and helpless and worthless.

[*"Please find her . . ."*]

Blue, brown and green studies of Grandpop and his garden: peppers (white blossom to black skillet) and tomato plants and basil. A beat-up ice-cream truck with Farsi lettering and primitive drawings of Daffy Duck licking a soft swirl. The bottle cap factory in conversation with the railroad tracks beside it.

Canvas without frames, stretched to the limit for love—*"What do you mean she didn't come home?"*—not commerce; all three rings of the circus caroming off of Basilio as he tried to decide what might ransom a distant cousin he didn't even know he had five weeks ago.

"The *calamares* ink bubbles up . . . *trémulo* deep green on the top," he'd told Nieves in ridiculous Spanish, showing his work the same day she arrived.

"*Chipirones,*" she laughed, reaching toward Pepper Plant Portrait No. 4, Basilio grabbing her wrist before she touched it, gone.

"I cooked them for Grandpop and tried painting with the ink."

"*Repugnante,*" said Nieves, laughing louder, a great laugh filling the studio in her absence.

Basilio was in love with her—fucked-up, lick turpentine off the work bench and listen to the same song forty times in a row (*"we could be married . . . and then we'd be happy . . ."*) LOVE.

He put the tarp back on the ceiling and left the house with a cup of cold coffee leftover from the morning, remembering . . .

How she watered the pepper plants in bare feet as the sun disappeared behind the bottle cap factory, hundreds of broken windows orange and on fire; made big pots of *caldo gallego* on a stove in the basement that hadn't been used since Basilio's grandmother passed away (making too much, the glut curdling and Basilio had to dump it before Grandpop got sick.)

And began keeping time with the young mother across the alley, engineering the affair with no visible effort after Basilio had tied himself in knots trying to learn the girl's name; stealing her lover's wedding rings to buy dope, getting locked up not a mile from Grandpop's front door.

Three balloons of dope in one pocket (they looked like gumballs, red and yellow) and what was left of the clumsily thieved rings in the other.

"If I had any lawyer friends I wouldn't be here," said Elisabeth when Basilio knocked on her basement door. "Take the car if you need it."

177

He parked it three blocks from the old City Jail—a 19th century castle of black stone at the corner of Van Buren and Madison, the old cells turned to offices where mothers and grandmothers and girlfriends and bondsmen and attorneys and preachers sought the release of people charged with violating the laws of the City of Baltimore.

High above the 1859 turrets loomed the bland, beige monolith of the penal colony that had overtaken the near east side of downtown, a cranny here and there for a carry-out or a body shop or the rare old-timer who didn't get out.

[What kind of municipality puts their penitentiaries downtown?]

Just as entrenched: the tent city beneath the Jones Falls Expressway [disciples of the Ashcan School could not have envisioned this], where, as he walked toward the labyrinth of corrections, Basilio heard snatches of conversation between hoboes and the hopeless in the Catholic Worker soup line.

They were all talking about the same thing: How a dozen prisoners waiting to be processed had run away when a bread truck lost control on Madison Street and rammed the jail, news so fresh there wasn't a reporter on the scene.

"Whole gang of 'em runnin' like cockroaches in the kitchen when you turn on the light."

"But that white girl walkin' slow, just mindin' her bidness while they chased everybody else. I seen 'er, mmm, mmmmm, mmmmmmmm!"

The city choppers were overhead now, two of them circling downtown. Basilio yelled to be heard: "What white girl?"

The men who'd been talking looked him over and turned away. Basilio took out $10.

"What white girl?"

"Don't go in and ask about it," offered a lady bus driver there to see about her grandson. "If she was with the ones that got away they'll keep you for collateral."

The raggedy man closest to Basilio reached for money and he drew it away.

"What did she look like?"

"You know," said the second guy, stalling as he tried to remember. Basilio put the money back in his pocket on the tip of the lie and headed back to the car. He was stopped by a former nun [you could always tell, somehow you can always tell which middle-aged women had left the convent but not the faith] downtown to protest for more schools and less jails.

Pointing west toward Charles Street, she said: "Dark hair in a bob, round brown eyes, torn jeans and a yellow t-shirt."

[A short three years and a second chance later, Basilio would remember this Samaritan—her short-cropped gray hair, white Fordham t-shirt and simple wooden cross (had it been a whistle, she'd have looked for all the world like a gym teacher)—would remember and never forget and one day, racing around the decades as he now ran for E's car, make it his business to find her.]

It was while driving in circles downtown and the housing projects that boxed it in that Basilio had an epiphany that would not bear fruit until the last week of his life. With both eyes out for his cousin, a third began cataloguing the bare walls of abandoned buildings as he moved deeper and deeper into the 'hood, canvases of brick filling the space between seek and you shall find.

Upon the right one (not today and probably not tomorrow and maybe never if he didn't move faster than the wrecking ball), Basilio would paint his masterpiece. He had 47,000 boarded up and crumbling homes to choose from and a notion of what the work would look like.

In deep water now, well beyond the boundaries of the Holy Land, he feared she might have been safer behind bars en route to deportation; prayed [Jesus as fire extinguisher, the humility of Dorothy and the ego of Jimmy at the other end of the rosary] that she'd already found her way back home, Elisabeth there to welcome her with a kiss.

Passing the ruins of Schmidt's Bakery on Laurens Street, Basilio stared up at the broken and rusting skylights and saw the mural that would cap an improbable career: His reflection in the dark circles beneath her eyes.

No, not her.

You think you know—Basilio's dreams absurd, impossible to carry out—but you don't know.

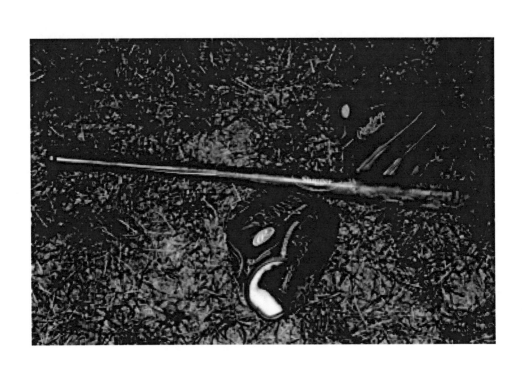

NINE INNINGS IN BALTIMORE
[1990]

AGITATED, SO FRUSTRATED and angry his skin itched, Basilio left the house on foot and an empty stomach a little after 6 p.m. He was looking for reefer. If not that, booze and someone new. Trouble enough to last through morning.

Something/Anything.

"I might not be much," he heard himself say, walking along the railroad tracks that ran from the bottle cap factory down to the coal yards of the industrial harbor. "But I'm all I think about."

How sick Basilio had become of Basilio. He watched a coal car on the tracks tip its load onto the wharf and wished he could do the same with himself: dump the shit and roll away clean and empty.

It was August 27, 1990, a night he'd remember to his distant grave.

Uptown, the Orioles were getting ready to play the Yankees at Memorial Stadium. There, twenty years earlier, he'd seen Dave McNally hit the only grand slam by a pitcher in World Series history. Basilio had cared at the time (deliriously so, as only a twelve year-old can) and it was a memory he'd committed to canvas more than once. But he didn't think much about it anymore.

He was a broke-ass artist who painted signs and houses and cartoons of monkeys eating banana splits on the side of ice-cream trucks to stay just one step behind instead of two. And hadn't given a shit about baseball—or much of anything, even his palette and the hole he'd cut in the roof of his studio—for a long time.

Not since Trudy left, Grandpop died and Nieves disappeared.

A crusty, almost-empty bottle of Fundador (Spanish turpentine, a holdover from the days when Grandpop still had friends who visited) was in the basement back home, gathering dust behind a flour sifter. Basilio wished he'd brought it along. Finish it off and smash the bottle against the rails.

He and Nieves had walked these tracks together in the first days after she'd arrived on short notice from Spain, making the last few months of Grandpop's life a miracle with food and stories from a village the old man had left seventy years ago. Basilio, for whom she'd made life a nightmare, would always be grateful for that.

And then he and Nieves and Elisabeth walked down the Chessie line—Elisabeth skipping across the ties, Nieves balancing on the rail— as he led them to a handful of waterfront dives that hadn't been torn down yet, places he could trade some lettering—OPEN DAILY—for a cold beer and a ham sandwich.

And then Nieves and Elisabeth started walking by themselves and Basilio stayed home.

"Grandpop . . . tell me about playing soccer in the land of baseball."

"*Donde esta Nieves*?" he answered. "Turn off the light and lock the door when you go out."

There was a time, when he still drew with No. 2 pencils and crayons, that Basilio could have told you about every Oriole from the owner who ran a local brewery to the groundskeeper who raised tomatoes beyond the foul poles.

One evening after his parents had gone to bed; he grabbed the phone book instead of his homework and—with a patience that now failed him—looked up the name of every player and coach on the team.

Eventually, he reached Mrs. George Bamberger, wife of the longtime pitching coach, and blurted: "I think George should tell Earl to use Moe more." Mrs. Bamberger said she would pass the tip along. After their third conversation in a week, she politely told Basilio not to call anymore.

A few years after that (goodbye crayons, hello blonde hash), he was outside of the stadium with a bunch of friends from Transfiguration High, all of them stoned before an afternoon game. He saw a kid about his age wearing a No. 7 jersey with the name "BELANGER" across the shoulders headed toward the good seats.

Basilio had always been quick, could remember things and spit them back with a little mustard. For the longest time (before he got to the part in life where the answers were more than mere fact) this passed for being smart.

"Belanger means warrior in medieval French," he told the kid.

"No," said the boy. "It's from the French *boulangerie*—it means bakery."

"Are you sure?"

"Positive. He's my father."

[Mark Belanger, a chain-smoking shortstop who won eight consecutive gold gloves across Basilio's childhood—a thin and flawless fielder known as "the Blade"—died of lung cancer at age fifty-four.]

Tonight, Basilio had banged the heavy receiver of Grandpop's rotary phone—black steel and Bakelite, Eastern 7-5254—against the kitchen wall, chipping the plaster, rolling the dice for nearly an hour without getting anyone. None of his guy friends had pot or Valium or a little bit of this or some of that.

[It was Nieves who was the addict because Nieves used needles.]

And none of the women who'd been orbiting Macon Street since Basilio had moved in with Grandpop were home or interested or able to lather up enough hogwash to get away. Up until tonight (Monday, a tough day for shenanigans), there'd always been another song on the broken record.

If a man answers, hang up . . .

Basilio veered off the tracks, passed the ruins of the Standard Oil refinery (back in the 1940s, his mother's grandfather had lost a foot there) and scuffled through the side streets and alleys toward Miss Bonnie's bar on the edge of the gentrified harbor.

It was hot and window air conditioners dripped condensation onto small squares of backyard concrete. A woman with a rag around her head used a hose and a broom to sweep trash down the alley where it would fall into the sewer grate and make its way down the Patapsco to the Chesapeake Bay.

Several miles to the north, up on 33rd Street, "play ball" was about to ring out behind a great coliseum of brick and limestone, a memorial to the dead from America's World Wars upon which hung 317 handmade stainless steel letters.

"Time will not dim the glory of their deeds . . ."

Trudy was going to the game with her father and India, the daughter born to her and Basilio about the time the wheels were coming off. Approaching the stadium, his granddaughter's hand in his, Trudy's father pointed to the wall of words and said, "Pop Pop made those letters."

"All by yourself?"

"Almost," said Pop, who liked Basilio but was not upset that Trudy was no longer married to him. It bothered him more that she was raising India by herself in the city.

Sometime tonight, between the first pitch and the last out, Basilio would become a father again and India would have a half-brother she wouldn't meet until she had children of her own. By then, Memorial Stadium would be long demolished, newer wars were remembered in silence before ballgames and lost to the winds were most of the letters Pop had made with twenty other men.

Big Ben McDonald was on the mound for the Birds. By the time he was about to throw the first pitch of the game, Basilio was well into his second beer at Miss Bonnie's. And you didn't have to read the sports page to know that the Yankees were cocksuckers and always would be.

-o-

After being fired from every job he'd ever had [even the longshoremen's union couldn't protect him], Ted the Clown's work boiled down to two suspect skills: bumming drinks at Miss Bonnie's Elvis Bar and putting curses on people (usually Bonnie's customers) who told him to go fuck himself.

"That clown is bad for business," said Bonnie, but she never barred him and her new clientele, young people from outside of the neighborhood, expected to see Ted at a corner stool, white face and grease paint and a shot of cheap brandy between soiled thumb and forefinger of a gloved hand.

["Clowns always wear gloves," said Ted, who'd picked up a few things about the craft he practiced so carelessly. "Even Mickey Mouse."]

Though Bonnie didn't believe in Ted's horseshit, she was pleasantly surprised a few weeks ago—"Damn near stupefied," she said—when an evil eye the imp put on Old Lady Kasha led to the bitter invalid's long hoped for death.

Kasha's tiny rowhouse was next door to Bonnie's and Ted stood outside of it on the sidewalk, fixing his rheumy eyes on the sack of spoiled potatoes in the hospital bed on the other side of a storm window.

"Trizzle, trazzle, drazzle, drone," he chanted. "Time for this bitch to go home . . ."

Poof!

So long, Kasha.

Good riddance to a dry, vengeful stick of Krakow wood who had outlived all of her relatives and few friends; no one happier than Bonnie Sobotka, the barmaid who lived atop the tavern that was her livelihood.

"I'll be goddamned if she didn't just shrivel up and die," said Bonnie. "Like Ted dropped a house on her."

The trick was followed a week later by a miracle that Ted had nothing to do with: the aimless pothead Basilio Boullosa being struck sober while bellyaching to Bonnie over his second 8-ounce draft of Old German.

"Look at that," he said.

"Look at what?" asked Bonnie.

On the wall in a far corner, above a man listening to the ballgame on a 9-volt transistor radio next to his beer [1-to-0 New York, top of the third] hung a painting of a ballplayer; oil on canvas in a flea market frame. It was one of the few images in the bar not of the King: a pitcher with a handlebar moustache and baggy gray knickers throwing a ball skewered with forks toward home plate.

A fork ball—ha, ha, ha—the work of a longtime regular named Ronnie Rupert, a house painter who'd lived across the street from the saloon all of his sixty-two years. Rupert liked Basilio and when he wasn't holding forth on baseball they talked about art.

"See how he made it look like the forks are spinning with the ball. I'd give anything to be able to do that."

"Anything?"

Basilio shook his head, sipped his beer.

"You're better than him," said Bonnie.

"Maybe when I was a kid," he said, no longer able to ignore a certainty closing in on him since he moved in with Grandpop: living with Trudy wasn't the problem, the obligations of fatherhood were not the problem, nor was the fact that there were only twenty-four hours in a day.

"I smell a rat," said Grandpop at breakfast one morning. "And I think I'm looking at him."

"What is it hon, what's eatin' you?" asked Bonnie. "You ain't been right all summer. Where's all your little girlfriends?"

"I don't know, Miss Bon. Everything is gray."

"I know."

Basilio pushed his glass toward Bonnie for a refill, looked up and held the barmaid's gaze. She took the glass off the bar and told him something she'd never told anyone in fifty years of serving booze. Opinions like this were not good for business but Bonnie had never loved anyone—not her kids or any of her five husbands—as much as she loved the mixed-up kid with paint on his pants.

"You're an alcoholic."

-o-

Basilio sits in an empty ball field a block from Bonnie's front door: a new creature unrecognizable to himself. Boullosa without booze, artist sans sativa. Less than half an hour into a sober ride that would last (one step forward, two steps back) the rest of his life.

There were bright stars in the sky, wonder and clarity; and the hint of a breeze off the harbor though not a cool one as a shape on the avenue—white pancake face shining beneath a streetlight—came into focus.

"What's the score, Ted?"

"Here's the score kid," said Ted, fishing around in the folds of his dirty pajamas for one of Bonnie's pink bar napkins. "Call came to the bar not two minutes after you left."

Basilio looked at Bonnie's scrawl on the napkin—"says it's important"—but didn't recognize the out-of-state number.

Ted was a short man, a gnarled *gonif* in a goof suit, not much taller than a cross-legged Basilio on the ground and, as the clown offered him a belt from his half-pint, Basilio saw himself standing above him.

"No thanks."

"No thanks?"

"Leave me alone, Ted."

-o-

Walking along Eastern Avenue, the napkin next to a joint in his white jeans [the ones with the 1970 World Series patch on them]; Basilio flicked the unlit reefer into the street.

Some lucky bum might find it in the morning light, it might get squirted down the gutter and into the sewer by an old woman with purple ankles and a hose and a broom. Or it might lie there until the next thunderstorm.

If Trudy wasn't the problem and lack of talent wasn't the problem and Grandpop (who'd worked as a machinist at the shipyard for forty years without such worries) wasn't the problem, then maybe, just maybe, Basilio was walking in step with the problem down the Avenue.

He was humming a tune to himself—*I hope you never had'em and I hope you never do . . .*—wondering what he was going to do with himself now when a dented gray Chevy pulled to the curb.

"Yo, Ringo, whaddaya doin' walkin' the streets?"

"Officer Friendly," said Basilio. "Where you going?"

"Got a fresh one in Waverly."

"Up near the stadium?"

"Close enough to hear the roar of the crowd."

"Can I go?"

"Sure," said the detective, pushing open the car door.

-o-

Zero Baubopolis, born the same year as Basilio, was a star of street and stage.

A police department phenom, he'd made homicide detective in less than three years on the beat in East Baltimore.

As a member of the Baltimore's first family of clowns—both priests and fools, subtle and disciplined practitioners of the ancient art with roots in Egypt and Greece—Zero and his siblings owned a storefront theater along the rows of restaurants in Basilio's neighborhood.

Zero lived in an apartment above the boards, where he worked out with weights, practiced yoga and gave private lessons to women of a certain age who were drawn to the muscular Greek with the purest of motivations: They wanted to make people happy.

He spoke with a faint accent, even though English was his first language, and showed his students how genuine whimsy could lower their blood pressure and improve the immune system.

"What are you painting these days?' asked Zero, turning north on Patterson Park Avenue. "Nothing better to do on a Monday night than come see a dead body?"

"Thought I'd take in the game."

"The game?" asked the cop, punching the radio. "Half over, isn't it?"

Basilio shrugged. As Zero searched for the play-by-play, he stopped on the news of Stevie Ray Vaughan's death that night in Wisconsin, the dead man's blues playing behind a reporter's description of the helicopter crash that took the guitarist's life.

"Man," said Zero. "I hear he just got clean too."

"I prefer Johnny," said Basilio.

Zero looked at him—*what?*—and Basilio said quietly, "No disrespect, but I prefer Johnny Winter."

"Hard-headed Ringo," laughed the cop, turning east for the lights of Memorial Stadium. "Always going your own way."

Zero pulled into the player's lot and used his badge to get Basilio right up to the turnstiles.

"Aren't you going to be late?" asked Basilio, thanking Zero as he got out of the car.

"They'll still be dead when I get there," laughed the cop.

-o-

The game's announced attendance was 24,589 with no one at the gate when Basilio arrived with the Yankees batting in the top of the eighth. He walked in uncounted, climbing a concrete ramp to the cheap seats when centerfielder Roberto Kelly hit a home run to make it 3-to-0, New York.

He found Trudy and their daughter in Section 34 of the upper deck. India sat with cotton candy between her mother and Trudy's father, a Sparrows Point steelworker with enough seniority to avoid recent layoffs. The crowd was beginning to thin.

"Daddy!" cried India. "You made it."

Basilio and Trudy had been separated for almost two years. All that was left for official divorce was a brief court appearance at which Basilio's presence was not necessary. Trudy was expected to sign the final paperwork by the end of the week.

India scooted down the aisle to hug her father and he took the empty seat next to Trudy with his daughter on his lap. He said hello to his father-in-law and asked Trudy if she'd go with him to get a hot dog.

India: "Can I go?"

Trudy stood up—oh brother—with India ready to follow. Nobody's dummy, Trudy's father gently held the girl back.

Basilio asked India if she wanted a hot dog and she asked for more cotton candy. Trudy said "no" as India, with a frown close to tears, watched them walk away.

In the tunnel leading to the concourse, a young hot dog vendor with Robert Plant hair—a guy Basilio sort of knew who sold hash in the bleachers—gave Basilio a nod, raising his eyebrows in a way that said he was open for business.

Basilio kept walking, saying to Trudy: "I've changed."

"You showed up in the eighth inning."

"I'm different Trude," he said as they got into the line. "Something happened to me."

"Well I hope it's a good thing. India is going to need you."

"When hasn't she had me?"

The old curtain had fallen, just like that. Trudy changed the subject as they made it to the counter.

"Two hot dogs, two beers and a cotton candy," said Basilio, handing the cashier money he would have spent at Bonnie's. He turned to Trudy with the cardboard tray of food in his hand and asked for the last time.

"Please Trudy, don't sign the papers."

"I'm sorry," she said. "Just stay and watch the rest of the game with us."

Basilio handed the tray to her and disappeared into the concrete cavern that led to the street, the first steps of his five-mile walk back home accompanied by the roar that greeted a worthless Mickey Tettleton double.

Walking east on 33rd Street, the night still hot, Basilio knew a few things he didn't when he left the house that evening, things he wouldn't be able to explain to himself, much less Trudy, for years. He was no longer who he'd once been yet he was somehow aware of what he'd always been.

Never again would he ask Trudy to give it another try. Tomorrow he'd make two calls: one to India to see if she wanted to go to that night's game—just him and her—and one to the number on the forgotten napkin, a vaguely familiar voice on the other end telling him that he now had a second child, a boy.

AUNT LOLA
[1993]

THE GATE TO Aunt Lola's yard hung limp on broken hinges, closed with a piece of rope. Basilio let himself in from the alley and walked over cracked concrete to her back door. It was nearly dawn on Christmas Eve, stars fading into a gray, cloudy sky, a sea bag of gifts on his shoulder.

He paused before knocking, staring in as Lola moved around the kitchen in her housecoat, sipping coffee. She didn't hear him when he rapped lightly, so he watched a moment more.

Post-war metal cabinets thick with brown paint and wrinkled decals of horses; an old Oriole stove—a tank without a thermostat—next to a top-of-the-line Kenmore fridge, a mourning gift from Lola's kids when their father passed away the year before.

On the wall, next to a one-week-left-in-the-year calendar from Our Lady of Pompei, a studio portrait of the original Bombacci sisters—Mary, Stella, Anna, Francesca and Amelia—unsmiling in old country sepia before dispersal to orphanages, servants quarters and, inevitably, America.

During the Great Depression—when being poor meant nothing more than not having money—the sisters had populated the alley with children, a score or more of first cousins that included Basilio's father, son of Francesca, and Lola, daughter of Anna.

Now, Basilio and Lola, whom he called "aunt" out of respect, were the only ones left in the 600 block of South Macon Street.

The rest were dead or scattered in a grass-is-greener hopscotch that began in an alley once known for homemade wine and rosebushes before skipping to Dundalk and then Rosedale and White Marsh and now out to the God-forsaken, subdivided pastures of Harford County.

Lola's children had tried for a year to get her out of the house and Basilio, who made ends meet painting seafood on the sides of refrigerated trucks and didn't own a car, sure wasn't hiking out to Fallston to celebrate Christmas Eve.

Lola came to the door and pulled the curtain, her face creased with lines he'd drawn a thousand times over, wisps of Francesca, gentle to the point of naiveté, alive on the other side of the glass. She squinted, recognized him and unlocked the door as he plucked something from his bag, the satchel immediately lighter by half.

"Hey, hon," said Lola. "Whatchu doin' up so early?"

"Giving out presents," he said, stepping into the warmth of fresh coffee, dishwater and oil heat and holding a heavy, long-handled cookie iron in front of her. "This one had your name on it."

In the long moment that Lola puzzled over the well-worn contraption, Basilio realized he hadn't been a boy for a very long time. His daughter was grown and on her own; his parents had slowed to a ritual of soup and salad at 2 p.m. every afternoon no matter what day it was; and no one put out shallow, dime store dishes of celery dribbled with olive oil and black pepper before holiday meals anymore.

"What is it?"

"What *is* it?"

Lola felt around on top of the washing machine that stood between the door and the sink and found her eyeglasses.

"Good God," she said. "I ain't seen one of them in many a year."

As she poured coffee for him, Basilio opened the flat jaws of the *pizzelle* iron to show what was engraved there: the Miraculous Medal of Our Blessed Mother on one side and a busy weave of diamonds on the other.

Miraculous: A floral "M" in a constellation of petitions, the initial interwoven with a cross surrounded by 12 stars.

Twelve stars: a dozen men on the road sowing truth no one wants to hear.

Truth: Spare parts and broken hearts in an East Baltimore kitchen nearly a hundred years after their ancestors had found warm beds, full plates and simple work in the shadow of a great bottle cap factory.

"Where'd you get it, kid?"

"Where do you get anything in the Third World nation of Baltimore?" laughed Basilio. "From some dummy who didn't know what the hell it was."

He set the iron across a newspaper on the table, yesterday's headlines confirming his cynicism, and looked around the spotless rowhouse, Catholicism a lesser devotion than prayers said on your knees with a bucket and a scrub brush.

192

Aunt Lola didn't have a tree, but carols were playing on a plastic AM radio and she'd taped Christmas cards to the spokes of the banister in the middle room.

"What the hell am I gonna do with a pizzelle iron? Hang it on the wall."

And, just before Basilio could say that it wasn't a bad idea—hang it on the wall, put up a small shelf and light candles—something better occurred to him.

"I don't know, hon."

"How hard can it be, Aunt Lol?"

"I turned many a pizzelle iron, but one of the cousins picked up on the recipe, not me."

"No one wrote it down?"

"Didn't have to," she said. "So nobody did."

"We can do it," he said, drumming his fingers across the plastic tablecloth. "I watched 'em do it, you did it every year. Eggs, sugar, flour and butter, like everything else."

"Got plenty sugar," she said. "But baking powder, baking soda—I don't keep that stuff around no more."

"The store does," said Basilio, getting up to peek in the fridge, empty except for a small carton of milk, a big jug of water and two meatballs in a dish of tomato sauce. An expensive night light.

"There's some vegetable oil in the cabinet," she said. "But the main thing . . ."

". . . is the anise," said Basilio.

Lola moved to a roll top hutch, Pennsylvania Dutch stenciling on the lacquered wood, and found a crusty brown medicine bottle, bone dry.

"Don't let 'em give you extract, it's too weak," she said, handing him the bottle. "*Oil* of anise. Same as what you're holding."

Lola went for her change purse but Basilio was already at the door, a good year of selling tacky paintings to tourists behind him: Mr. Boh throwing a baseball, Mr. Boh scrubbing marble steps, Mr. Boh eating a pile of steamed crabs.

"Be right back," he said, picking up his seabag on the way out the front door, counting the houses as he passed them, remembering who used to live in them.

Mr. Kugler, "the German" who made beer in his basement, put on lederhosen to hike in Patterson Park and was head chef at the bottle cap factory down by the railroad tracks when it employed a thousand people.

Miss Helen, a tough Polish lady who shucked oysters in cold packing houses on Boston Street, worked as hard as any man and would tell you without being asked, "We didn't have no women's lib in them days, we just worked . . ."

His grandparents' house was in the middle of the block and he remembered the Christmas Eve forty years earlier when he'd lost a flying Beatle doll—John—above these tarred roofs; a toy enjoyed for a moment before it disappeared into the cold night sky.

How he'd cried!

Never imagining that a couple of miles down the salty river would find him living on Macon Street the way his widowed grandfather had before him: alone.

Two blocks up, he hit Eastern Avenue and turned left toward the old Chessie underpass, built in 1930 when the factory was supplying millions upon millions of crimped, cork lined "crowns" to bottlers around the world. A train rolled by as he walked beneath the trestle and he stopped to absorb the feel of it, remembering stories of Depression era kids being sent to pick up loose coal to throw in pot-bellied stoves: cheap coal that burned dirty and every now and then blew up a house.

The train passed and he moved into the Highlandtown shopping district, reaching into his bag to give away a baseball cap–the mighty cartoon bird orange, freshly laundered and smiling—to a boy young enough to be happy about it; a repaired rosary to a Salvadoran woman pushing a stroller with two kids in it—he laid a little holiday Feliciano on her and she smiled—unloading everything he had in a short walk to DiPasquale's near the corner of Gough and Conkling.

Sometimes during this annual ritual, passing out unwrapped oddities that people would have stepped over if they hadn't been presented as gifts, he'd see the very thing he'd given away—a plastic action figure or a ball with a few bounces left in it, a redistribution of something more impossible than wealth—lying in the gutter alongside the spot where he'd offered it.

At DiPasquale, around the corner from the Zannino funeral home where his grandfather had lain, Basilio ordered a double espresso from the girl behind the deli counter and drank it down, his duffel no longer a St. Nick sack but a grocery bag as he grabbed what he needed and resisted the urge to linger.

At the register, he took out the anise bottle and asked if they could refill it for him, the way Lola said they did back when you got anise at the pharmacy. Studying the bottle like an Indian arrowhead, the cashier chuckled and handed it back to him with a clear, plastic bottle of anise, just as small and $5.95.

In Basilio's wake, someone was buying ricotta and someone was getting hauled out to a hearse. On an opposite corner, Mr. Stan was selling last minute inventory at his custom foam shop: pierced hearts and holly for the cemetery and twinkling lights for fake trees. One goes and the whole string goes out.

"Got it," said Basilio, walking back in the house without knocking.

The kitchen table was covered with wax paper and an empty aluminum spaghetti pot sat on the counter. Aunt Lola was leaning up against the washing machine, counting on her fingers.

"I think I got it, too," she said. "It'll all come back when I start working the dough."

She cracked a half-dozen eggs into the pot and tossed everything else in after them, pouring out a couple tablespoons of the anise oil, Basilio holding the pot steady as she leaned over it with an electric mixer, the beaters nicking the edges.

And then, she took a dab of the dough and fashioned a small cross from it, sticking the icon to the back of the stove where they'd see it as they worked.

"My mother always did that," she said. "For luck I guess."

Basilio turned a knob on the stove and put a match to the front burner, the oven as old as the railroad underpass, bought at Bolewicki's and in the house for years before Lola moved in on her wedding day.

The iron lay over the open flame—"good and hot," said Lola, "it's gotta be good and hot"—and soon she was dropping small balls of dough between the scored jaws. The first few were pale prototypes; trial and error and an almost good one for every three that weren't right at all.

"Let me try," said Lola, taking the iron and dipping under the weight of it. "My God it's heavy."

Basilio held her wrists in his hands, they were soft and pudgy, like the dough, and helped her turn the iron. They made a keeper and flipped it onto the wax paper, the cookie flat and crisp and light brown around the edges, the "M" raised in perfect legibility.

The day, she'd been up since 3:00 and couldn't get back to sleep, had worn Lola out and she sat down, pooped.

"I'm gonna rest my eyes a little bit," she said, moving to the couch in the front room, a crocheted pillow under her head. "Just a couple minutes."

That minute was all it took for Basilio to get the ambidextrous hang of making the cookies by himself, as though the iron and the dough were brushes in his hand: open, plop, squeeze long enough to say a "Hail Mary," turn the iron, sing a verse of "God Only Knows," open, pluck, repeat, repeat, repeat as Aunt Lola breathed in the warm aroma, the licorice scent of the anise perfuming her dreams.

Awake, we recognize and remember the mystery of more than ten thousand smells through a thousand genes and a thousand receptors. They come together the way letters make words and words make sentences. Asleep, the gift multiplies and the receptors that told Lola pizzelles were piling up in the kitchen had bonded in the shape of a teardrop.

Science promises that in the future, smell may be restored to those who've lost it; a day when appetite, fear, and longing will be given back to people unable to follow their nose.

Until that day . . . two dozen pizzelles on the table, three dozen, four.

As pictures moved in Lola's gray head—glimpses of trucking company at Foster and Oldham when it was a pasture, the day when her mother unwittingly burned up the rent money by hiding it from her husband in the oven—Basilio turned the iron and stared into the alley.

Out there in the weeds and litter, he saw moments when he'd been taken into small, dark bedrooms crowded with heavy furniture and crucifixes large enough to plant on Calvary, vanity tables turned to altars for sick old ladies as the Bombacci sisters fell away, one by one.

He never remembered their names, could never tell the difference between Aunt This One and Aunt That One, the rooms smelling of death and Noxzema as the aged brushed their hair below 3-D collages of the Sacred Heart, frames of bleeding butterfly wings that scared and transfixed a boy no taller than the post at the end of the bed.

"Come here, kid," they'd say in broken English. "Let me look at you."

For taking five small steps from the foot of the bed to the head with a little nudge from behind, for letting his cheek be touched, Basilio would get a quarter. Remembering what a long, hard road those steps had been, he decided that when Lola woke up, they'd retrace them together.

A couple of hours later, Lola found the table crowded with cookies; the aluminum pot, rimmed with crusts of dried dough, soaking in the sink.

"Good Lord, how long was I sleeping?" she said, nibbling the edges of a pizzelle. "What are we gonna do with all these cookies?"

"Give 'em away," said Basilio.

"Sounds good to me," she said. "I slept good."

They packaged the cookies in deco tins Lola found in the basement, dusty things once packed with Goetze's caramel creams, Esskay sausage and Utz potato chips, old drums she rinsed out and layered with the last of the wax paper.

As Basilio passed her stacks of cookies for the tins, Lola counted them: four dozen, five dozen, six dozen, "seven dozen, just like I thought we'd get from what we whipped up," she said, eating another cookie as Basilio picked up the phone and asked for a cab.

"Where we going?

"Fallston."

"Fallston!" laughed Lola, happy to take a ride. "Wait'll they get a load of us! Should we call and let 'em know we're coming?"

"Nah."

The cab honked out front and they walked out the door, Lola in front with one tin, Basilio behind her with two more, his sea bag empty on the kitchen floor; the cold sharp and the late afternoon sky heavy with the possibility of snow.

"I dreamt the bottle cap factory was on fire again," she said as they got in the cab. "That cork burned for a week when we was kids. Didn't think they'd ever put it out."

"It's gonna be new again," said Basilio, telling the cabbie to ride by the factory on the way out. "Just like the old American Can building over in Canton."

"Canton, sure, over in Canton. But not here."

"I'm just saying, hold onto your house Aunt Lol. It's going to be worth a lot of money."

"Where the hell am I gonna go?" she said, a month away from her seventy-fifth birthday. "I'm going straight from here to Zannino's."

The cab turned for the Interstate, over the river and through the woods with pizzelles warming Lola's lap through the bottom of the tin.

THE GANGES OF BALTIMORE
[1995]

"You always love the city you die in . . ."

—Tom Nugent, trouble maker

SIDE ONE

THIS IS A five-sided box of clear glass made of broken transoms and shattered diner china salvaged in alleys from the slums of West Baltimore to the rubble in the east.

It hangs on spider silk, a half-bubble off plumb, deep in the bleeding heart of the Holy Land.

In 1995, from Thanksgiving weekend through the last day of the year, Basilio Boullosa received a series of letters from one of his few peers, an artist who'd abandoned Baltimore to live alone in the woods.

X-rays written on scraps of paper stained with paint, dirt and glue, rings from coffee cups and marijuana ash.

Sent to 21224: *"Dear Ringo . . ."*

Posted from 21520: *"Hettleman."*

Bragging letters, pissed-off letters and crying letters; a self-absorbed dirge for things Hettleman professed to care nothing for.

"Don't miss it at all . . ."

If not his mind, then surely Hettleman's talent—substantial, acknowledged for a moment and then forgotten—was failing him.

Hettleman made his splash assembling reliquaries: shrines to Irish railroad workers near Fourteen Holy Martyrs, black oyster shuckers along the harbor rim, household saints and scraps—half-a-handkerchief, a missing house in the middle of Smallwood Street—from his own family.

Basilio lived in a reliquary inherited upon his grandfather's death.

He slept in the bed where his father was presumably conceived and shaved before a wooden medicine cabinet whose mirrored door bore a log his grandfather had kept with a carpenter's pencil, tracking the life of each razor blade—when purchased, how many shaves he'd gotten out of it, when it was time to buy a new one. The last date was from the summer of 1989.

Basilio boiled eggs in a sauce pan his grandmother bought on Eastern Avenue a few days before her wedding. He stretched canvas and built frames on his grandfather's work bench, worried over the rosebushes in the backyard and weaved all of it into portraits of women who'd come to visit over the years before going on their way.

"*Dear Ringo,*" wrote Hettleman. "*Do you remember how we met?*"

Long time ago, whispered Basilio.

"*. . . it was your first one-man show. First time I'd ever been to Miss Bonnie's. She sure must have liked you to take down all that Elvis for your work. That rich broad bought the painting of your grandparents in bed when they were young.*"

Grandmom and Grandpop, thought Basilio, closing his eyes to see them as they were in the painting, half his age and entwined in the bed he slept in every night.

"*Deep blues and dark greens,*" wrote Hettleman. "*The money goes in a day—we spent some of it on hash that night. Blonde like the attorney who bought the painting. We both could have nailed her that night. When you sober up the money is gone you wish you had the canvas back.*

"*Still sleeping in that bed?*"

I am.

Basilio hadn't seen Hettleman in years and rarely thought of him before the missives began landing from the other side of the state.

"*Out here, man, the air is pure out here and the soil is rich . . . I'm breathing like I haven't breathed since I was a kid.*"

Basilio—lost in sauce-stained cook books his lover brought over when she could get away—never wrote back.

SIDE TWO

If a great man were to paint a landscape of two hundred miles between the City of Baltimore and the far reaches of Western Maryland, where might the line fall between braggadocio and despair?

"*Instead of watering down the gesso,*" wrote Hettleman, "*I rub it into planks of wood and work on top of the swirls.*"

New work by Basilio—a dirty wineglass on a zinc counter—leaned against the wall near the door. He would sell it cheap for quick Christmas money and turn forty by spring. The longest relationship he'd had beyond an extended adolescence with his daughter's mother did not last five months.

The vestibule door was made from a dozen panes of pink milk glass, each framed with wood painted to look like wood: undulating striations of brown and gold made with a craftsman's comb, one of ten thousand inherited relics.

The door the same, save for a new generation of nicks and chips—one long scratch from an especially large painting carted to market the day before—as it was when Basilio the boy waited for guests to arrive on Christmas Eve. The holiday had not been celebrated on Macon Street for more than twenty years.

Outside, the aluminum storm door with the letter B encircled in the center creaked. Basilio had begun waiting for the sound that announced the day's mail since the arrival of Hettleman's first, unexpected letter.

Bills, junk, and a supermarket circular dropped against octagonal tiles, the shadow of the mailman passing the curtains as the storm door banged closed.

Basilio stepped gingerly across tangled strings of lights and scattered ornaments to get the mail. He sifted it on the couch (nothing marked *correo aereo*, there never was) and stopped when he saw Hettleman's hand across a smudged envelope that had been used before.

He'd spent the morning mopping the floor, pushing all of the ornaments that hadn't been broken to the side. Now he lay stretched out on a couch where a few hours ago Aubergine had moaned with one leg in her jeans and one leg out. She'd lost half-a-cup of blood; he a third.

"Dear Ringo—

"This county issues the fewest number of building permits in Maryland. No dope, no murders, no beggars, no bullshit."

It was the day after Thanksgiving and Basilio—pained and exhausted in the front room, staring at the vestibule over the top of the letter—wondered if he should get up and make another turkey sandwich from the carcass Aubergine brought for soup.

"I should have done this a long time ago," wrote Hettleman. *"Don't miss that shithole at all."*

Basilio was preparing for a one-man show at Bonnie's Tavern—big pieces, frames made of scavenged wood, scratches on the door from hauling them out to the car.

[He might sell a painting. Maybe two. And if the mood struck him—

she was pretty, if she was sad, if she was old and remembered when Baltimore was Baltimore—he might give one away.]

Basilio made more money painting provincial Christmas scenes on decorative pillows—Baltimore the most provincial of cities: big-hearted, duckling ugly—than he did telling the story of Life on Earth as it is Idiosyncratically Lived along the Crumbling Holy Lands on the Patapsco.

"My studio is a stand of ancient hemlocks, sky high," wrote Hettleman. *"They filter the light before it reaches the old barn planks I'm using. Natural sunlight, Rings. Won't paint by anything else."*

Basilio wondered if Hettleman was painting at all.

"You know what's really weird? Everybody out here is white. I mean everybody. The town sits under a big hill they call Negro Mountain but there aren't any black people. You think you know what it means. But you don't. You don't know until you move to a place like this. You can forget that you grew up in a black city . . ."

Piss and bravado in Western Maryland.

And blood on the tracks in the 600 block of South Macon Street.

-o-

Since they'd met under the whirligig at the Visionary last summer—Aubergine chaperoning her daughter's field trip, Basilio looking for colors—his lover had brought the best version of herself to his door, one in opposition to a day-to-day life she no longer recognized.

This morning, as always, they were on each other before she had time to take her coat off.

Aubergine dropped a bag holding potato and parsley salad, mumbling "Walter Hasslinger's recipe," as Basilio smothered her words with his mouth. Any trace of the Baltimore that was gone pleased him. Anything they could share together pleased her in turn.

Basilio waltzed her across the maze of decorations on the floor as buttons and zippers broke loose, tossing her gray beret across the room just before they fell onto the couch.

It was great, it always was, great until they rolled from the couch to the floor and Aubergine screamed like a teenager in childbirth; stabbed in the soft, dimpled flesh of her rear-end with the ice-pick point of a steamed crab shell, a holiday ornament painted by a hand far less patient than the one decorating pillows.

The ornament was precious to Basilio, a bauble from a moment bigger than all that had occurred on Macon Street, more than the story told in the brushstrokes of the green and blue painting that Hettleman liked so much.

[Every Christmas since Grandpop died, Basilio promised to put the shell in a safe place—better to protect it in a china closet than hang it on the tree—and every year he let it sit out until December rolled around and hung it on the tree.]

The wound ran deep and Aubergine refused to go to the hospital.

Since the whirligig had spun: buckets of spousal hogwash lathering friction burns across her shoulders, bruises on her thighs, books laying around the living room by authors no one had ever heard of and a receipt for $28.95 worth of rotisserie chicken (all of Aubergine's appetites were blue-ribbon) in a part of town her husband only knew from maps.

But stitches in your ass from a puncture wound delivered by a Christmas crustacean?

"Jesus," said Basilio, running for a towel, stepping on the same shell in his bare feet—"FUCK!"—his blood pooling with Aubergine's on the floor.

Blood on the rug, on strings of blinking lights that Basilio had plugged in before she arrived, in the grooves of the hardwood floor.

Blood running down Aubergine's leg as she ran up to the bathroom where after sex they rested in a claw foot tub below a skylight; where during the Depression newlyweds had washed their dinner dishes when Grandpop rented out the second floor.

Dime-sized drops of blood that Basilio wouldn't notice for years and then, on his hands and knees when he couldn't get the colors to mix the way he wanted, when Aubergine's successors walked out, he'd assume it was dirt or chocolate.

Aubergine left Macon Street limping, her backside daubed with the last drops from a twenty year-old bottle of mercurochrome that Grandpop had used on shaving cuts and a thick wad of paper towels affixed with masking tape.

Basilio lay on the couch with half a crab shell upon his belly, the bloody rug in the backyard where it would be rained on, crapped on by birds, baked in the sun and one day thrown away.

"I'm in heaven, Rings . . ."

Basilio pinched the bridge of his nose with the envelope, tears smearing Hettleman's penmanship.

"Come see me when you're tired of getting shit on in the Third World."

SIDE THREE

The second week of December, into a house whose every baseboard bore painted canvas—histories within histories, the covers of Long Playing record albums, endive trampled among a thousand odors—came a package.

"Dear Ringo . . . I made you something . . ."

Wrapped in newsprint on a bed of straw, lay a mask—unyielding and crude.

Painted to resemble flesh that looked like wood, it had eyeholes, an opening for the mouth and twine attached behind the ears.

"Made it out of some cereal boxes that blew out of the trash and got rained on in the field," wrote Hettleman. *"I set them next to the wood stove in the kitchen and when they dried out, I saw your face."*

"Whose face?" demanded Basilio, walking the mask to the basement where a pot of cabbage had simmered since morning.

Basilio stirred the pot and contemplated Hettleman, a man with his troubles behind him making a witch doctor mask out of soggy cardboard in the wilds of western Maryland. And remembered the day he watched as a crab shell was transformed from garbage to gem.

Remembered is not quite the right word, since he thought about her—and all she'd done with him, to him, at him and for him in fourteen weeks on Macon Street—all the time. No matter who was in his bed or sitting for their portrait, he thought of her.

Nieves Boullosa Caldas of Galicia, named for snow in a land of hot springs, a distant cousin close enough to touch, on Macon Street just long enough to reverse the tides.

She fished a crab shell from the trash in the backyard, squirted it off with a hose and across its back painted a winter scene of a stone *horreo*, snow dusting the cross at its peak. Nieves worked with a focus Basilio had rarely seen, patiently drilling the point of a safety pin through the carapace to make a hole for twine.

A summer of extreme memories more than seven years past yet not much evidence of it: a hurricane that roared down the alley in the last months of his grandfather's life. A few notes left on the kitchen table saying she had gone out, a glass earring he attached to a broken rosary and a pair of bright yellow shorts on the line she had every intention of retrieving.

Basilio had offered her everything: a backyard just wide enough for two trash cans and his grandmother's rosebush—arms spread wide: all this can be yours—and in return was told that Grandpop was still alive and what right did he have to make such a proposal?

My heart?

Take my right eye.

Basilio stirred the pot—his mother's recipe, there'd be plenty of time for Spanish meals between now and the *caldo gallego* on New Year's Day—and sat down in a basement perfumed with the scent of cabbage and peppercorns.

Kapusta.

Hettleman had stopped working with canvas because he didn't like the *"give"* of it, said he was using old boards and cabinet doors, things that *"held their own."*

"Yeah, Rings . . . this one is you!"

Having Lithuanian mothers—one on either side of the Messiah—had connected Basilio and Hettleman early on. They'd supported each other's work, followed Nugent like field mice and stayed up past dawn smoking pot and drinking beer in the alley behind Miss Bonnie's bar.

Hettleman's mother grew up near Druid Hill Park. Basilio's came of age around the Hollins Street Market, dead since Basilio was thirteen, run over on a supermarket parking lot with an arm full of groceries.

He was ashamed to admit—which he hadn't, not to Aubergine or any of her predecessors—that he missed Nieves more.

He'd never made a picture of his mother but he had a few photographs of her, kept one in a drugstore frame next to the stove. It showed her as a kid during the Depression, posing in a kiddie wagon and holding the reins of a goat in front of the Hollins Street Market. It was the source of a great family story.

She'd seen one of her girlfriends posing on the goat and cried until her mother fished out enough quarters, dimes and nickels to buy a pork chop dinner so that the crybaby (known in the family as "Squeaky Oil Can") could have what she wanted. Not so much to have what she wanted. Mostly so she would shut the hell up.

And the crab ornament crumbling to dust in an old Noxzema jar in his grandparents' bedroom, the only proof that Nieves had ever been on Macon Street at all.

On the sink, the mocking mask: What are *you* looking at?

Not long after Nieves disappeared for good (early on, he jerked between wondering if she was really gone or just lost), Basilio overheard a man talking about his daughter at a bus stop.

"I'd kick her ass," he said. "But it would be like kicking myself . . ."

How much of Hettleman's anger had leeched into the mask?

Rain on cardboard, heat on rain, paint on heat, Hettleman on paint, resentments chewing on Hettleman.

"You live in your grandparents' house . . . my bubbie's place on North Smallwood Street? Jesus Christ, Rings. She used to chase the little *schvatzas* with her broom like a crazy woman. They thought it was a game and laughed so hard no one bothered her. Last twenty years of her life she was the only white person for a dozen blocks in every direction.

"All those years I could have been lighting candles and eating good. Instead I was just fucking around. Some half-ass artist. Fuck that. I'm not fucking around anymore."

Basilio set out a bowl (Limoge, rosettes with gold leaf, 1950) and spoon (stainless) while scanning Hettleman's grievances.

The night cramps in his legs, how Bubby Klein was knocked down and robbed after she got too old for the chase; how Highlandtown might have taken a beating for fifteen minutes but Reservoir Hill had been in the toilet for more than forty years by the time Hettleman came to his senses.

Envy, anger and a hollow vengeance worthy of Bobby Fischer.

"I hate that I didn't move in and take care of her like you did with your grandfather . . . I fucking myself . . ."

Hettleman knew well the one painting Basilio was known for—"her hair was black, as black as an olive"—and he was at Miss Bonnie's the night the rich lady bought it. But did he know that it is easier to admire the picture than to be in it?

Basilio left the letter on the table and walked on a still-tender foot to the mask. It lay on a drying board between the sink and stove.

The cabbage bubbled slow and thick, the color of the corridor where Basilio was told his mother's injuries were fatal. The stew smelled like the mess Nieves left in Grandpop's old bedroom when she disappeared.

Basilio picked up the mask with his left hand and stirred with his right, permanent indentations on the tip of his index finger and the inside of the middle one from years of gripping pencils and brushes.

Basilio brought the mask to his face and stared into the holes. Not *through* but *into* . . . deep into Grandpop's funeral a half-dozen years ago. At the wake, Basilio stood next to his father with one eye on the door to see if Nieves would show.

A Spaniard—even one as fucked up as Nieves, a half-click away being

207

one of the all-time greats in a life where any difference is all the difference—is a Spaniard. And in her heart—the foot vein is connected to the ankle vein—she loved Grandpop more than dope.

She walked into the funeral parlor at the corner of Conkling and Gough looking like shit and Basilio left his father's side for the first time in three days. He moved quickly but not quick enough as Nieves knelt at the casket, made the sign of the cross, nodded to Basilio as though to an acquaintance and fled into a car at the curb.

Basilio saw it all as though they'd buried Grandpop that morning.

As though . . .

BANG!

The pot of cabbage flew off the stove—Basilio struggling to pry the clammy mask from his face—and struck the photo of his mother riding the goat, cracking the glass. The pot hit the far wall and fell, viscous broth and bits of potato in puddles on the floor.

This very thing—pots sailing off of stoves like cannon balls—supposedly happened now and again; once to the best friend of Basilio's grandmother. He'd heard them talking about it at this table in this basement when he was a kid.

"Frances, I'm telling you, it *shot* off the stove and gave me a black eye."

But he'd never believed it.

Aubergine in the détente of counseling she neither needed nor wanted.

Nieves in the wind.

The mask fell into the mess on the floor, it's edges beginning to fray from the acid in the cabbage.

He picked it up—dripping, stinking—set it on the table and cried: "Come back . . ."

But one wasn't talking and the other never listened.

SIDE FOUR

Christmas Eve in the 600 block of South Macon Street.

The mail came late, the storm door banging as Basilio dressed for dinner, waiting for his daughter.

Then to Cousin Donna's for the meal: empanada the Galician way; calamari from Ikaros up at Eastern and Ponca; pasta with tuna; smelts, thin lengths of celery in shallow dishes of olive oil and cracked black pepper; crusty bread soaked in wine and sprinkled with sugar.

At the center: salted cod baked in fresh cream and bread crumbs.

Bathed and shaved, Basilio opened Hettleman's letter with one of Grandpop's penknives while walking upstairs to dress. He unfolded it on his grandmother's vanity and read while buttoning his white shirt, his grandfather's cuff links—mother of pearl inlaid with an onyx B—next to the Noxzema jar.

"*Dear Ringo,*

"*How'd you like the mask?*"

[Loved it, thought Basilio. Couldn't get enough.]

"*Remember what Nugent used to tell us when he was bombed and shitting his pants at Bonnie's and she'd run us out and tell us not to come back?*"

[Maybe you, thought Basilio, but Miss Bonnie never ran me out.]

"*He'd preach: 'Everything profound loves a mask . . .'*"

The mask hung in a window upstairs, Hettleman's pigments—something like cochineal mixed with lead white—holding its own against the early winter sun.

"*Skin is reflective,*" wrote Hettleman. "*It mirrors everything.*"

A shimmering 360: Grandpop's cufflinks; the cobalt Noxzema jar; a portrait of the Sacred Heart of Mary made with butterfly winds by a long-dead relative in Argentina; silver vanity mirrors, also like wings, spotted with gray.

On the bed, an unopened gift from Aubergine, forgotten when she'd hurt herself, found when he went looking for the last rolls of his grandmother's wrapping paper. Basilio made a triangle knot in one of Grandpop's old ties, a short one from the '30s, ox-blood with cream swirls, and moved toward the bed, Nieves' bed when she lived here but never Basilio and Nieves' bed.

"*I hope the mask didn't piss you off,*" wrote Hettleman. "*If it did, don't toss it. One day it will hang at the Visionary . . .*"

And Basilio laughed—*his* laugh—as high as a pigeon.

The Visionary!

He ran a comb through his thinning hair and paused to open the gift from Aubergine. She had found a can opener, the same vintage as Grandpop's tie, the kind that worked on elbow grease. It had a smooth wooden handle, painted red down to a rounded white tip. If she had left it in the basement during one of their dinners, Basilio would have assumed it had been there for sixty years.

He laid it next to the comb on the dresser, shoved Hettleman's letter in his pocket and went downstairs.

On the couch—floor gleaming, tree twinkling, door open to the vestibule—Basilio sat with Hettleman's letter and waited like he used to on Christmas Eve when the dinner was held here, two dozen people in a narrow basement kitchen where Basilio now ate most of his meals alone.

The basement where his grandmother's lady friend, Miss Leini, sipped coffee from a bowl, a scar from a deep cut across her brow, and told his grandmother—almost blind, naïve in her blindness—how a stewpot flew off the stove and knocked her to the ground.

The letter was one more in a recent flurry from Hettleman and Basilio had filed them chronologically in a wire napkin holder. Each letter, even the amusing ones, revealed a Hettleman a little shakier than the last.

"Did I ever tell you about the Christmas ball factory? I bet some of your relatives worked there . . . it was up by the bus yard on Ponca Street."

[Basilio didn't know and it nettled him. He remembered walking his grandmother up to Ponca Street to visit Miss Leini. But a Christmas ball factory? Three blocks from his house? It pissed him off to learn it from Hettleman.]

"It was my great-grandfather's business, Bubby Klein's father. The goyim called him 'the Old Jew.' I think some of my relatives even called him that when they didn't think there were any kids around."

Basilio had once done a series of paintings based about things he'd heard when the grown-ups didn't think children were afoot.

That's how he'd learned that his mother had had a few "highballs" when the car hit her; that his grandfather had been deported as an illegal during Prohibition; and his grandmother was Miss Leini's only friend because the proper society in a neighborhood of shipyard workers and housewives shunned the orphaned Greek—so good looking it caused pain in others—for living as she pleased.

"They worked the line the way their husbands worked at Bethlehem Steel. Like their men who walked out the gates with enough steel to build a destroyer, these broads robbed us blind. They had to be able to letter and draw," wrote Hettleman, who'd doodled reindeer and elves in the margins. *"Trite greetings, glue and sparkle . . . usually in script but lettering too, simple stuff."*

Basilio glanced at the front window, listening for the sound of a car door.

"My father worked in the factory on summers and weekends. All women, Polish and Italian, a couple of Greeks. Some blacks when he couldn't find anybody else, but not for the lettering. All of them could draw, though. More people knew how to draw then."

Basilio considered the ancient balls on the small plastic tree in the front window, the ones he'd found wrapped in newspaper in shoeboxes the first Christmas after Grandpop's death.

Happy Holidays, Merry Christmas, 'tis the Season . . .

God Bless Us.

Everyone.

"The God-fearing Catholic women of Highlandtown eating meatball sandwiches on the line and robbing us blind one Christmas ball at a time!

"One day, a flat-chested woman (she wasn't Polish or Italian, my old man said the other women called her "American" but she was just a hillbilly), one day, Rings—no-tits Fannie had a rack! My father gives it squeeze and—crack!—two of the biggest balls they made, one green and one red, broke like stale crackers. Christmas falsies!

"My Dad was just a kid, helping out over the holidays, Rings. He had no interest in the Hebrew Piano, he wanted to be like us. Or maybe he wanted to be like you. I have some of the stuff he did before he knocked up my Mom and had to get married.

"He was a natural born cockhound, Rings. The shit you can't teach. I bet he got as much pussy as Sinatra. Of course it was Baltimore pussy, but hell, the worst I ever had was great."

Nice talk, chuckled Basilio, nice talk on Christmas.

"But Fannie could draw . . . she could draw, Rings—you know what I mean—so the broken bulbs came out of her bra and out of her pay and she got to keep her job."

The car Basilio was waiting for—he knew the sound of his daughter's mother's exhaust—stopped outside and he waited for the vestibule knob to turn.

Now it was Christmas.

On the way out—trying to do nine things at once, his arms full of presents, car keys in his mouth, receipt for the paid-in-advance calamari between his fingers—Basilio shoved Hettleman's letter in his pocket.

The wind caught the pages, sending the missive sailing across Macon Street toward the railroad tracks where the bottle cap factory used to be.

SIDE FIVE

New Year's Eve, 1995.

Up from a very late nap, Basilio walked up two flights of stairs to his studio on the third floor, a new letter from Hettleman in one hand—the last he would receive—a cup of black coffee in the other.

"I'm so fucking broke, Rings, I ain't got change for a grasshopper and that's a pizzy ant and two crickets . . ."

Basilio laughed, settling in for a night at home on the last night of the year. Not because he was broke (he was, having sold just enough paintings and some sign work to get through Christmas) but just because.

"In the middle of nowhere, dead ass, bent-dick broke," wrote Hettleman. *"Who you gonna sell a painting of Memorial Stadium on the back of a hubcap to out here? No one. Fucking nobody."*

Basilio entered a long, open room; paint spattered across bare floorboards, a hole in the ceiling. He hugged a wall in the darkness to the middle of the room, a deckhand on a rowhouse schooner; a length of heaving line holding a tarp across the opening in the roof.

As he loosened the line from a cleat on the wall, the tarp dropped to the floor.

Swoosh!

Above his still-groggy head—waking up on the far side of 10 p.m.—a large, squared hole opened onto a sharp, crisp night, clouds sailing like nocturnal zeppelins through chilly moonlight.

Wind knocked over an unfinished portrait of Aubergine, her blood in the brown of the birthmark on her shoulder. As it fell, it knocked over an incomplete portrait of her predecessor.

[He'd opened the roof once for Nieves, not knowing that she had come up on her own all the time while he was out of the house, expertly dropping and replacing the canvas tarp, stealing a peek at the view before she began stealing from Grandpop.

The one and only time they'd been intimate (that's how Basilio preferred to think of it) had occurred here, under a gaping hole on the anniversary of the Day the Beatles Met Elvis; Grandpop out for a late summer walk with the young mother across the alley who ran interference the way Basilio's grandmother once did for Miss Leini.]

He stood directly beneath the hole and looked up.

New Year's Eve had become a night to mull the accomplishments of the past year, pushing work by degrees from the studio to the vestibule and out the door, never finishing all he'd attempted; a night to sketch a plan for the year ahead.

An annual date with solitude for when you were as chronically mixed up in other people's domestic strife as Basilio had been since he was a teenager, New Year's Eve was a difficult night to be out in the world.

Pathetic?

What are *you* doing New Year's Eve?

Basilio sat on a threadbare Persian carpet and looked up at Nieves spread across the ceiling like a crow, the ones that dive-bombed *la tornaratas* back in Galicia, her pale, thin face spreading out in vapors of red and gold from the edges of the hole.

He'd made the mural in the wake of her brief and turbulent time on Macon Street; Elisabeth's husband—only half the pussy that Aubergine's husband was—banging on the kitchen door with his fist.

"Do you know where they are?"

Basilio invited him in for a drink.

"I wish I did."

"I bet you do, asshole," said the cuckold, slamming the gate on Grandpop's fence so hard it fell from its rusted hinges.

-o-

Basilio put a pillow under his head and stretched out. With a sip of coffee, he took the letter from his pocket as the studio—one large room, from the street out front to the alley behind him—absorbed the cold from open sky.

Hettleman: *"It's full-on winter now and I'm late working the berries. Possum haw, good for the bluebirds.*

"Those beat-up little seagulls still pecking away at frozen French fries on Pratt Street?"

[Basilio thought of the one he'd seen that morning—filthy gull struggling under the weight of a chicken wing—when he'd walked to get a paper to see what he'd be missing tonight.]

"Wanna know the truth, Rings? My ass is dragging. You play make-believe with the ponytail of the month beneath those cathedral skylights and all I've got is a shard. A dented oyster bucket missing a handle.

"I didn't leave Baltimore because of Smallwood Street or the fuck ugly hotel they put up that blocks the Bromo Seltzer tower. Let Nugent write those stories. What did he used to tell us when we were getting high in the alley behind Bonnie's?

213

"You always love the city you die in. I never knew what he meant until now."

Basilio had known since August 27, 1988.

"I left when my dog died," said Hettleman. *"Crying on the steps, 101 degrees at 10 a.m. and one more mutant—why this guy, why that moment, I don't know cuz I seen it a million times. One more retard eating shit out of a box and dropping the trash on the sidewalk as casually as wiping his ass.*

"I snapped, Rings. It was leave Baltimore or kill somebody."

Basilio knew the feeling, doubted there was anyone in the city that didn't. The week Grandpop died—week fifteen of Nieves in the wind—he planted two pink dogwood trees in front of the house and had Petrucci the bricklayer build planters around them at the curb.

And then stood sentry over the saplings, watching from the front window with all the vigilance he'd once used to stare across the alley at Elisabeth's house; watching to make sure no one fucked with them.

Once he caught the local urchins—kids whose mothers shepherded them with admonitions like "eat your grilled cheese motherfucker"—jumping on the thin branches and hanging like monkeys, limbs snapping like chopsticks.

Basilio had fantasized about shooting them from the branches—he had not yet thrown Grandpop's .22 pea shooter into the harbor—and rehearsed his testimony.

What does Baltimore City need more, your honor?

Strong, beautiful trees—shade and color and a filter for the air; birth and rebirth for spring beats death—or another mouth to feed in juvenile prison?

Both the trees and the kids survived and Basilio never told anyone of this most shameful of all lusts, hovering just below his desire for Nieves.

"I began packing the truck on the spot," wrote Hettleman. *"Moe still warm, in the back of my truck in a broken dresser drawer. And then I lit out for the territories, one last drive by the missing tooth that was my Bubbie's house."*

Basilio stroked the carpet beneath him as Hettleman described the Baltimore heat—Calcutta, the Serengeti, New Orleans on Labor Day—weather as different from the one pouring through the hole in the ceiling as kale is from corn flakes.

"I jumped on the expressway at North Avenue and ran to the

headwaters of the Falls. Ten miles north of chicken bones getting washed into the storm drains and dumping into the harbor where Maggio used to catch rubber balls with a crabbing net.

"Parked the truck and carried Moe to the riverbank. Water was a little cleaner up there. Set the drawer down and took off my clothes. I waded in and poured the Falls over my head with a sauce pan just to say I'd done it.

"Didn't do any of the authentic stuff. Just waded in, held my nose and went under."

And people think I'm nuts, thought Basilio. Sections of the Jones Falls were easily as filthy as the Ganges. He held Hettleman's letter to the sky, the words translucent.

"Moe as dead as Smallwood Street and the dresser drawer—the cabinet gone to splinters . . . I was going to save it Rings, was going to glue it, clamp it, strip it and stain it, was gonna, was gonna, was gonna . . .

"The dog in the dresser, easel rags tucked around him on all sides. Took him to the water's edge, doused it with turpentine and dropped a match . . . nudged Moe out into the current and he burned beautiful, absolutely beautiful headed down to the harbor . . . just like a proper Hindu . . . wouldn't George—what is life anyway, Rings, what the fuck is life—wouldn't George have loved it?"

Basilio took a sip of coffee, now cold. "Viking, you idiot . . . not Hindu."

"So Moe sails toward Pratt Street and I fill an old oyster jar with river water, put the jug on the passenger seat and roll away . . ."

Basilio rubbed his eyes. There was stirring on the street and a premature string of firecrackers popping in anticipation.

In the summer—many humid summers down the road from *the* summer—a ballgame on the radio would help Basilio measure how long he'd labored over the precise constellation of freckles across Nieves' nose.

Keep going to the fifth inning, the black and orange of perennial doormats bleeding into portraits of women, Grandpop and abandoned buildings. Two more outs 'til the 7th inning stretch. Extra innings and he could get the down along the curve of her ears and the little chunk of flesh missing from a knife-game back in Vigo.

Across the ceiling, he painted Nieves spreading like vapor from each right angle of the hole, the rippling mercury of Luna making her teeth shimmer against splintered wood.

Black eyes—"I got a crow on a wire," wrote Nugent in his Library of America edition, ". . . ever look into a crow's eye? Think about a hunk of black ice . . ."—and wings of orange.

This bird has flown.

"Nothing out here," wrote Hettleman. *"Nothing I want to paint . . ."*

The story of the cremated mutt impressed Basilio in a way Hettleman's art never did. Someone shot a gun in the alley, premature but not by much. A gust swept through the hole and rattled the mask where Basilio had arranged it to stare at the house where Elisabeth used to live, his grandmother's Fatima rosary weighing it down from the same nail in the wall.

He held it in front of his face and looked himself dead in the eye, holding his own gaze for a long moment, as if trying to decide whether or not to take a hit of acid.

[Once you get on that bus—cabbage stew all over the floor, the stink of it in the cuffs of your pants—you don't get off until it runs out of gas.]

Basilio brought the mask to his face and counted the moments left in the year as Nieves shook herself loose from the beams and sat cross-legged at his feet.

"Nice mask . . ."

Basilio struggled to sit up, caught a splinter in his palm.

"Hettleman made it."

"Never heard of him."

"Where'd you go?"

"O Camiño de Santiago."

"What?"

The edge of the mask cut into his jaw as he tried to freeze her face in front of him.

"I didn't go anywhere."

Basilio had neither seen nor heard from Nieves in more than six years, not since Grandpop's funeral when she showed up dressed in black—frayed cuffs of a men's dress shirt buttoned at the wrists—and looking like shit.

Now, the harder he tried to see her, really see her, the more the roads she had traveled in the last six years rolled out before him.

Living it up in New York, a belle of hipster Brooklyn.

In the back of a white Chevy Impala squealing through the streets of Mexico City.

Kicking up grain after grain of desert.

And right here, as Basilio confessed to a ghost that she is the love of his life, right here in the Holy Land with seconds to go.

A bang of pots and pans on the street, the rat-a-tat-pop of firecrackers as Nieves took Hettleman's letter from Basilio and read it aloud.

"I love Baltimore," she said, sailing away through the hole in the ceiling, the letter falling back upon Basilio's chest with the first flakes of a light snow as the New Year erupted. "No one can say I don't."

Selected stories for this collection were previously published in the following:

"Aboard the Miss Agnes" appeared in *Port Cities Review,* 2013

"The Aishe Cooper Story" appeared in the *Loch Raven Review,* 2012

"Junie Bug" appeared as "Rolling With the Seasons," in *The Edinburgh Scotsman,* 2010

"The King of a Rainy Kingdom" published by Macon Street Books, 2008

"Granada in the Drink" appeared in *Little Patuxent Review,* 2011

"An Alley Most Narrow" appeared in *Maryland Life Magazine,* 2009

"Room 829" appeared in *Smile Hon, You're in Baltimore,* 2010

"The Johnny Winter Dream Sequence" appeared in *Smile Hon, You're in Baltimore,* 2011.

"I Know Why I Was Born" appeared as "Christmas Eve" in *Orlo & Leini* (Woodholme House), 2000

"Too Rolling Tookie" appeared in *Out of Tune* (Hilliard & Harris), 2006

"Wedding Day" published in "Storyteller" (*The Baltimore Sun*), 2001

"The Fountain of Highlandtown" published as Fiction Award winner by the Baltimore Artscape Festival, 1994

"The Long Vietnam of My Soul" published by Macon Street Books, 2013

"Aunt Lola" appeared in *Style Magazine* (Baltimore), 2005

"The Ganges of Baltimore" appeared in *Nimrod International Journal of Poetry & Prose,* 2012.

PHOTO CREDITS

If you enjoyed *Tales From the Holy Land*,
check out these other titles from
Perpetual Motion Machine Publishing . . .

Also, make sure to sign up for our newsletter
for up-to-date information on publications,
submissions, and contests.

http://eepurl.com/VFcB5

www.PerpetualPublishing.com
pmmpublishing@gmail.com

SO IT GOES:
A Tribute to Kurt Vonnegut

Kurt Vonnegut was a man who pushed his imagination off a cliff and followed it for the whole drop; a man who was able to write the most cynical material, yet make you die of laughter at the same time. We have been enjoying his brilliance for over 50 years now, and it's time we showed how he's affected us. Stories by Jonathan Balog, Tony Wayne Brown, C.M. Chapman, James Dorr, T. Fox Dunham, Rachael Durbin, Brady Gerber, James W. Hritz, K.A. Laity, Sue Lange, Christian A. Larsen, E.E. King, Joseph McKinley, Thomas Messina, Frank Roger, Mike Sheedy, Philip Simondet, Michael Lee Smith, Jay Wilburn, Eli Wilde, James Wymore, and Aric Zair.

THE RITALIN ORGY

BY MATTHEW DEXTER

"If you want to understand a society, take a good look at the drugs it uses. And what can this tell you about American culture? Well, look at the drugs we use. Except for pharmaceutical poison, there are essentially only two drugs that Western civilization tolerates: Caffeine from Monday to Friday to energize you enough to make you a productive member of society, and alcohol from Friday to Monday to keep you too stupid to figure out the prison that you are living in."

-Bill Hicks

As a young teacher trying to inspire and save advisees from expulsion, Nick Neary immerses himself into the secret rituals and lives of his students, entering a world of excess beneath the campus that threatens everything, including himself. As a dorm parent, Mr. Neary battles his obligations to inform the deans about the ills he has witnessed with his visceral urge to crawl deeper into the clandestine underbelly to learn more. The Ritalin Orgy is the unmitigated truth of decadence, degenerates, and the debauchery which encompasses America's most prominent prep schools.

Long Distance Drunks
A Tribute to Charles Bukowski

Charles Bukowski had a very distinctive style. He wrote in a simple and often cruel, unforgiving voice. A typical story would involve isolation, alcohol, writing, hookers, and gambling. He wrote about the scum of the city. He became the scum. His words were scum, and it was all so damn beautiful.

LONG DISTANCE DRUNKS is an anthology consisting of short stories and poetry that pay tribute to the old blue bird himself. Told in the same voice and style as Mr. Bukowski, this book is a homage to his legacy.

Featuring short stories and poems by Eli Wilde, T. Fox Dunham, William Barker, Brett Williams, Jonathan Balog, Gabino Iglesias, Craig Wallwork, S. MacLeod, Michael Bailey, Will Viharo, Jacob Haddon, Teri Louise Kelly, Joe Clifford, Tom Pitts, John Mitchel, Kyle Hemmings, Justin Hyde, Jay Wilburn, Vincenzo Bilof, and Richard Thomas.